Assa...

"A potpourri of spices, ... of murder—Pepper and her crew serve up a tantalizing mystery and a fragrant treat for the senses."

> —Connie Archer, national bestselling author of
> the Soup Lover's Mysteries

"There's a savvy new amateur sleuth in town . . . Pepper Reece. *Assault and Pepper* is a smart blend of zesty characters, piquant spices, and scrumptious food. Set against the intriguing Seattle backdrop, this well-plotted whodunit is the perfect recipe for a great read."

> —Daryl Wood Gerber, national bestselling author of
> the Cookbook Nook Mysteries

"Leslie Budewitz writes . . . with a dash of humor and a half-turn of charm that will leave readers smiling."

> —J.J. Cook, national bestselling author of
> the Sweet Pepper Fire Brigade Mysteries

"An iconic Seattle setting, a smart and capable heroine, and a *spicy* investigation . . . What mystery reader could want more? Budewitz combines it all with effortless finesse."

> —Victoria Hamilton, national bestselling author of
> the Vintage Kitchen Mysteries

"Set in Seattle, this is the perfect read for a few hours of pure enjoyment." —*Suspense Magazine*

"Parsley, sage, rosemary and . . . murder . . . will add zing to your reading."

> —Barbara Ross, author of the Maine Clambake Mysteries

Guilty
as Cinnamon

LESLIE BUDEWITZ

BERKLEY PRIME CRIME, NEW YORK

**BERKLEY
PRIME
CRIME**

**An imprint of Penguin Random House LLC
375 Hudson Street, New York, New York 10014**

GUILTY AS CINNAMON

A Berkley Prime Crime Book / published by arrangement with the author

ISBN: 978-0-425-27179-7

PUBLISHING HISTORY
Berkley Prime Crime mass-market edition / December 2015

PRINTED IN THE UNITED STATES OF AMERICA

10 9 8 7 6 5 4 3 2 1

Cover art by Ben Perini.
Cover design by Lesley Worrell.
Interior text design by Kelly Lipovich.

Penguin
Random
House

For the real-life Sandra,
who lent me her name,
with thanks for
decades of friendship and inspiration

Acknowledgments and Historical Note

In my student days at Seattle University, and later as a young lawyer working downtown, I spent many happy hours in the Pike Place Market. I also drank many cups of tea in the tiny Market Spice Shop in the LaSalle/Creamery Building, where it's been since 1911. My Seattle Spice Shop is not that shop, nor any other actual business. But if I have captured some of the flavor of the Market, then the magic of the tea is still working.

I have done my best to be faithful to the city of Seattle, but a city is not a stagnant thing. Shops and restaurants open and close. Buildings come down and go up. Public works projects run into obstacles—sometimes literally, as in the case of Big Bertha, the machine tunneling near the waterfront so the Alaskan Way Viaduct can be relocated underground. If the city on the page does not quite match the one you know or remember, please forgive me.

I've taken a few liberties with the Garden Center Building in the Market and the Pittman Automotive building on Western to create Pepper's shop and loft. I've also moved the King County Archives to the King County Courthouse to make sleuthing more convenient, and rearranged the Festival schedule at Seattle Center. The building on Lower Queen Anne that houses Ashwani's restaurant and the future Tamarack is fictional. Ripe, the First Avenue Café, and Magenta, Danielle's flagship, also exist only in my mind, although Ripe draws loosely on my memories of a café that anchored the old Seafirst

Building, now Safeco Plaza, twenty-some years ago. The Seattle Mystery Bookshop, where Jen works, is real—and if you're in Seattle, you must go explore its treasure shelves.

The tales of ghosts in the Economy Market and the Butterworth Mortuary, and of young Jacob, who haunted the bead shop, are drawn from *Market Ghost Stories* by Mercedes Yaeger.

In writing this series and my Food Lovers' Village Mysteries, set in northwest Montana, I discovered "kitchen lit." A few favorites: *Blood, Bones & Butter* by Gabrielle Hamilton. Gritty, moody, and mouthwatering. Plus Chef Hamilton introduced me to the Negroni, and to a scam I've adapted on these pages. *Sous Chef* by Michael Gibney and *Back of the House: The Secret Life of a Restaurant* by Scott Haas take the reader behind the scenes in high-test kitchens. On a trip to Seattle, my husband found *The Joy of Mixology* by Gary Regan, which inspired Pepper's cocktail recipes; it also provides fun facts about the origins and proper serving techniques for zillions of drinks. Cheers!

For spice history and trivia, I've drawn on *The Spice and Herb Bible* by Ian Hemphill, *The Scents of Eden: A History of the Spice Trade* by Charles Corn, and *Spice: The History of a Temptation* by Jack Turner, as well as cookbooks and food lit in my own collection.

Thanks to my husband, Don Beans, for sharing his knowledge of Indian music, and to our friend Ashwani Bindal for lending me his first name. My Facebook fans Katrina Elkinton Powers, Karen Wakeland, and Jill Jofko named the fictional Ashwani's restaurants.

Penny Orwick and Mike Lancaster lent me their ski condo for several key days early in this book's gestation, and again as I neared "The End." Thanks to you—and to the mountain songbirds and pika who kept me company.

Hugs of thanks to Katherine Nyborg for the insider's tour of Seattle Center. Once again, Lita Artis and Ken Gollersrud provided ground truthing, moral support, and a home base during research trips. (By research, of course, I mean eating.) Marlys

Anderson-Hisaw and Derek Vandeberg fill me in on retail doings, and sell my books in a village bereft of a bookstore. Naturally, I made the mistakes all by myself.

Thanks to my agent Paige Wheeler at Creative Media Agency, Inc., my editor Robin Barletta and all the crew at Berkley Prime Crime, and the booksellers, librarians, reviewers, and bloggers who have championed the Spice Shop Mysteries. Most especially, thanks to my readers, who have fallen in love with my characters and traveled to the Northwest with us on the page.

And always, thanks to Don, aka Mr. Right, for unstinting encouragement, enthusiasm, and all-around good taste.

Seattle Spice Shop Checklist

Everyone you need to cook up a mystery!

THE SEATTLE SPICE SHOP STAFF

Pepper Reece—owner, ex-law firm HR manager
Sandra Piniella—assistant manager and mix master
Zak Davis—salesclerk by day, musician by night
Lynette Cobb—salesclerk who calls herself an actress
Reed Locke—part-time salesclerk, full-time college student
Kristen Gardiner—part-time salesclerk, Pepper's oldest
    friend
the job applicants—oh, for the right one!
Arf the Dog

THE FLICK CHICKS

Pepper—she'll never tell you her real name
Kristen—she knows, but she knows enough to keep her
    mouth shut
Laurel Halloran—deli owner, caterer, houseboat dweller
Seetha Sharma—still a bit of a mystery

MARKET MERCHANTS, RESIDENTS, AND FRIENDS

Ben Bradley—ace reporter
Jim and Hot Dog—men about town
Fabiola the Fabulous—graphic designer

Jen the Bookseller and Callie the Librarian—Pepper's former law firm employees

Vinny—the Wine Merchant

Hal—ghost scholar

IN THE BIZ

Tamara Langston—aspiring chef-owner of Tamarack

Ashwani Patel—owner of the Indian restaurant next to Tamarack

Alex Howard—chef, businessman, rule breaker, heartbreaker

Danielle Bordeaux—successful restaurateur, Tamara's business partner

Tariq Rose—a line cook in Howard's employ

Scott "Scotty" or "Glassy" Glass—Howard's longtime bar manager

SEATTLE'S FINEST

Officer Tag Buhner—aka Bike Boy, aka Officer Hot Wheels, Pepper's former husband

Detective Cheryl Spencer—homicide

Detective Michael Tracy—homicide

One

An ancient token of friendship as well as an ingredient in the anointing oils Moses used, cinnamon is one of the oldest-known spices, well traveled and heavily traded.

"PARSLEY POOP." THE INDIAN SILVER CHANDELIERS HANGING from the Spice Shop's high ceiling swayed, their flame-shaped bulbs flickering. The crystal candelabra they flanked burned on defiantly. As I stared up, unsure whether to curse the Market's hodgepodge of ancient and modern wiring or the fixtures themselves, all three blinked, then went dark.

"Cash register's got power," Sandra called from behind the front counter. "And the red light district's open."

I glanced over my shoulder at the miniature lamp perched on the Chinese apothecary that displays our signature teas and accessories. The red silk shade glowed steadily, a beacon in the back corner.

"Better call the electrician," I said at the exact moment as my customer asked, "Where's your panel?" and Lynette, my newest and most annoying employee, said, "I'll check the breakers."

At the very next moment, the ceiling lights came back on, bright and steady.

Kristen started whistling the theme from *Ghostbusters* as she unwrapped a tall roll of paper sample cups for our special tea, black Assam spiced with cardamom, allspice, and orange. Any day now, we'd start serving an iced version alongside the hot brew made in the giant electric pot that looks like a Russian samovar.

"Don't those ghosts know they should be sleeping this time of day?" Whether Sandra Piniella, my assistant manager, believes in ghosts, I don't know, but she holds the wisecrack sacred.

This was one of those undecided mornings, common in a Seattle spring, that could turn gloomy or glorious, and the shop needed lights. I shrugged and turned back to Tamara Langston. I would let nothing—not even the magical, maddening Market—interfere with the prospect of becoming chief herb and spice supplier to this promising young chef, on the brink of launching the city's hottest new bar and restaurant.

"Gotta love old buildings," Tamara said. "The power in our new space has been giving me fits, too."

"Tell me more about your plans."

"Ingredient driven. Simple, yet adventurous. Food I love, prepared and presented in a way you'll love." An all-inclusive "you," meaning anyone passionate for a great plate of food. Tamara vibrated with intensity, her presence boosting everyone around her to a higher frequency.

Maybe that's what disrupted the lights. Like people whose personal magnetism stops watches and messes up computers. I'd known a few in my decade-plus as a law firm human resources manager, before buying Seattle Spice in the venerable Pike Place Market.

The chef was a fair-skinned blonde in her early thirties, roughly ten years younger than I. Thin and wiry—from hard work, not workouts—her features were too intense to call pretty. But she buzzed with an irresistible energy.

"Not vegetarian," she continued, "but we will champion vegetables. And cocktails. We'll pour the best gin in town."

"I'm sold. We can get anything you need. Our supply networks circle the globe." I gestured to the map on the wall, speckled with pushpins showing the sources of our hundreds of herbs and spices. In the year and a half since I'd bought the place, I'd worked hard to expand our offerings. To not follow trends, but set them. Peppers were hot, as was almost anything new. Especially the new *and* hot.

I like to think beyond that. So did Tamara.

"Tamarack is all about flavor," she said, her small hand, scarred by burns and knife blades, opening and closing as she pumped her lower arm. "Both bold and subtle. Spicing should complement the food, not dominate it."

Music to my ears. "Love the name. Where's the space?" She hadn't said. Restaurateurs often keep plans under wraps as long as possible, then leak a few juicy hints, aiming to pique curiosity and build buzz.

"Lower Queen Anne." She kept her tone low and cagey, though we had no other customers at the moment. "Next to Tamarind, the Indian place. I'm spending every spare moment there. The architect came up with the coolest design—woodsy but light filled. Like the best picnic you ever had, but no rain and no ants."

Tamarack was a joint venture with Danielle Bordeaux, the visionary owner of half a dozen of Seattle's favorite eateries and drinkeries. If I played this right, we might get her business, too.

"Great concept. Good location—near the Center, Queen Anne, Magnolia." Near money.

"Aren't you worried that the names are too similar—Tamarack and Tamarind?" Sandra swept by, a giant jar of Turkish bay leaves in her plump arms.

"I like the synchronicity. Our image will set us apart." Tamara's luminous green eyes shone. "Not to mention the line streaming out our door."

"Isn't that space haunted?" Black Sharpie in hand, Lynette paused in her task of checking items off a delivery list.

"Ghosts, shmosts," Tamara said.

"Let me give you a sample of those Ceylon quills." True cinnamon, my finest grade, still called by the ancient name of the island where it originated. I pulled a jar off the shelf and carried it to the front counter.

"Alex giving you a hard time about leaving for a competitor?" I twisted off the lid and reached for clean tongs. Tamara's silence snagged my attention and I looked up.

"I—haven't told him yet."

Behind her, Lynette straightened, glancing from Tamara to me.

"I want to get all the details in place first," Tamara said, the words breathy and rushed. "Finish the build-out. Nail down sourcing. Recruit the key staff."

I read between the lines. "And you don't want to tell him until you're ready to draw another paycheck."

The creases in her forehead and the red stains blooming on her white flour cheeks told me I'd guessed right.

"Our lips are sealed. You don't honestly expect him to be surprised, do you? Or behave rashly?"

As lead sous for the First Avenue Café, the flagship of Alex Howard's restaurant empire, Tamara knew the man well. He bought his spices from me, even after I'd ended our fling—too fast and furious to call it a relationship—last September. Tall, dark, hawkishly handsome, and one heck of a chef, he boasted the legendary temper and bravado as well as the cooking skills. Rumors of his cutthroat business practices swirled through Seattle's food community, but he'd always been fair with me.

In business, at least.

"Not a chance I'm willing to take," she said. I reached for her shopping basket brimming with fresh produce, but she tucked the samples into her own green-and-white-striped tote. The quills were for her, not the Café. "I'm dying to try your ghost chiles. Alex makes a terrific relish out of them, but he won't let anyone else handle it, so I'll have to work up a recipe myself."

From under the counter, I drew a canister of the double-bagged devils. *Bhut jolokia*, better known as *bhut capsicum*, the ghost chile, is a naturally occurring hybrid from the Assam region of northeastern India that blasts the top off the Scoville heat scale. "Alex uses the dried whole pepper, but I've also got a powder. Kinda like ground lava."

"He mentioned an oil."

"Right. An experiment he and I tried one night. We extracted the capsaicin by roughly grinding dried peppers, heating them in oil, and straining it off. The result was a gorgeous, fiery red-orange oil. He made the relish by adding a few drops to a medley of fresh peppers, white onions, and cilantro. And fresh corn, if I remember right." A big "if"— tequila had also been involved. Like Alex, I don't let my staff handle the peppers. I pack them after hours, wearing a respirator and elbow-length gloves. A fleck landed on my eyelashes once and fell into my eye. I stuck my head in the sink and wanted to leave it there. It's the one task that makes me wish for a commercial warehouse, an option I reject at every suggestion. I like running a small show. "You sure? Farmers in India smear it on their fences to fend off elephants."

"If he can handle it," Tamara said, "so can I."

I dropped the peppers into her tote. Confidence is more than half the battle in retail, the legal world, and the restaurant biz.

She scribbled in her notebook, its spring green cover matching the stripes on her tote, and added a quick sketch. "I'll wait for your price list, then make some decisions."

"Great. End of the week." I held out my hand. Her grip was firm but not overpowering—capable of wielding a meat mallet or embracing a delicate filet of sole.

After Tamara left, the brass bells on the door chiming behind her, Sandra and I restocked our Spice of the Month table. This month's star: cinnamon—half a dozen varieties, ground and sticks. Supporting players: recipe cards suggesting sweet and savory uses, and a few favorite cookbooks. No one, it seemed, had written the definitive book on cinnamon. I'd searched online, scoured publishers' catalogs, and consulted cookbook collectors. All wasn't lost, as the hunt had been a great excuse to reread a few favorite mysteries, including *Cinnamon Skin* by John D. MacDonald and *Cinnamon Kiss*, an Easy Rawlins outing by Walter Mosley, both now on display.

A customer stopped to watch us. "Cinnamon in April? I think of it in autumn."

"It's a year-round spice." Truth was, I'd ordered a special crop of Ceylon cinnamon that had been delayed at customs and didn't arrive until after Christmas. And then, with our staff changes and other hoo-ha, we hadn't gotten around to celebrating cinnamon until now. I took the lid off a small jar and held it out. "Take a whiff."

"Sold," she said. I handed her off to Sandra, who held up a copy of Joanne Fluke's *Cinnamon Roll Murder* and shot me a meaningful look.

"Right," I said. "C'mon, boy. Break time."

Arf, the black-and-tan Airedale bequeathed to me last fall by a former Market resident, popped up from his bed behind the counter. Technically against the Market rules, no one seems to mind—dogs are commonplace down here. I snapped his brown leather leash onto his LED-studded collar—a gift from the street men, in appreciation for the warmth my staff and I try to show them—and grabbed a scooper bag.

If any food known to woman is unavailable in the Market,

don't tell me. Indulgence may be a hazard of the job, but I make up for it by walking. Walking the dog, walking to and from my loft a few blocks away, walking, walking, walking for nearly every errand.

That's my story, anyway.

In the last few weeks, Sandra and I had become cinnamon roll aficionados. (Lynette, nursing a dream of returning to the stage, declined to participate in the interests of her figure. Kristen, my BFF, and college student Reed, both part-timers, joined the finger-licking fun when they were around, and with Zak, a broad-shouldered, six-foot musician, on staff, we never had to worry about leftovers.)

My current fave featured croissant pastry instead of yeast dough, cream cheese frosting, and raisins. Big enough to feel like you've indulged, but not so big it ruins your appetite for the rest of the day.

After Arf stretched his legs and other parts, and greeted his two- and four-legged pals, we fetched a box of rolls from one of the Market's yummy bakeries and headed back to the shop.

"We can give you your money back, if you insist, but the manufacturer won't refund ours. You must have cranked it too hard." I wasn't two feet inside the door when Lynette's retort—her tone harsh as her words—shattered my vision of a sugar-and-cinnamon orgy.

"To your bed, Arf." His nails clicked on the plank floor as he trotted behind the counter. "I'm Pepper Reece, owner of the shop. How can I help?"

The customer, a trim white woman in her forties with thin lips and a tight face, explained that she'd bought the nutmeg grinder from us a week ago. The second time she used it, one of the screws holding the blade in place snapped. "I did not crank it too hard," she said, her words clipped. "And it was not inexpensive."

"I am so sorry. Things break occasionally for no obvious

reason. We'll refund the full price and give you a new grinder, at no cost." A generous offer; that's what it takes to mend a broken relationship. I reached for another style. "Would you like to try the same model? Or this one? You can see it works a little differently. It's what I use at home."

She chose the second, more expensive version and left with a smile on her face.

After Lynette finished helping a customer who'd come in during Grinder Gate, I invited her to join me in my office. Not much more than a closet with a chipboard remnant jammed over two file cabinets for a desk, a few shelves mounted above, it was strictly utilitarian—and the closest thing I had to a private woodshed.

When Tory left last fall, leaving Sandra the sole employee who'd been here longer than me, I knew she'd be hard to replace. But I had not anticipated such a major pain in the anise. Lynette was my third hire in that slot, an unemployed actress who changed hair and makeup like most of us change underwear, and who could flip the charm off and on like a power switch.

And it turned out, she did not take direction well—at least, not from me. She'd pushed both my HR skills and my patience to the limit.

"What do customers and umpires have in common?"

She reddened. A small sign on the shelf behind me said it all: EVEN WHEN THEY'RE WRONG, THEY'RE RIGHT.

"I don't believe that." Her voice quavered, her eyes searching for anything to look at but me.

"You're an actress." I folded my arms. "Pretend."

Two

🌿

In 1971, the people of Seattle voted to establish the Pike Place Market Historical District and a Historical Commission to preserve the "physical and social character of the soul of Seattle," in the words of the Market's saviors.

—Alice Shorett and Murray Morgan,
Soul of the City: The Pike Place Public Market

I SPENT THE REST OF THE MORNING TRYING NOT TO glower. It doesn't actually help. And it creates wrinkles.

If I fired Lynette, would I find a better candidate? She'd learned our spice talk and sales patter like scripts and delivered them with dramatic flair. But she stank at personal interaction and improv—and low-dollar, high-traffic retail is fast-paced ad-lib.

I sat in my office, flipping through the short stack of job apps on hand and studying the online inquiries. Nothing promising. Anytime you ignore your doubts and hire because you're desperate, you regret it. As Lynette had just proven.

Breathe, I told myself. *Breathe and think.* You own the joint. What can she do—she knows she's in trouble.

I sighed and dug my phone out of my apron pocket. We

had to get fully staffed before tourist season. The Market feeds the city, but it also entertains millions of visitors who stroll the arcades and cobbled streets every year, most of them between May 1 and October 15. I texted Laurel Halloran—good friend, Flick Chick pal, veteran chef and caterer: Help. Send job candidates. And gin.

Then I called an employment agency I'd used in my HR days, managing support staff for one of the city's largest law firms. When it imploded, taking my job with it only a year after my divorce and move to a downtown loft, I'd shocked everyone, including myself, by buying the Spice Shop.

Spice has added flavor to the Market since shortly after its founding in 1907. In the fervor surrounding the campaign to save the Market from redevelopment in the early 1970s, hippie chick Jane Rasmussen threw her lot with capitalism and started this shop, just down the street from a competitor. Why she thought the Market could support two entirely separate, unrelated spice merchants, I didn't know—but she'd been right, running this one for forty years until she sold to me and retired to the San Juan Islands.

Time to prepare for the inevitable. I brought up the Craigslist job postings. "Food/beverage/hospitality" covered it. Lynette seemed to have misread the job as part of the "hostility industry." I checked the right boxes, pasted in my standard ad copy, uploaded a picture, and voilà! Copied the listing and e-mailed it to a few contacts.

"Hey." Zak's booming baritone broke my reverie. I glanced at the clock. Five minutes to noon.

"Hey, big guy." I slid back my chair and gave him a half hug. Tall, muscled, a few months past thirty with a shaved head and arms full of tattoos, Zak worked weekdays so he and his band could rock the weekends away. His eyes darted nervously to the clock. I trust my staff to request time off only when necessary, no questions asked, and no one had abused the privilege. He'd asked for a rare morning free, and I appreciated his conscientiousness. "Right on time. Quiet morning. Cinnamon rolls out front."

"Umm, thanks." He stashed his pack in the tiny cupboard. "Delivery just came. Gotta get to work."

"Hey, boss." Sandra stuck her head in, the space too small for the three of us. "Guy to see you. And he's cute."

Zak trailing like a bodyguard, I headed out front. A man in slim black pants and a black jacket over a white shirt, a black leather messenger bag in hand, surveyed our shelves of colorful jars and tins. He wore his light brown hair in a classic square cut, longer on top and combed back. Professional, but stylish.

"Ben Bradley," he said when I offered my hand and my name, a touch of Chicago in his pleasant tone. He flashed an ID card from the weekly paper and gestured at the Spice of the Month display. "Looks like I'm in the right place. Hoping you have a few minutes to talk about cinnamon. The Cinnamon Challenge."

"One of the stupider tricks bored high school kids have found to amuse themselves. But, better than dropping bowling balls off bridges."

"Can I quote you on that?" He flashed me a genuinely sweet smile I couldn't help return.

For the next few minutes, I gave him the cinnamon spiel: its origins, its role in ancient burial rites and trade. "Some call it the spice that launched a thousand ships, referring to the Age of Exploration. Cinnamon is one of our biggest sellers. Nearly every kitchen has a jar, even in homes where no one cooks." In my mother's "brown bread phase," when our family had shared a big house with Kristen's family up on Capitol Hill, she baked with whole wheat flour, honey, molasses, the barest minimum of salt, and liberal doses of cinnamon. Fortunately, my mother had been an excellent cook despite the strictures, which hadn't lasted long. She flew out of them with a vengeance, embracing butter, cream, and well-butchered meat like a pig embraces mud.

"The Challenge," Ben prompted. "It's sweeping the high schools."

"Not again," I said. He was about five-ten—three inches taller than me—and clearly a regular at the gym. I gestured to the mixing nook, a built-in table and benches in a raised corner of the shop. Perfect for reviewing price lists and sourcing options with our commercial customers, for staff gatherings, and, yes, for mixing and testing our custom seasonal blends. We sat. "Cinnamon does contain coumarin, which can be toxic to the liver in high doses. But a dash or two in your coffee or on your oatmeal isn't going to hurt you."

"What about those cinnamon rolls?"

I drew the box closer, and we plucked out the last two. "It's the cream cheese and sugar that'll get ya."

He grinned, then swallowed before asking his next question. "What about medicinal uses? I've heard it can lower high blood sugar and blood pressure."

"Not my expertise, and I don't give medical advice. But you're talking about extracts, which are generally considered safe. On the other hand, trying to swallow a tablespoon of dry, powdered cinnamon—the Challenge—is just dumb. It won't kill you, unless you're allergic. You'd probably sneeze most of it out before you could swallow it."

We moved on to culinary uses—far more fun.

"You know, this place is fascinating. I'd love to do a feature interview, bring in a photographer." He closed his notebook and gave me a wink. "And get the scoop on how a woman named Pepper ended up running a spice shop."

"Destined for my job, like you."

He slid out of the nook. "Not spelled the same. And how do you know him? Watergate happened ages before you were born. Besides, nobody reads the *Washington Post* out here."

Barely a year before I was born, but I didn't say so. The

Ben Bradley in front of me couldn't be more than thirty-five to my forty-two going on forty-three. "Hey, he was legendary. Besides, my mom had a crush on Robert Redford. And Dustin Hoffman. I've seen *All the President's Men* at least a dozen times." She likes to say she named my brother for Carl Bernstein, while my dad insists he's named for Carl Yastrzemski, the Red Sox left-fielder, but in truth, Carl is a variation of an old family name.

"Maybe you can show me around the Market. Give a newcomer the insider's view."

I peered outside. The rain had held off. Sandra and Kristen eyed us like a pair of fifth graders plotting a trick on their teacher. He was young, but cute. And they were convinced I needed a new man in my life. Despite a few fun dates over the winter, nothing had ripened into a relationship. Turns out I kinda like being single—most of the time. Okay, some of the time.

"Sure," I said, grabbing my shopping bag and a jacket for insurance. We made the tour into a walking lunch, starting with pizza at DeLaurenti's. At Rachel the Pig, the Market mascot that stands guard beneath the iconic sign and clock, we stopped to ogle the fishmongers flinging whole salmon through the air, and I bought a filet for dinner. We ambled up the Main Arcade, past the daystallers who haul in their produce, art, and crafts season after season.

We stopped to chat with Angie Martinez and taste raspberry and strawberry jam from her family's Central Washington orchard. Tried honey from the beekeeper in the adjacent stall and checked out Herb the Herb Man's crops. Tulips, daffs, lilacs, and other spring bloomers filled the flower sellers' buckets. Too soon for aconite, thank goodness. Not their fault that on sleepless nights, bundles of their purple blossoms crowd my dreams.

Early produce filled the tables, and I picked out gleaming white scallions, peppery arugula, and fresh spinach. Pondered radishes: classic red balls or a slender white-tipped French variety that I'd discovered last year? Pointed at a bundle of orange, red, and purple carrots. Ben made a face at the purple roots, until the farmer scrubbed one clean and handed it over for a taste test.

"It's sweet." His eyebrows dipped in surprise. "Orange inside."

"Purple Haze. Very popular in Seattle, birthplace of Jimi Hendrix." I paid the farmer and tucked the veggies in my shopping bag.

As we reached the end of the Arcade, I glanced west to Puget Sound and the Olympic Mountains. A hint of clearing. *Nice.* The skies, the walk, the company—all nice.

We crossed the cobbles of Pike Place, the Market's main thoroughfare, on our way back to the Spice Shop. A familiar whizzing sound snagged my hearing. My jaw tightened. Beside me, Ben stiffened reflexively, as people often do at the sight of a uniformed police officer. Even one on a bike.

"Hello, Tag," I said flatly. "Is there a problem?"

"You tell me." He stretched one long leg, in sleek black spandex, to the cobbles, the other foot on the pedal. "Seattle's finest, here to serve."

"Ben Bradley, reporter, meet Tag Buhner, beat cop. My ex-husband." I sent Tag an unspoken message to play nice. We'd worked our way back to being friendly, even going out together a few times to catch up, but he had a history of not being so friendly to men who showed any kind of interest in me.

Ben extended a hand. Tag, Ray-Bans gleaming, ignored it, flexing his fingers in their black gloves.

"Thanks for the interview and the tour, Pepper. I'll call you about the feature," Ben said to me. Then, with a slight nod, "Officer."

"The future?" Tag drawled as Ben walked away.

"*Feature*, as in newspaper." I pushed past him into my shop, the brass door bells chiming like a call to prayer.

Sandra and Kristen stood shoulder to shoulder, conspiratorial looks on their contrasting faces—one round and olive skinned under a dark pixie cut, the other narrow, her fine bones framed by straight blond hair.

"I liked it better when you two didn't like each other," I said.

"We never didn't like each other," Kristen protested. "We just had to find common ground."

"Like you and Mr. Reporter," Sandra said. "Until Mr. Cop showed up."

"Let's Google him." Kristen whipped out her phone.

"Don't you have work to do?" Not a customer in sight. Lynette had left for lunch, and Zak was unpacking the day's UPS delivery.

"B-R-A-D . . ." She spoke the letters out loud as she punched.

But Ben Bradley is too common a name for a good search, though we did find a few recent bylines.

"Check him out on Facebook," Kristen said.

"Enough of the proxy stalking. I can't date him. He's too young. Besides, my luck, he's married with three kids and a metal allergy that makes his hand swell up when he wears a wedding ring."

"Mr. Right's sister married a man ten years younger, and it's a match made in heaven." Sandra always calls her husband Mr. Right, in contrast to his predecessor, Mr. Oh-So-Wrong.

Business picked up a bit that afternoon. Kristen and Reed helped customers while Sandra focused on the new wedding registry we hoped to unveil shortly. Zak took the day's shipments to the mailing station. Lynette straightened shelves and sulked. I huddled in the nook with my laptop, working up Tamara's price list. Lively, intriguing choices. Consulting with chefs is great—I'm able to see what gets their juices flowing, and steal ideas for combinations to recommend. But helping new cooks is just as sweet. I love when a customer comes in asking for more of our special Herbes de Provence, after insisting she wouldn't know how to use them, or graduates from measuring out each half teaspoon to developing her own sense of how much of this, how much of that.

And it's all a lot more fun than mediating interoffice squabbles between legal assistants or counseling a stressed-out lawyer on how to work with a pregnant staffer whose bladder sends her to the bathroom three times an hour and whose fluctuating hormones plunge her into tears every afternoon at three fifteen.

The antique railroad clock over our front door had just struck four thirty when the door flew open so abruptly I half expected the glass to shatter.

"Alex. What a surprise!" If he needs a special spice or runs out between deliveries, he usually calls or sends someone down. He hadn't set foot in the shop in months.

His burning eyes said this was not a social visit.

He delivered his words like a crime boss in a Mafia movie. "I get that you don't want to be lovers. But I thought we were still friends. I am a loyal customer, and I counted on your loyalty in return."

Understanding crept in. "Alex, I sell to half your competitors, at least. Vendor exclusivity has never been part of the deal."

"I don't give a rat's back end about exclusivity. You knew an employee I took in and trained—an employee I trusted—means to cut my throat, and you didn't bother to say a word."

That was rich. The man who stood me up and lied about it protesting an insult to his honor.

"When to tell you was Tamara's choice," I said, ignoring the muscle spasm in my jaw. "She had her reasons for waiting, and I'd be out of business tomorrow if I ran around spilling my customers' secrets."

He leaned forward a fraction of an inch. I resisted the urge to lean back. "You knew," he repeated, as if I hadn't heard him the first time. "And you didn't say a word."

A stab of pain shot past my ear and into my skull, but I managed to keep from wincing. "When you were young and ambitious, did you tell your employers everything you were up to? Or wait until the time was right? You know Tamara. She had no intention of leaving you in the lurch. But she also didn't need to give you time to talk her out of it." Or to make her life miserable.

"This isn't about Tamara," he said, but I refused to listen.

"No," I said. "It's about you wanting to control other people. To run their lives for your convenience. Sorry, Alex. That's not my game. I'm happy to be your spice purveyor. But I am not willing to be your spy."

His jaw stiffened, and his eyes hardened to marble. After a long, unblinking stare, he flung his left arm out in a "we'll see about that" gesture. The back of his hand struck a tall treelike sculpture made of found metal objects that stood between the nook and tea cart. *The Guardian*, the sculptor had christened it. Dangling leaves made of silver spoons and forks struck gears and pipes, clattering like a busboy's nightmare.

A red scratch opened up on the back of his hand. Alex didn't notice. Shooting me one last burning glare, he stalked out.

"Whoa," Sandra said. Behind her, Lynette surveyed the scene, eyes flicking from me to the door and back like a drunken mosquito. "You okay, boss?"

How had he known?

My eyes burned as hot as after the ghost pepper incident, and my hands curled tight. To my surprise, the cramp in my jaw let go. I had stood up for myself. I had refused to back down.

Good girl, my inner cheerleader said.

But how had he known?

Sandra continued to study me, concern welling in her dark eyes. Lynette unplugged the samovar and rolled the red enameled tea cart—one of the few pieces I'd taken when

I left Tag—toward the front counter to empty the day's old tea into the big sink.

I frowned. More than an hour left before closing. Besides, that was Zak's job.

Zak hadn't returned yet from his mail run. Kristen was deep in conversation with an avid cook whose tastes run to Middle Eastern and North African cuisine.

The mental light burst on. And I could tell by the determined way she refused to look at me that Lynette knew I knew.

"No need to finish that, Lynette."

She shoved the tea cart toward the wall, and one balky wheel swiveled the wrong direction. The tower of paper cups crashed to the floor. The samovar teetered, and instinctively, Sandra reached out to grab it.

"No," I cried. "It's hot."

Too late. The samovar tipped over and hot tea splashed out. Sandra recoiled in pain. Lynette's mouth fell open.

"He deserved to know," she said, her voice thin and rushed. "He deserved to know that Tamara was planning to quit and try to take his best people with her."

"Leave," I said, dashing behind the counter to turn the cold water on full blast. I steered Sandra forward, not sure how badly burned she was, and plunged her hand into the sink. "And don't come back."

SANDRA was more stunned than hurt, the palm of her right hand a pale, puffy red. Dr. Ron Locke, Reed's father, had been tutoring me in basic homeopathy, and I insisted she take a dose of cantharis and cover the burn with calendula gel.

"Not your fault, boss," she said, sitting in the nook soothing on the cooling gel. In a show of sympathy, Arf rested his bearded chin on her black-clad knee.

"She overheard my conversation with Tamara," I said.

"After the nutmeg grinder incident, she felt humiliated and decided to get back at me." And when she realized I was onto her, she'd panicked, and Sandra had gotten in the way.

They call that collateral damage.

Reed mopped up the spilled tea, and he and Zak carried the samovar to the counter for closer inspection.

"See that?" Zak pointed to a long, fine crack in the ceramic interior.

Collateral damage can add up.

MOST weeks, Tuesday night is movie night. But two of the four Flick Chicks—Kristen and Laurel—had kid-related conflicts, so we'd canceled this week. I clipped on Arf's leash, tugged the collar of my pink-and-gray jacket up around my neck to ward off the early evening mist, and grabbed my tote and market bag, carrot tops poking out.

"Red or white, boy?" I asked my dog on the way to the wine shop in Post Alley. He did not reply. Silent is not my usual type, but it made a nice change.

Vinny Delgado—no clue whether his mother gave him the first name or he picked it up on the job—pointed to the treat jar and, at my nod, tossed a liver chew. Arf plucked it out of the air.

Oh, to be so easily satisfied.

"Wild world out there, from the looks of your cute mug," he said as I debated light reds. The old bromide "white with fish, red with red meat" doesn't take salmon into account. Plus I drink what I like.

"Short version, I'm hiring again." I chose a Côte de Brouilly Beaujolais and handed over a twenty. A blend rather than a varietal, the classic Beaujolais is full-bodied, tannic, and fruity. According to Vinny, it had recovered nicely from the popularity-driven quality crash a few years ago. "I fired Lynette."

"Excellent choice. The wine, I mean. But also canning that

wanna-be actress." He gave me back more bills than he should have. "Employee discount."

"You don't have any employees, Vinny."

"Thank God for small favors. Believe me, I know what I'm missing."

Have I mentioned I adore working in the Market?

And I equally adore living downtown. All the comforts of home and no lawn to mow. Of course, my four-legged roommate enjoys a bit of green grass now and again, so we swung by Victor Steinbrueck Park on the north end of the Market before heading home to my warehouse loft.

With my neighbors' help, I'd revamped what they charmingly call my "outdoor space" so there's enough room for a round black bistro table and two slim metal chairs in a vivid willow green. And a propane grill, three varieties of tomatoes, and potted herbs. My neighbors say skip the small pots in a small space—go big to make it feel bigger.

And by golly, it works. I raised my glass toward their silent veranda. They were celebrating their anniversary with a three-week trip to Paris. "Lucky dogs," I said out loud. Arf thumped his tail, as if in agreement.

I reached down and scratched his chin, behind the scraggly beard. He let out a soft, contented sigh.

After the day we'd had, we were lucky dogs indeed.

Three

※

*Pluviophile: (n) a lover of rain; someone who finds joy
and peace of mind during rainy days*

—Urban Dictionary

"I CAN WORK AN EXTRA DAY," KRISTEN SAID AT OUR
Wednesday morning staff meeting. More breathing room
in the nook without Lynette. "Until school's out."

"No summer classes for me this year," Reed said. "Pile
on the hours."

"Thanks. That's a big help. But we need another full-
timer. Eyes and ears open."

Sandra's right palm sported one small Band-Aid. "A
teeny, tiny blister," she said. "Worth the price to have this
place back to ourselves."

All heads nodded. Lynette's departure had been eagerly
awaited.

It amazes me how much good employees will endure without a peep, to avoid creating more trouble. Sometimes, you've
almost got to be a master of divination to understand what
they're thinking.

Zak scraped a bit of sugar off the butcher-block tabletop
with his thumbnail. He and Tory had deliberately kept their

romance from me, to prove that it wouldn't interfere with their jobs. It had, but in a good way. She'd left to pursue her art, and I was genuinely happy for them both.

Other employees let it all hang out, setting the place on fire with their hot words. Thank goodness Lynette had lashed out at me, not them—Sandra's blister aside.

And if Alex Howard chose to shop elsewhere, fine.

But the loss of the pseudo-samovar hurt. Electric versions are scarce, and I crossed my fingers that we could find another. For the short term, I'd borrowed vacuum pots from Ripe, Laurel's deli and catering company, as we had last fall when the samovar spent a few nights in a police evidence locker.

"Update me on the wedding registry," I said, returning to the morning's agenda.

"The computer terminal should be set up this week," Sandra replied. We'd created space along the back wall, using a repurposed entertainment center Kristen scored at a block sale on Capitol Hill. She and her family live in the house we grew up in, though it bears little resemblance to the hippie commune slash peace-and-justice center it had been in the '70s. It's a blast to work with women who share my love of antique and vintage, despite our wildly different tastes. Mine runs to diner style, while Sandra favors midcentury modern—the Space Age—and Kristen the Gilded Age.

We brainstormed our contribution to the Market's spring festival. After Tory left, I'd roped Laurel in to collaborate with Sandra and me on the spring spice blends, which we'd just shipped to our Spice of the Month Club members. A small display hugged one end of the front counter. We had ideas for future blends, and our new gift packs were selling well.

If only we weren't shorthanded. But being free of Lynette lightened the mental load so much that I almost didn't mind.

I clapped my hands playfully to signal the end of the meeting. "So, let's have a spicy day!"

"Pepper," Zak said when we'd all vacated the nook. "Can we talk?"

"Sure. I'm meeting a rep from the Historic Commission in"—I glanced at my shiny pink Kate Spade watch, the last splurge before I'd lost my law firm job—"five minutes. After that?"

His big bald head bobbed. So serious. Must want a raise, or time off for a band tour.

All manageable, if we were fully staffed. My young employees bring so much spirit to the job, but the trade-off is that their passions often lie elsewhere.

Oh, for someone who loves food and retail and wants to make spice a career. A younger version of Sandra. I closed my eyes and aimed a tiny prayer at heaven.

"The design, colors, and materials suit the age and style of the structure," the Commission rep said ten minutes later as we stood on the cobbles of Pike Place facing my building. "It's tasteful."

I smiled. The new sign—part of my effort to rebrand the shop and give it my own touch—echoed the logo the fabulous Fabiola had created last fall when I'd despaired of finding anything suitable. After a late-night brainstorm, I'd hauled my collection of '50s glass salt and pepper shakers to her Pioneer Square studio for a dash of inspiration. The tipping saltshaker logo that resulted now adorns our recipe cards, tea boxes, and aprons.

Never mind that salt is actually a mineral, not a spice.

We'd sold out of coffee and tea mugs featuring the design and were waiting for a new shipment of mugs and aprons. (I got the idea to add aprons to our stock when a customer asked where she could find one. I took mine off and sold it to her.)

"We appreciate that you're willing to shrink it a bit, to avoid safety concerns," he continued.

The salmon pink stucco building sports a flat Art Deco

awning in forest green. Very distinctive. Very Seattle. Regulations say signs must be mounted below the awning, but high enough that NBA players and other giants can stroll past worry-free.

"But with no historical evidence showing an exterior lighted sign or a shaped sign, we have to reject your application. Regretfully."

I hate the word "no."

"You said yourself, it's classic 1930s. LED, not neon, but it looks like it could have been there." I fought to keep the pleading tone out of my voice.

"But it wasn't. I'm sorry, Pepper."

I might hate hearing "no," but I understand the need to maintain the Market's historical character and appearance. Without it, the soul of Seattle would be one more outdoor shopping mall. But I'd developed an almost irrational craving for a classic Art Deco neon sign in place of the usual flat wood rectangle.

"Not your fault." I held out my hand. The tips of his fingers brushed mine, as if shaking hands would mean acknowledging he could have fought harder for an electric sign if he'd wanted to.

Inside the shop, Zak came up behind me. "Pepper? Is this a good time?"

The sign. The samovar. Lynette. The wonky wiring that had sent the chandeliers blinking. Could I please hide in my office and pout? Call Fabiola and whine?

But when an employee needs to talk, then by golly, you've got to talk. Or listen, which is usually what they mean.

"My timing stinks," he said, perched on the folding chair I keep in the corner, his big hands dangling between his knees. "Now that Lynette's gone. But I'd already had two interviews when they called me in Tuesday morning and made the offer."

My ears pounded like I'd been underwater and surfaced too fast.

"It's only assistant producer, but they train. It's an opportunity I've wanted for a long time."

What had I just reminded myself about young employees following their passions?

"You know what it's like for a musician and a painter," he continued. "Tory's getting shows and sales, and my band works steadily, but this is a great job. One of the best recording studios in the Northwest."

"Can you give me two weeks?"

He nodded, visibly relieved. The space wasn't big enough for him to stand and fold the chair at the same time, so he backed out, then stashed the chair. "Thanks, Pepper. You've been a great boss. I can't tell you how much—"

I held up my hand. Not to stop him from expressing his feelings, but to keep me from blubbering mine.

THERE is no accounting for taste. On some crazy days, we crave the comfort of scrambled eggs with tomatoes and fresh chives, baked custard with a sprinkle of nutmeg, or a gratin of macaroni and cheese with herbed bread crumbs.

On other equally difficult days, only explosions of flavor and spice will do.

So, after a day that left me a mountainous to-do list and zero idea where to begin, I drove to Lower Queen Anne, then traipsed up First Avenue North to meet Laurel for Indian food, still wearing my Spice Shop black pants and T-shirt. I'd never eaten at Tamarind, but Tamara's mention of it had gotten me in the mood, and Laurel said his samosas and his paneer with peas and chile-tomato sauce were classic North Indian fare.

Next to it stood the future home of Tamarack. At the moment, the space radiated negative charm. No quirky, appealing exterior features. Not even a handwritten sign announcing the coming attraction. The black-and-white hex tiles outside the door were dirty and chipped. Brown paper covered six windows trimmed in peeling white paint. An equally blank glass door stood slightly ajar.

Curiosity called. I pushed the door open and took a step in.

To a Big Empty. The interior had already been cleared, and framing for new walls had begun. A thick layer of grit covered the floor.

"Tamara?" I stepped over the threshold, greeted by a loud mechanical hum from the back. She wouldn't be able to hear me. I squeezed between a pile of two-by-fours and a stack of Sheetrock. The place had potential—that deceptive, expensive word I knew well from my loft build-out.

She hadn't gone far—her green-striped tote sat on top of the lumber.

I called out again, slowly turning around. The place smelled of sawdust and—what? I shook off a childhood memory that came from nowhere. A slightly musky, barklike scent, with notes of something sharper. I cocked my head. *Cinnamon—here?*

I opened my mouth to call Tamara's name. Stopped, wordless, at the sight of a silver sneaker laced in lime green lying on the clean-swept floor.

Behind a pile of white plastic pipe, Tamara Langston lay on her back, a panicked expression on her blue-gray face, her eyes red, her fingers flash frozen like the claws of a Dungeness crab.

The dull humming screamed in my ears.

Four

In Indian cooking, cinnamon is considered a sweet
spice, used in both curry and garam masala to balance
the pungent and hot spices.

—Ian Hemphill, *The Spice and Herb Bible*

A GOOD CHUNK OF MY CHILDHOOD REVOLVED AROUND
the Church, or rather, redefining it. My parents believe
deeply in God and good works, but my father practiced the
zen of hard work and my mother the art of family maintenance. Our extended household, which included Kristen's
family and assorted others who came and went, formed the
hub of the Catholic Worker Movement in Seattle, supporting
pacifist causes of all types, including the free meal program
at the Cathedral.

As she baked, washed, swept, and weeded, my mother
had hummed and chanted chamber music, her medieval
harmonies the soundtrack of my young life. Though we
chopped and stirred in the Cathedral's basement kitchen
several days a week, we climbed the stairs to the nave only
a few times a year, for choral concerts. I'd held my mother's
hand and imagined the angels listening to such songs as they
built the heavens.

And so, when I least expect them, those angelic tones slip into my consciousness, uniting the seen and unseen.

They surrounded me now, until the dispatcher's voice jerked me back to reality.

"Wait for the officers outside," she said. It didn't seem right to leave Tamara, but I knew the routine.

"There you are." Laurel zoomed toward me the second I emerged. "Pepper, what's wrong?"

I dragged myself to the wrought iron bench in front of Tamarind. Rubbed my damp right eye. Told her what I'd found, grateful for a kind ear.

Minutes later, EMTs and SPD officers swarmed the scene, blocking the sidewalk and half the street. The officers worked out of the same precinct as Tag, and their faces looked familiar, but this was a different sector and shift. I agreed to stay put, wishing the bottled water in my bag was gin. The officer on door duty kept a casual eye on me.

"Oh cra—cardamom," I muttered under my breath as a familiar duo stepped out of an unmarked car. Why did Spencer and Tracy have to catch this call? (Yes, they've heard the jokes, and no, they're not amused. In my experience, homicide detectives are rarely amused.) Spencer and I clicked the first time we met, but for reasons I've never figured out, Michael Tracy and I rub each other the wrong way.

"Ms. Reece," he said, as if my name were sand caught in his teeth. "Ms. Halloran." Behind him, Detective Cheryl Spencer—model perfect, as always—stepped into the construction site. A white van marked KING COUNTY MEDICAL EXAMINER joined the virtual parade of official vehicles that blocked traffic, removing any doubt that Tamara Langston, promising chef and restaurateur, had, in police jargon, expired. Like a carton of milk.

My stomach turned sour.

"Suppose you tell me," Tracy said, standing in front of

the bench and taking full benefit of his temporary height advantage, "how it is that you found another body?"

Laurel's fingers tightened on my arm, and I suppressed the urge to say "Bad luck." "She—Tamara—the victim." The words scraped my throat raw. "She was a professional acquaintance. She's—she was opening a new restaurant here and came to see me about spices. She mentioned the Indian place next door, and that got me in the mood for curry. I got here first and the door was open, so . . ."

"Mm-hmm."

"We planned on doing business together. I wanted to see the layout."

"Hmmph." Tracy's rumpled camel jacket stretched a tad less tightly across his chest and stomach than during our regular encounters last fall.

"I was late," Laurel said, "or I'd have gone in, too."

He ignored her, his small, dark eyes intense, perpetual sags beneath them. "So you decided it was okay to just march right in."

I sighed. "I called to her, but some mechanical thing was making a ton of noise. She'd left her bag, so I knew she hadn't gone far. And then—"

And then it was too awful and my throat clamped shut. My eyes stung. I felt Laurel's hand on my back, her stricken gaze on my face.

Spencer emerged from the no-longer-empty shell, and Tracy joined her for a whispered conversation. He strode inside, and she crouched in front of me, her manicured but unpolished fingertips on my knee. "Pepper. Sorry to see you under these circumstances. Tell me what happened."

I told her, bit by excruciating bit. Cheryl Spencer's vibe, to borrow a word from my mother's tongue, is as different from her partner's as her appearance. The tall, slim blonde is cool as a 1940s movie star, while Tag describes her short, stocky black partner as a fireplug who doesn't get pissed on often enough.

But, far as I can tell, they are solid with each other.

Behind her, the crime scene crew went in. The body came out.

Heels rapped on the concrete. The air hushed and I looked up. A graceful woman of about fifty with artfully colored hair and a stylish teal raincoat stopped before the open door, eyes and features stone-still. She was one of those people who command a space, who fill it up with their energy. Like them or not, you can't help notice them and be impressed. And I had no idea who she was.

Laurel charged forward. "Danielle." She took the woman's hands in hers. So this was Danielle Bordeaux, a legend of the local food scene. "I'm so sorry, but there's been an accident or—well, we don't know what happened. Tamara's—gone. Dead."

Danielle Bordeaux stiffened. She stared. She surveyed the crowd—Detective Spencer, me, the EMTs repacking their unused gear, the ME's crew stowing theirs, patrol officers guarding the perimeter, neighbors and after-work gawkers on the other side of the yellow tape. Detective Tracy blocking the doorway. And finally, her attention landed on Laurel.

"What are you doing here? And what do you mean, dead?" Underneath the question, her voice held that same command note her posture conveyed. A voice used to being in charge. Used to the hurried, hassled minions responding in unison, "Yes, Chef," "Firing two filet, one sea bass, Chef," "Sorry, Chef."

She let Laurel lead her to the bench, and I gave up my spot. Spencer ignored the rapid-fire questions and sat beside her. The detective has that matter-of-fact empathy that lets you know she's ready for any reaction, any demand, anything you throw back at her, all the while maintaining the sharp watchfulness of the veteran cop.

Danielle did not fall apart. She let the news sink in about as long as she would pause to reflect on simultaneous orders from two six-tops, a four-top, and a VIP two-top.

Spencer's tone was kind as she said Tamara had probably been dead before I found her, that there were no visible injuries, that we'd have to wait for the ME's preliminary opinion. "Did she have any illnesses that you know of?"

Danielle's features—long, straight nose, full lips, slightly hooded eyes—darkened briefly, and she shook her head. "She called me an hour ago and asked me to come down. We'd noticed odd sounds and flickering lights a few times, but no one could find the cause. Tamara thought she had an answer. Chefs learn how to fix things," she said, answering the unasked question why Tamara would poke around with the wiring. "One service call can kill your profit margin."

A man in a long white apron pushed his way into the circle, forcing me to step aside.

"What's going on? I've got a restaurant to run here."

We'd never met. I vaguely recalled seeing Tamarind's name on a list of former Spice Shop customers, though why or when we'd lost that one, I had no idea. A handful had departed when I took over, lacking confidence in an owner who had no experience in spice, retail, or even in the food business. Others had seen the change of guard as a chance to change their loyalties. No surprise, and I hadn't let it bother me.

A vague feeling surfaced that I ought to call on him and solicit his business, followed by an equally vague feeling that I shouldn't.

Detective Spencer stood and flashed her badge. "We're investigating a suspicious death, Mr.—?"

His head jerked back, and his wide mouth fell open. "Pa-Patel. Ashwani Patel. Chef and owner of Tamarind. Death? Suspicious? Who? Where?" He glanced at the boarded-up building, and when he spoke, I had to lean in to hear the low, raspy words. "No—not in there? I told her to stay away." He noticed Danielle. "I told you it was haunted."

Danielle pursed her lips and waved a hand. "Patel, everyone knows you've been spreading rumors for years to drive off the competition. Why you think a trash heap next door is better for business than a bustling hot spot, I can't imagine."

They locked eyes, hers hard and clear, his red rimmed and puffy. I suspected he'd once been handsome, with his burnished skin and black hair flecked with silver, but he now looked both a little doughy and a little overbaked.

Behind him I glimpsed a blonde in a white apron—one of his cooks?—and a tiny Indian woman in a deep red sari who stared straight at me. I swear, she winked.

"The rising tide theory," Patel said. "Well, we'll never know, will we?"

The theory that a little competition improves business all around. After seeing close-up how the two spice shops in the Market boost each other's bottom line, I'm a believer.

"Let's talk inside, Mr. Patel," Detective Tracy said, ducking out from behind the yellow tape and leading the man toward his own front door.

Was that distrust or disgust on Danielle Bordeaux's striking face?

Or neither? I shivered. Nothing like finding a body to fire up the imagination.

Five

*In the Middle Ages a pound of ginger was worth a
sheep, while a similar weight of mace could buy three
sheep or half a cow.*

—Charles Corn,
The Scents of Eden: A History of the Spice Trade

"HOW CAN YOU CALL YOURSELF A FOODIE? LOOK AT THE
state of your fridge."

Spencer had cut us loose a few minutes after Patel's interruption. We'd given Danielle our sympathies, climbed into
my Mustang, and zipped back to my loft on Western Ave, a
few blocks south of the Market.

"I shop for a day or two at a time. And we were eating
out." I peered over Laurel's shoulder. "Oh, I spy appetizer
potential."

She backed away from the fridge, leaving it to me. "Just
give me comfort food. And red wine."

Laurel's husband, Patrick, an assistant U.S. attorney, had
been shot and killed in the backyard of their home on Queen
Anne Hill three years ago, when Laurel and their son, Gabe,
were away on a school field trip. Unsolved to this day, and

I knew by her strained tone that Tamara's death had reopened the wound that might never fully heal.

Laurel had called Gabe, just to hear his voice, while I took the dog out. Now, I piled a few vegetables on the salvaged butcher block that tops the peninsula and opened the freezer. "How about a ready-to-bake vegetarian lasagna from Ripe? I hear their food's pretty good."

She grinned at the reference to her own place, a breakfast and lunch favorite that also provides takeout for the downtown working crowd, then plucked a Washington-grown Sangiovese blend from the wine rack. "Hand me that corkscrew."

I did as instructed. Laurel perched on a tole-painted wooden stool Kristen and I had found on one of the junk shop tours she calls "antiquing." We'd been hunting treasures for her top-to-bottom redo of the Capitol Hill house, but I'd scored a few prizes of my own. Arf padded across the loft's wood floors to the kitchen corner and lapped water from his stainless steel bowl. I punched on the oven, then sliced a day-old baguette and brushed on olive oil. "These can toast while we're preheating."

"And drinking." She slid a glass toward me. "To the memory of Tamara Langston."

Shame on me, but I would have liked to forget Tamara lying on the floor of the construction site a little while longer. I raised my glass but didn't drink. Didn't trust my throat to work right.

Instead, I rinsed beans and greens. My place is classic loft, the west wall a bank of twelve-foot-high windows—why, on the fifth floor of a 1920s warehouse, I've never known, but they bring in a ton of light. And when the old double-layer viaduct that carries the highway above the waterfront comes down, they'll give me killer views.

Meanwhile, there's a concrete wall forty feet from my living room, traffic whizzing by behind it. The mezzanine above the bed and bath gives a peekaboo view of Puget Sound and the Olympic Mountains that's stunning this time of evening. But we needed to feed our grief. In minutes, I pulled out the toasts, slid in the lasagna, and assembled a platter of white bean and arugula crostini topped with sun-dried tomatoes.

We carried our wine and appetizers to the windows, climbed out the one that serves as a door, and sat at the bistro table. Despite the traffic noise, the greenery and new furniture—and the virtual forest on my neighbors' adjacent veranda—created the sense of a tiny alcove outside a Greek hotel or in the south of France.

The wine scraped across my throat, raw with unshed tears. The tension in my neck and shoulders heightened momentarily, then began to recede, like the shadows around the edges of an old-time movie.

"Do you really think it's homicide?" I said. "I mean, Spencer called it a suspicious death, and they have to treat it as a crime scene until they know what happened. But there wasn't a mark on her."

Laurel put a hand on my leg. My black yoga slash work pants smelled like spice. "You did everything you could, Pepper."

"Danielle said she'd called about an hour earlier. That means she was alive not long before I found her." Police would use phone records to pin it down. The ME would weigh in. And I would never know, because they would never tell me, whether I could have saved her by showing up a few minutes earlier. Whether anyone could have.

"The detective asked—" I said as Laurel started "I've never seen—" We both stopped. I raised my glass to my lips and said, "You first."

"I've never seen Danielle at a loss before."

"How do you know her?" I crunched into a crostini. The slice of sun-dried tomato on top of the beans slid off the bread and landed on my thigh. One more reason to wear black.

"We were line cooks together ages ago, when I was still

doing the cook-all-day-and-never-sleep thing." She still works long days, but it's different when it's your own place.

"Two women in one kitchen? Unusual, back then."

She refilled our glasses. "What made it different was that we were both on the line, not relegated to salads or pastry. Some guys gave us a hard time, but Chef didn't care as long as we could cook and keep up. And we both did."

"And you both left."

"I quit to have Gabe, and opened Ripe when he started school. Danielle started her own place, too, then another and another. My niche is good, fresh, fast. Hers is creating the concept and managing it all."

I swirled the wineglass under my nose. Earthy. Hints of cherries, vanilla from the oak barrels, tea leaves, and a touch of cinnamon. "Did you like her?"

Laurel took the last crostini. "She did her work and stayed out of mine. That was all that mattered."

The oven timer buzzed, and I stepped back in through the window, carrying the empty platter. On his occasional visits to the loft, Tag gives me grief about the lack of a real door to the veranda, but that's one feature I won't ever change.

"If she died from natural causes, it was something sudden. A brain aneurysm," I said when I'd returned with the lasagna and settled into my green metal chair. "Or a heart condition, like those athletes who just drop dead."

Laurel served us each a generous piece. "Because she wouldn't have been planning a new business if she knew she was ill."

"Exactly." I took the first bite. "This is delicious."

"I'll tell the chef."

Not easy to laugh with your mouth full.

Laurel's longtime baker had fallen in love with a Bainbridge Island brewer and given notice of her intent to head off to other yeasty doings, so we commiserated over staff shortages. Her deli-style setup requires counter staff rather than full-serve waitstaff—easier in some ways, tougher in others.

"Oh geez. Forgot to tell you. The Cinnamon Challenge is going through the schools again, including Gabe's." I told her about Ben Bradley and his questions.

"I know better than to say Gabe would never do anything so stupid," she said. "But soccer and school keep him pretty busy. Cramped as we are on the houseboat, it's going to feel empty when he leaves."

"Boat living will be good training for dorm life." Laurel had bought a houseboat on Lake Union after Patrick's death. Her soccer-star son had passed up all three local schools in favor of a scholarship to Notre Dame. But encouraging the chick to fledge and watching him fly away are two different things.

We finished dinner and wine, giggling about my employees researching Ben on Google, and Laurel called a cab. Arf and I traipsed downstairs to wait with her, then took a quick spin around the block. Walking the dog at night never worries me—no one wants to bother a woman with her own personal guardian.

Funny how a day, or an event, changes your perspective. We walk every evening, and it's much the same, one night to the next. But tonight, the air felt different. As though the loss of one person—a woman I barely knew—had changed the world.

Back in the loft, Alf settled onto his bed by the windows—he's got another in the bedroom—and worked on a chew toy. I cleaned up the kitchen and made a cup of decaf spice tea, the shop's own blend. They say the olfactory sense is the most closely linked to memory, and it always is for me. The scent transports me back to childhood, when my mother often took Kristen and me along on Market shopping trips and let us sip the special, grown-up treat. Not until after I'd bought the shop did I wonder if I'd been groomed for the job all along and hadn't recognized it until after a fifteen-year detour into another career.

While the tea steeped, its fragrance filling the air, I tuned in to a late-night pop and jazz show on public radio. *Why*, I wondered, *had I caught a whiff of cinnamon in Tamara's building*? We sell more cinnamon in winter, for holiday baking, but it's popular year-round. Our most popular spice.

We sell so much of it, the smell must have gotten stuck deep in the fibers of my nose. In my clothes, maybe—friends say spicy scents waft off of me, even when I'm away from the shop and out of my work clothes.

I changed into jammies, then settled into my red leather reading chair with my tea and *The Servant's Tale*. My obsession with medieval mysteries began with a box of Brother Cadfael paperbacks my mother had left in my storage locker in the building's garage. I'd worked my way through all twenty novels and a short-story collection. Jen at the Mystery Bookshop, a former paralegal in my firm, had recommended Margaret Frazer's Sister Frevisse series, set in a fifteenth-century English convent, as a follow-up. One book and I was hooked. A niece of Thomas Chaucer, son of Geoffrey, Frevisse had left her parents' life of pilgrimage for one of solitude, prayer, and devotion.

Or so she thought.

But she'd learned a lesson that I was struggling to grasp: Death intrudes wherever it will.

Six

❦

In 1851, Doc Maynard suggested the new town on Elliot
Bay in Oregon Territory be named Seattle, after the
Duwamish Indian chief Sealth—said See-ALTH or
See-AA-TLE. Sealth may well have been horrified—
members of his tribe had a superstitious dread of
having their names mentioned after death.

—Murray Morgan,
Skid Road: An Informal Portrait of Seattle

THURSDAY DAWNED—I USE THE TERM LOOSELY—SO GRAY
and drizzly that I felt lower than a termite's tits, as my grandfather used to say. And that was before remembering that
I'd found a dead woman twelve hours ago.

"Holy nutmeg," I swore as my foot snared the edge of
Arf's bed. My right shoulder slammed into the bathroom
door frame, and pain shot up my arm. I clutched it and
caught sight of my reflection in the mirror.

Part of what my friends and relatives call my "Forty
Freak-out" had been to chop off my meticulously cut brown
hair and trade it for a spiky, gelled do that says cutting-edge
on good days and bedhead gone wrong on bad.

"A shower will fix it," I told the mirror before it could

tell me I looked like Sleeping Beauty's evil stepmother with a hangover and without her wig.

Buying the loft less than a month after I left Tag had been uncharacteristically impulsive, and I had never regretted it. Despite all the challenges of build-out, the ongoing frustrations with the developer, the uncertainty over the Viaduct, and the "reimagining" of the waterfront, I absolutely, seriously heart the place. Everything in it I love and chose on purpose.

Between the sleepless night, memories of Tamara, and all the problems at the shop, I'd almost forgotten how much I love the loft. But while the shower heated and I rubbed my shoulder, my gaze settled on a playful bit of "shower art" I'd found in the Market—a turquoise fairy godmother in a pink frame, with the slogan "I will rescue myself, thanks"—and the burdens eased a bit. By the time I'd dried off and pulled on a fresh pair of black pants and a matching T-shirt, I was a new woman.

Even if my hair still looked like I'd stuck my finger in a socket.

Arf, on the other hand, is almost always in a cheery mood. The greetings from the Market regulars as we dodged puddles and drips on our way up the long steps from Western to Pike Place were intended as much for him as for me.

I'd stayed up too late reading, slipping into bed well after midnight. At two thirty A.M, Tamara had appeared to me draped in Sister Frevisse's white wimple, silver sneakers poking out beneath the hem of a nun's dark gown. "Time for Lauds," she'd urged, but I knew it was a dream. No way would a chef get up in the middle of the night to pray, even if she was dead. Mercifully, she let me sleep through Prime until my alarm—the modern version of prayer bells—rang at six thirty.

But it's impossible to grump my way through the Market morning chaos, even in the rain. Especially in the rain, when people keep on doing what they do despite the damp and chill.

Their steadiness and commitment remind me that what we do here matters. At the law firm, my job was to take care of the people who did the real work. Important in its way, but I'd often felt like an invisible cog.

Here, though, we're all hands-on.

At the well-placed bakery at the top of the steps, I ordered a latte and an applejack and leaned against a pillar to wait. This may be my favorite part of the day in the Market, watching the flower sellers and farm vendors, their wares so fresh they're practically still growing. At eight, they'd already been going a good hour. Farther north, the arts and craft vendors get a more leisurely start.

My coffee appeared on the countertop without a word from the blond waif working the espresso machine. A new face—with so many bakeries and coffee shops in the Market, I like to spread my business around, and I sometimes lose track of who works where.

A poet, this one. Instead of my name, she'd written on the cup:

For the lovely lady with the pensive eyes.

I bought a bundle of coral pink ranunculus to arrange with white lilacs and some foliage I couldn't identify for the mixing nook, and late paperwhites with orange centers for the front counter, where space is tight.

As I crossed Pike Place, the sweet floral scents mingled with diesel fumes from delivery vans and trucks. Clutching my coffee and the flowers in one hand, my jute tote over my unbruised left shoulder, I unlocked the shop door and crossed the threshold. I am struck every morning by the power of scent to transform us, in space, time, and memory. Sharing that may be the best part of my job.

Sandra and Zak arrived, shaking off the rain I'd just missed. I finished setting up the cash drawer, and we readied the space for the day. The coffee and pastry had brightened my mood, as had the flowers and morning routine. Good thing—Zak's resignation put us in double doo-doo now, and I needed a little caffeine-and-sugar-induced optimism.

In my office refuge, I texted Laurel—knee-deep in Ripe's morning bustle—to check in. Called two women who'd inquired about the openings. One had already found another job; the other would come in this afternoon. I called the Market office to check for job hunters, then e-mailed my old boss and texted a few former law firm employees I hoped would have the right contacts. Dithered over posting a HIRING sign. In the Market, signs tend to prompt inquiries from the curious but not the qualified.

Desperate times call for desperate measures. I dug out our sign to put it in the front window.

"Hey. I heard. It's awful. How are you?" Kristen wrapped her arms around me from behind.

I touched her hand. "Better, when I don't think about it."

She propped on the edge of the desk. Shop staff wear black pants, black or white shirts with the shop logo, and bib-front black aprons. Kristen always adds accents. I'd put the kibosh on the black-and-white feather boa that shed like a snake, and she hadn't worn the off-white muffler her daughter had crocheted since Sandra told her it looked like overcooked spaghetti. (In Sandra's defense, it did—and she hadn't known it was an eleven-year-old's first attempt.) Today, Kristen's silver infinity scarf triggered an instant replay of Tamara's silver running shoe.

It's not just scents that summon memories.

"I talked to my neighbor, but she can't work full-time." Kristen gave me an apologetic smile. "Any chance for short shifts?"

"Not with Zak leaving, too."

"Makes sense. I thought I'd start searching online for a new samovar."

"Perfect." I wheeled my chair back, careful to avoid her feet, and let her sit.

Kristen may have a weekly manicure appointment and a hefty credit card limit at Nordstrom's, but when it comes to a shopping challenge, she's pure terrier. She came in to help out after I bought the place, and loved it so much she'd stayed.

Speaking of terriers, time to take mine for a brisk walk. I changed my black climbers for ankle-high Wellies and headed out front. "Hook up," I said, and Arf sat, letting me click the leash on his collar.

Fat, angry clouds hung like bruises above the city, weighting down the urban steel, concrete, and glass with an extra layer of drear. The rain had stopped. Arf never minds a puddle or two, and my feet were prepared, so we strode up Pike Place to the park. He pooped, I scooped, and we paused at the wrought iron rail to watch the tugs and ferries ply the cold, gray waters.

On our way back, I noticed Alex's operations manager— Ops, he calls her. Her real name always escapes me. She rounded the corner of Pike Place and started up Virginia to First Ave, the woven shopping basket in her hand sagging with produce. Why was she making the supply run?

You ninny, I told myself. Someone has to fill in for Tamara, who'd hauled that same basket into my shop two days ago.

A sign that things were a bit topsy-turvy at the Café, after the murder of a sous chef. The heat of embarrassment crept up my throat as I realized I'd been too peeved by his tirade, after Lynette narked on Tamara's business plans, to call Alex and offer my condolences.

Shame on me.

"Hey, you own the Spice Shop, right? I'm the new chocolate shop." A petite strawberry blonde with freckles scattered across her fair cheeks stuck out a small hand. "Mary Jean Popovich."

"Oh, Down Under?" The name for the Market's maze of lower levels. "Pepper Reece. And this is Arf."

"I've been wanting to talk," she said, letting Arf sniff the back of her hand. "We're doing plain single-source bars and molded chocolates to start, but we're working on a truffle line, and I'd like to source some flavorings. Green tea, chiles, ginger. Maybe you can add some exotic touches."

"Sure. And you can suggest a good cocoa for a steak rub." Some amazing cross-pollination occurs when you cram hundreds of entrepreneurs into nine acres seven days a week.

Back at the Spice Shop, Kristen knelt before the bookshelves, duster in hand. She always cleans when she's frustrated.

"No luck?" I said.

"'I'm sorry, ma'am. That item is discontinued for lack of interest.'" She mimicked a snooty customer service rep. "Well, *I'm* interested."

"You call that restaurant supply service Laurel recommended?"

"They're checking their warehouse. Cross your fingers."

"Both hands," I said, echoing our childhood ritual.

Zak restocked the loose tea supply while Sandra helped a young couple choosing spices for their new kitchen. I heard Sandra say, "Wedding registry?" and watched the man blush while the woman turned her head slightly. *Not yet.*

I spent the rest of the morning making orders—we finally had a decent handle on inventory, thanks to months of measuring and tracking sales. Jane's eyeball method didn't cut it in the modern world. Restaurant and producer sales are key, and you can't be out when a chef or a pickle maker calls in a pinch.

Kristen and Fabiola had been urging me to expand the commercial side of the business. We rent a production facility a few hours a week to mix and package our teas, blends, and Spice of the Month Club mailings. Our own warehouse and equipment would make those operations easier, but the very idea makes my brain freeze. Capital and staff—a double headache.

Business picked up a bit after lunch, but was slow enough that I wondered whether we needed to replace both Zak and Lynette.

We did. No way around it.

Twice I reached for the phone to call Alex, and twice I chickened out. Condolences are not text-able. A teacher customer says her biggest challenge these days is to get kids to look her in the eyes and interact. *It's not just kids.*

Kristen left and Reed arrived. Outside, I stared at the awning, praying for inspiration, when Tag wheeled up. He dismounted, a bad sign, and slowly removed his sunglasses.

Another bad sign.

"Pep. Sorry, but I've got to cancel tonight." He fiddled with his glasses, staring at the wet street.

"Oh-kay. What's up?" I hate when he makes me fish for explanations.

He adjusted the strap of his glasses. "Um, well, I've got to, um." He exhaled a breath big enough to knock a smaller woman over. "We've made an arrest in your murder, and we're waiting for the search warrant. Hate like the dickens that you found another body and you're all mixed up in this, but I want you to know, I didn't ask for the assignment."

"Whoa, Tag." I held up a hand. We hadn't talked since yesterday, but no doubt the police grapevine buzzed about his ex-wife who kept finding bodies. I'd forgotten to tell him, which said a lot about our relationship. Or rather, our divorce. But that one word shoved everything else aside. "It's murder? For sure? And you're on the search squad?"

He sagged with misery.

I grabbed his arm. "Tag, what aren't you telling me?"

His eyes finally met mine. "You'll think I think he's an SOB who had it coming. I told you to stay away from him."

Shock shoved frustration out of the picture as I realized what he was going to say next.

"We've arrested Alex Howard," he continued. "We're charging him with Tamara Langston's murder."

TAG was right: I did think he thought Alex an SOB who had "it" coming—whatever "it" was. During my fling with Alex, Tag had made his disdain clear as gin.

But Tag had warned me away from Alex because he was a player, not because he was a killer. And since Tag had played around, too, I'd dismissed his attitude as jealousy mixed with protectiveness. Though I gave him no encouragement, Tag showed too much of both.

And ultimately, I'd ended things with Alex on my own, not because of Bike Boy's hints and innuendo.

After Tag left, I stood in the back of the shop, pondering. Had there been more to his caution? Cops hear all kinds of talk, and it isn't always easy to tell the true and false apart. And veteran officers sometimes develop what experts call hypervigilance and an overinflated ego with undertones of self-doubt and insecurity.

Their ex-wives have less sympathetic words.

Tag had told me more than he was supposed to—neither the arrest nor Alex's name had been made public yet—so back in the shop, I had to bite my tongue. But I've never been very good at keeping my emotions to myself.

"Sandra, you and Mr. Right want to go to a ball game? Tag had to cancel. Seats on the third base line." My father had rejoiced, in his quiet way, when big league baseball returned to Seattle in 1977, and we'd often gone to games as a family. I didn't want to go alone. Not tonight. Too many thoughts swirling in my head, too much acid roiling in my tummy, to enjoy myself.

"You bet," she said. "It would do him good—the job cuts at his work have him worried."

Kristen followed me to the back room. "Are you sleeping with him?"

"No! How can you even ask that? We're just friends." Not that Tag hadn't expressed interest, but he'd been a gentleman. Despite our recent evenings out, we weren't dating, exactly. More like trying to figure out what "just friends" means. We'd known each other twenty years, been married thirteen, divorced two. I like him. Don't trust him. Can't live with him. But we do have fun together.

"Because," she said, as if explaining to a two-year-old why she had to keep her diaper on at the park, "of the look on your face."

"It's not what you think." She thought I was upset over the cancellation, that work had won out over private life as it often does in cop marriages. In every marriage, far as I could tell. Even though we weren't married anymore.

"So, are you going to tell me?"

I looked her in the eye—she was my oldest, bestest friend in the world, and I owed her that—and told her the truth. "No."

Seven

Snakes and snails and puppy dog tails,
That's what little boys are made of.

—19th-century nursery rhyme

DON'T TELL MY FATHER I LET ARF RIDE IN THE MUSTANG.
I put a sturdy cover on the leather seat, but this car is his baby.
Bought it in San Diego from his commanding officer's widow
when he came back from Vietnam. Drove it to St. Louis to
see his parents, then to Seattle—the farthest city he could
reach in the Lower Forty-Eight—where it had lived a sheltered life ever since. He'd entrusted it to me when he and my
mother decamped for Costa Rica.

And I know it's not the safest place for the dog, but he loves
it. The skies had cleared, so I put the top down and the two of
us sped north on 99 toward Greenwood, Tag's spare house key
in my pocket.

"The tickets are on the desk," he'd said. "In the TV room,
on the first floor."

As if I didn't know where the TV room was. He'd hardly
moved a dish or chair since I'd left. I'd taken only a few pieces
of furniture: The Chinese apothecary he'd always complained

about that now stood in the shop. The two-tiered tea cart, in red-and-white enamel, also now in the shop. And a cedar-lined mahogany chest, one of the first antiques I'd ever bought—a reminder of the hope chest my grandfather bought my grandmother when they were courting, lost in the fire that destroyed their home the winter I was fourteen.

It's odd to walk into a house where you used to live. We'd bought the run-down bungalow from Tag's elderly aunt and spent all our spare time those first few years restoring it, adding modern outlets and appliances to the 1930s charm. We'd scraped and painted inside and out, congratulating ourselves for accomplishing such a major chore with only one spat, when Tag yanked the drop cloths off the roses before I finished the last window trim.

I climbed the steps and crossed the porch. Not the time to wonder what had happened to us. Not after Tamara's murder and Alex's arrest.

The oak door opened without a squeak. Inside, I punched in the security code—our wedding date. The sweet purple smell of lilacs mingled with beeswax and orange oil. Tag's cleaning service used the same products I always had. And a hint of—what?

In the corner stood the wingback chair his mother and I had redone—my first upholstery job—on one of the Persian rugs we'd found rolled up in the back of an upstairs closet. I stuck my nose in the lilac-filled Rookwood pottery vase—another family piece—on the dining room table.

Ah, that's the smell. I wrapped the blue cheese he'd left on the kitchen counter and tucked it in the fridge, between the bottles of Corona and the mustard.

I'd been here a few times since I left, making a pickup or drop-off. And once or twice this past winter for Sunday game day. *Go, Seahawks!* But I had not been alone inside since moving out.

Weird, weird, weird.

The tickets lay right where Tag had promised, on top of a small desk we'd found on one of our rare joint hunts. I stood at the foot of the stairs leading to the master suite we'd created from two small bedrooms and a bath best termed a water closet. *Don't do it, Pepper.*

I did it. What can I say? I'd sweated blood and tears over that project. My fingers trailed the smooth pine rail as I climbed, remembering the terror on Tag's face when an old storm window shattered in my hands and the shared relief as we realized I wasn't badly hurt, despite the blood spatter.

He'd swapped the double wedding ring quilt we'd been given for shirting striped linens and a navy comforter that went surprisingly well with the red-and-blue Persian rug and the unpainted fir floor. Tag did have a sense of style, despite his pokes at mine, but I sensed his mother's hand.

The closet door stood open. An icy spasm gripped my gullet. After I'd found him and the "parking enforcement officer" plugging each other's meters, half a dozen signs of trouble had fallen into place. Including the time I'd picked up the cleaning—usually his task—and noticed shirts I didn't recall him wearing.

My breath snagged in my throat as I realized I was standing in my ex-husband's bedroom searching for signs of Another Woman.

You left him, Pepper. For good reason, yes, but you left. He's entitled to move on.

Maybe he was dating and I was the Other Woman.

That I didn't know shouldn't matter, but it did. Meaning—what?

Meaning it was time to go.

I gave up the plan to cut peonies in the backyard—the garden wasn't mine anymore, either—and dashed outside.

"Good boy." I grabbed Arf's leash, and we trotted to the curb. I opened the driver's door, and he hopped in. For a small guy—about twenty inches at the shoulder—he's a heck of a jumper.

A few blocks away, I stopped for a light, my heart still in high gear. *What were you doing, Pepper?* What had I expected—booby traps for intruders? But that wasn't the kind of danger I'd faced.

The danger of my own uncertain heart.

A movement at the bus stop caught my attention. A slender black kid grooving to his earbuds. No—not a kid. One of the line cooks from the First Avenue Café. Tariq something. We'd met when I'd dropped off Spice Shop deliveries, and a time or two when I'd joined Alex and the staff for family meal.

I waved. He frowned, trying to place me, and approached, tugging one bud free.

"Tariq, right?" I said at the same moment he said, "You're Posh. No, Pepper. That's it."

Alex had dubbed me "Posh Spice" when he heard I grew up on Capitol Hill. No matter that my family were neither the landed old school nor the moneyed new aristocracy, but part of the hippie invasion forty years ago.

"Hop in. I'll give you a lift downtown."

Arf jumped into the backseat, Tariq slid in, his pack in his lap, and the light changed. A car honked, and I shifted gears. Urban ballet.

"You work the line, right? Meat side?"

"Yes, ma'am. Started in the Eastside joint, moved over here a year ago when Alex shuffled kitchen staff." His torso rocked back and forth as he spoke. "Original paint?" At my look of surprise, he added, "I like cars."

"I'm sorry about Tamara," I said. "Must be rough on all of you."

Tariq stopped rocking and snapped his head toward me. "You found her."

My hands tightened reflexively on the wheel and my jaw pinched as I turned onto Highway 99, aka Aurora Avenue, and merged into the zooming midday traffic. "Mm-hmm."

"Sucks," he said, sitting back and gazing forward. "She was going places."

An innocent word choice? Staff changes are a constant in the biz, but her death only a day after her firing would be a serious blow to morale. Still, they knew the boss was a show-must-go-on, keep-the-customers-happy kind of chef.

How would they respond to Alex's arrest? Would Ops close the joint, or bring in a chef from another restaurant?

It occurred to me that Tariq might not know about his boss's arrest.

I slowed for a light and stole a glance at him. The earbuds hung around his neck, the cord snaking down his white T-shirt to his pants pocket. His head rested against the seat, eyelids half closed, long lashes nearly brushing his cheeks.

"Might be better if you hear the news before you get to work," I said. "The police have arrested Alex. They plan to charge him with murder."

Did Tariq gasp? The traffic noise made it impossible to tell.

Off the highway, I worked my way toward First Ave. Tariq did not speak, his lips parted, eyes wide and unfocused.

"We're in luck." A bus drove away, and I slid to the curb, not worrying about the police cars parked in front of the Café. Tariq reached blindly for the door handle, and I put my hand on his arm. "Let me know if we can help."

He nodded and slammed the door, then reached back to touch Arf. He loped across the street and down the hill to the side door, the delivery entrance. Ops, the accountant, and the front of the house manager stood on the sidewalk. Some kitchen staff leaned against the stone wall; others milled nervously. Evicted, temporarily, while the cops did their thing.

Scott Glass, the Viking-bearded bar manager Alex called Scotty or Glassy, paused in his pacing long enough to notice me. He drew long and slow on the cigarette gripped between his thick fingers.

I pulled into traffic.

Not my circus, not my monkeys.

I spotted the job applicant the second Arf and I jogged in the shop's front door. My stumble down memory lane, combined with Mission Tariq, had made us late, and I'd splurged on a parking spot in the Market garage rather than run the Mustang home and dash back.

First clue: the leg warmers. Who wears leg warmers? Not even dancers, anymore.

Second clue: the schoolgirl skirt. The yellow, gray, and turquoise plaid did not remotely coordinate with the rainbow-striped leg warmers. She'd topped it with a pale yellow blouse sporting a Peter Pan collar and a navy jacket.

The Market is a magnet for free spirits.

Third clue: her kohl-eyed, openmouthed gape at the shelves crammed with round jars, square jars, and ancient painted tins full of culinary and aromatic treasures.

Alas, she did not glance at the door or me, suggesting retail instincts yet to be honed. But we could work on that.

We sat in the mixing nook. She "*loved*" our tea. She'd "*never tasted anything like it.*" Spices were "*so fascinating.*" She spoke in italics. I asked about her retail experience. The answer was hard to decipher, but seemed to boil down to a talent for thrift store shopping.

"What do you enjoy cooking?"

She caught her lower lip in her teeth. "Umm. I don't cook much."

Ah. That would be okay, if she conveyed the slightest interest in food. After all, that's what brings customers in. But she didn't.

I trotted out my standard questions. How would you respond if a customer interrupts while you're helping someone else? If they ask to use the bathroom? If you suspect a customer of shoplifting?

What's the difference between oregano and marjoram?

Actually, that question is less important than the others. I can teach spice knowledge. I can't teach patience or tact, though the willing student can learn. And I can't teach temperament.

She might have had it, but lacked the life experience to cope with the wildly unpredictable world of the Market. Every job has its quirks and quarrels, but let's just say every day down here is a full moon.

And, despite her avowals otherwise, I suspected she'd be a temporary hire. This sounded like fun, the pay was decent, and wouldn't it be cool to work in the Market? Maybe that was the best I could hope for. But what I wanted—needed—was a food lover fired up about foodie retail.

Or who at least took it seriously.

"I've got a few other people to talk with"—happily, the lie did not set my pants on fire—"before I make a decision. If you get another offer before you hear from me, give me a call."

She gushed her thanks before dashing out.

Retail: fun and easy, except when it's not.

Leg warmers.

Sandra was thrilled to get the baseball tickets. It's fun to treat your employees.

Hold on to that thought. I'm a big believer in reaching for the positive, no matter how minor, when it seems like the world is falling apart. Those tiny things keep us afloat.

An hour later, Sandra, Reed, and I clustered around the terminal for the new gift registry. The tech had taken us through its paces, showing us how to register hopeful giftees, create wish lists, and enter purchases. All that was missing was the software that would link the registry to our inventory system, triggering a memo to me when we had more requests for pepper mills than we had in stock.

To Reed, it was a shiny new electronic toy. To Sandra, a gadget she was both afraid to touch and eager to master, so she could help more customers. To me, dollars out and, my fervent wish, dollars in.

"Now all we need are brides," I said. Our ads in the spring bridal magazines would appear any day now. They'd cost a pretty penny—one more worry.

The front door opened and I turned, half expecting a vision in white beaded satin, trailed by her dazed-but-happy mother.

But no. Our consolation prize was the Dynamic Duo. Starsky and Hutch. Cagney and Lacey. Batman and Robin. Andy Griffith and Barney Fife.

Turner and Hooch.

I suppressed the urge to share my smart-assery—as I said, in my experience, homicide detectives aren't big on humor. Instead, I pasted on my bland-but-pleasant HR smile, anticipating more questions about my grim discovery at the building site.

You know what they say about assumptions.

So I nearly lost my socks—and my lunch—when Tracy slid a folded paper out of his inside jacket pocket.

"We have a warrant," he said. "For your sales records."

Whatever I might have expected, it wasn't that.

"Not all of them," Spencer said. I followed her wary gaze as she assessed the crowd, or lack thereof. "Quiet in here."

"Midafternoon on a wet Thursday barely into April. What records? And do I get to ask why?"

Tracy handed me the warrant.

"*Bhut capsicum?* You're joking, right? Who cares who bought ghost peppers? When you walked in, I expected more questions about—the body. Then I decided you wanted evidence related to Alex Howard, since you've arrested him." They exchanged looks, wondering how I knew, and I sent Tag a mental apology for squealing. "But you think—you think ghost chiles killed her?"

Their silent, impassive faces spoke volumes.

"I suppose it's possible, physiologically. But you'd need a ton of the stuff." The papers shook in my hand as I scanned the list: my purchases and sales, and the dates and amounts of all transactions. "It would take more than I've sold at any one time. Diners crave heat these days, but chefs don't keep a lot on hand. Peppers go off quickly."

No double entendre intended.

"What I mean is, we sell it dried, not fresh, right? With a dried spice, the balance of oils is critical. It can't be measured. The lighter volatile notes deteriorate faster than the darker or lower notes, and the flavors turn sharp and bitter. You'd think that wouldn't matter, with all the heat, but it does."

"I didn't know that," Spencer said.

"We can gather sales data for commercial accounts. But individuals buy the stuff, too, and we have no way to track that." I couldn't imagine someone buying an ounce at a time and hoarding it, pepper shopping like meth makers hopping from pharmacy to pharmacy snapping up Sudafed.

The crazy stuff people do.

"Read the damn warrant." Tracy was losing patience.

I read it once more, with feeling. They wanted more than sales info. They wanted my stock. *Holy patchouli.* I read on. They wanted all records of my sales to Alex Howard's company. My brows creased.

"Am I under suspicion?" Tracy ignored me. Spencer gave me the same bland smile I'd given her. "I'm guessing not, or you'd be conducting a broader search. And you wouldn't let Tag help search Alex's place."

Tracy's gaze sharpened to a point, and even Spencer looked a tad surprised.

"Well, you can have everything we've got on hand. Zak, would you—"

Spencer extended one hand, palm out in the universal stop sign, then pulled thin latex gloves out of her jacket pocket. "Mr. Davis, kindly direct us to the containers without touching them."

He glanced at me, and I nodded, then we watched the detectives bag and label my complete supply of *bhut capsicum*, aka *bhut C*. I wasn't worried about the loss—not a big seller, and we could get replacement stock in a few days.

But my insides squirmed at the thought that one of my customers might have used my product to kill another customer. That Alex might have used my peppers to kill Tamara.

And that he'd only known she was planning to leave because my employee had ratted her out.

I swallowed back vomit and poured myself tea. Gripping the cup stilled my shaking hands.

He would have discovered the truth eventually. He'd have been furious no matter when the news became public.

Listen to yourself. You think he did it. I forced myself to take a sip, to stop my internal shivers. It didn't work.

How would you kill with peppers? Force someone to breathe pepper dust or ingest them? Stick their head in a plastic bag full of ground particles? I pictured Tamara lying on the floor of her future restaurant. Her hands, her expression, all said she'd fought her attacker, but other than scuffed footprints, I'd seen no physical evidence of a struggle.

My meth lab comparison might not be too far off. If they'd found chile powder on Tamara's body, could the crime lab compare it to various supplies and determine the source stock? Of course, my competitors probably bought from the same importer as I did.

That smell. Had my nose fooled me? Not cinnamon, but ghost peppers?

Spencer noticed my furrowed brow. "Something you want to tell us?"

I shook my head slowly. "Reed and I will put the sales and purchase data together. Should take—how long?"

My youngest employee's hands trembled as he read the warrant. "Three hours?"

Spencer handed me a list. "Are we missing any spice merchants that you can tell?"

I read slowly. Were all my competitors getting the third degree, too? "No, but restaurants and retailers get their stock from all over the country. They don't necessarily buy local." Particularly true of ethnic restaurants. If you're buying your mango pickle from an importer in Los Angeles, you might get your cardamom pods there, too.

The door opened, and Mary Jean the Chocolatier charged in, clearly On A Mission. "Pepper, I just *love* your shop. Where did you find that old map? And that clock. Being on street level instead of hidden Down Under—" She stopped abruptly, as if realizing the couple standing next to me weren't ordinary customers.

Sandra to the rescue. I couldn't hear what she said, but Mary Jean stared at me and the detectives with a mix of surprise and awe. Eyes bulging, she nodded rapidly to Sandra, then scurried out the front door.

"We'll let you get back to business," Spencer said, her voice warm. "Your cooperation means a lot."

It meant staying late while Reed downloaded the info off our computer system, checking it, printing it, worrying over it. It might mean helping find Tamara's killer. And it might mean putting a man who'd been a loyal customer, if not a loyal friend, away for a long time.

Oh, Alex. Why can you never use your chefly discipline in the rest of your life?

"Don't forget," Tracy said, one hand smoothing the front of his jacket, tiny crumbs falling to the floor. "All the records, on time. Or there will be consequences."

Good cop, bad cop. The cliché lives.

My staff fell in beside me, like a row of suspects in a lineup, as we watched them leave.

"The world, she be a strange place," Sandra said.

"Thanks for running interference with the chocolatier. What did you tell her?"

"The truth. Sort of." She paused. I waited. "I told her the police regularly consult you on murder investigations."

That would set Market tongues wagging.

Eight

Don't look back. Something might be gaining on you.

— Satchel Paige, Hall of Fame pitcher

REED AND I WORKED WELL AFTER CLOSING UNTIL I SENT him home, his shaggy-on-purpose black hair tugged and tousled. More tedious than difficult, compiling the records required much finger twisting, cross-referencing, and screen shifting that left us both cramped and bleary-eyed.

A few restaurants keep late hours, but the Market was largely deserted when Arf and I emerged at half past seven. I needed food, and we both needed to stretch our legs, so we ambled down to the waterfront and Ivar's Fish Bar at Pier 54.

"Fish and chips," I told the man behind the counter.

I zipped up my jacket and tried not to worry. But I'd walked down here to think, and sometimes the line blurs.

Even on a coolish, dampish Thursday night in April, the waterfront hummed. Traffic sped by on Alaskan Way. Ferries chugged across the Sound—one blew its horn to signal "incoming," and a few minutes later, a dozen cars clanged off Pier 52 and disappeared into the city.

A pride of teenage boys leaned over the rail between Ivar's

and the ferry terminal, ogling the *Leschi*, the city's newest and shiniest fireboat. Good to see kids still dream of being firefighters and not just computer programmers. Although fire departments need IT whizzes, and computers catch fire, so there may be some crossover.

I carried my dinner to a table overlooking the water, the harbor with its giant orange cranes to the south. Arf sat beside me expectantly. "Good boy. Two chips. Here's the first." He took the potato in his mouth, then lowered himself as if to savor the treat, though I knew it was already sliding down his gullet.

I hadn't had a dog since kidhood, but the adjustment had been fairly easy. Sam, his former owner, had bounced between SROs—single room occupancy units—shelters, and the streets. Arf had been a faithful companion, always alert and on guard, but he'd relaxed a few notches since joining me in loft living.

While Sam had always kept him clean and well-groomed, regular meals of good-quality food had turned him from scrawny to healthy, and I had to keep track of the treats my Market neighbors offered. And limit the fries.

Sam had gone back to Memphis, and his sister had sent a Christmas package stuffed with jars of BBQ sauces, tins of hot spice rubs, and other Tennessee treats. Her card said he'd settled in well, the voices quieter lately, but that every time she suggested he consider another dog, Sam said there weren't no other dog for him.

I understood.

Somewhere in the depths of my tote, my phone chirped. I let it go to voice mail, enjoying the salt air on my cheeks and the hot cod melting in my mouth. Alex's arrest must have been announced in time to lead off the six o'clock news. Kristen had called me at five after six and every five minutes thereafter until I texted her back, saying, *I know—I'm okay—working late—tell you more tomorrow.* Laurel had shown more reserve, calling once to say she'd heard, call her if I needed to talk, and what a relief it must be to Tamara's family to have a suspect in custody.

Tamara. I knew nothing about her family or friends. She and I had only met a few times. She'd served me a bowl of curried clams, perfectly spiced, when I made a delivery during family meal, when the staff eats. She'd come into the shop with Alex around Christmastime, and I'd thought of her as his human shield—an excuse to deflect personal conversation while he browsed, brainstorming new combinations.

And then, two days ago.

Egad. That had only been two days.

What else did I know about her? Ambitious. Single, I suspected—no wedding rings and no mention of a husband or kids. Was a cat prowling an empty apartment at this moment, hungry and afraid?

Alex had been furious with her, and with me. But who else might have done the deed? Not to blame the victim, but if you'd ticked one person off enough to kill you, you might have made others mad, too.

I sipped my Coke and stroked Arf's head. Fought off the rumble rising in my chest, the dizzying feel of being back in the construction site, her body stretched out before me. That sensation of fear after the fact.

And then, a wave of relief that I'd ended my involvement with Alex. Because it seemed clear that no woman's influence could have stopped him from acting out his rage, the deep sense of betrayal that Tamara's departure triggered. Or had it been her failure to confide in him that set him off?

I poked at the corner of my eye. Breathed out long and slow. Slipped the dog another chip.

"We're okay now, aren't we, Arf?"

We finished our dinner on Ivar's deck, the salty, green smell of the water and its undertones of diesel mingling with the scents of hot oil and fish. The Coke bubbles tickled my nose, and the cod tickled my tummy. The dog let out a noisy sigh and leaned against my leg.

We were okay.

I kicked off my shoes and hung my jacket on the coat tree inside my door. Plopped my tote on the table behind the couch. Arf sauntered over to the wall of windows and tucked himself into his bed. (Lucky dog—beds everywhere he goes.)

Me, I poured a glass of the Sangiovese Laurel hadn't finished last night and curled up on the soft caramel couch. My book was on my nightstand, so I reached for the latest issue of *Saveur*, then remembered the phone messages. Stretched for my tote, half falling off the couch in the process.

And I'd barely touched my wine.

I remedied that problem, then leaned into the big cushions and studied the little screen. A few messages and texts that could wait till tomorrow. A reply text from Kristen, telling me to watch the news.

The last call had come from an unknown name and number. I frowned and punched the button to listen.

My blood froze. Alex, an edge of anxiety in his voice. "Pepper, you've heard the news. They've thrown me in the slammer. I need your help. I know that sounds crazy, after the way I blew up at you. But I'm innocent."

Innocent was the last thing Alex Howard was. Not guilty of murder, maybe, but hardly innocent.

He rushed on. "I saw what you did last fall, when everyone else was convinced the wrong person was guilty as sin. Gotta go. Visiting hours Friday morning, Pepper. Please."

A magic word from the mouth of a difficult man. I tossed the phone aside, refilled my wineglass, and dug for the remote in the basket on my packing crate coffee table. I so rarely watch TV news that I didn't remember which channel showed who when.

The TV—a smallish flat screen—hangs above the gas fireplace in the corner of the living room, making it visible from everywhere in the loft except the bathroom and the far back of the kitchen. Local news hasn't been the same since Jean Enersen retired. First female TV anchor in the country, she'd led the nightly reports since the year I was born. This new guy might be fine, but he isn't Jean.

"Tonight, we bring you news of an unexpected arrest. Tamara Langston, sous chef at the famed First Avenue Café, was found dead Wednesday evening at the site of a new restaurant she planned to open on Lower Queen Anne." The screen switched from a talking head to footage of EMTs carrying Tamara's body out of the construction site. I hadn't noticed the cameras or reporters. "Police initially refused to state how she died or whether foul play was suspected. This afternoon, they made an arrest."

The cameras shifted to Alex, hands cuffed in front of him, being led out the side door of his building. I sank onto the couch, clutching the remote. "Alex Howard, a nationally renowned chef and owner of several of the city's best-known eateries, was arrested outside his headquarters in downtown Seattle. A police department spokesman says he will be charged with first-degree murder in Langston's death, but was unable to provide details on the murder or the cause of death. More as this story develops."

In the background, I glimpsed Scott Glass and a few other employees.

"Holy moly." Arf lifted his head at the sound. "It's okay, boy."

It was most definitely not okay.

I lowered the volume, letting images of a bus accident on I-405, a mayoral press conference, and a flooded storm drain in West Seattle roll by. Sipped my wine, the deep, fruity notes leaving a slightly tannic taste on my tongue and throat.

Why ask me for help? Because of what I'd done last fall,

he'd said, when I forced my help on a person who hadn't wanted it. I'd been a bit of a terrier, convinced police had it wrong.

And I'd been right. Naturally, Detective Tracy considered my actions intentional interference with an official investigation. That he still had to hold his nose to look at me made Sandra's wisecrack to the chocolatier about him "consulting" me particularly rich.

I knew what Tag would say about Alex's plea, and not just because he dislikes on principle anyone romantically interested in me. Kristen, too—she was always polite when Alex came in, but she has no patience for anyone who hurts her friends.

Laurel, for all her sympathy for the victim, champions justice for the wrongly accused as well. She's never been keen on Alex, but I could almost hear her advice: "What matters is what *you* believe, Pepper. Is he calling on you for the right reasons? Or is he lying to you?"

Lying, or using me? I had no sway with the police, despite what he believed.

Truth was, I didn't know why he'd called. Desperation? For some reason, he trusted me—though I did not trust him. But a liar isn't necessarily a killer. Thank goodness. Because we all lie a little.

He'd lied a lot.

I needed to know who'd killed Tamara. Because I found her and that linked us forever. And if she had been killed with my peppers, I had to know who and why.

Could I dig around without being committed to Alex's cause? Assuage my own guilt while probing his?

Arf made a moaning noise in his sleep, his front paws scrabbling the canvas bedcover, one leg kicking out behind him.

"It's okay, boy," I said in a reassuring tone, not knowing whether it was or not. Because who knows what dogs dream of?

Nine

Sugar and spice and everything nice,
That's what little girls are made of.

—19th-century nursery rhyme

I DELETED THE FIRST THREE MESSAGES ON THE SHOP phone Friday morning. No, I did not want to "share my story" with the NBC affiliate, nor the ABC station, nor the CBS channel.

But my finger hesitated when I heard the fourth message. "Pepper, it's Ben Bradley. I just heard you found the chef's body in the restaurant. I'm so sorry—that must have been awful. I hope it's not presumptuous, but if there's any chance you'd like to talk about it, for the paper, please give me a call."

"Please," he'd said. "The magic word," my father had called it when we were kids. Alex had used it, too, last night. I'm a sucker for the word "please."

Later. After I make up my mind how involved I'm going to get. Because even the magic word has its limits.

I hopped a bus to the jail and breezed through the security line. I'd made enough trips here last fall to know the routine.

Nobody looks good in felony red. It's a peculiar shade,

designed to clash with every skin tone. On Alex, with his olive complexion and morning-after-arrest stubble, it reminded me of those dried pepper garlands people bring back from vacation in Mexico and hang in their kitchen, then forget to use or dust.

"I spent two hours explaining myself to high-priced lawyers who claim they believe I'm innocent, but they sure as hell don't act like it," he said, his voice low, worried but seductive. His knuckles were white as he gripped the phone, his dark eyes boring through the Plexiglas between us.

I had not stayed up late. I had left the restless dreams to my sweet dog. It had only taken me two glasses of wine and three slices of brie on seasoned flatbread crackers to convince myself that I could guard against manipulation. That I could use helping Alex as an excuse to dig up info to help me find Tamara's killer. That I could draw lines in the sand and solve my problems. If I helped free him or jail him, I could live with either outcome.

Drawing those lines wasn't so easy, sitting here before him. But I had one distinct advantage: I could walk out anytime.

"So here's the deal. You have to be honest. One hint that you're lying to me, that you're whitewashing the teeniest detail, and I will not come back. I won't lie for you, and I won't withhold the truth."

He glared at the ultimatum. His jaw tightened almost imperceptibly, then he nodded once.

"Tell me what happened," I said.

"Nothing." He sensed my sternness and backed down. "Okay. Tuesday, when I found out that Tamara was planning to leave, I was upset, I admit. Partly at her—after all the opportunities I gave her, she buddies up to my chief competitor to open a joint in a neighborhood she knew I had eyes on."

Alex owned four or five restaurants, but I'd had no idea he wanted a foothold near the Center.

"You should have seen it coming. She was young, talented, ambitious."

"You know me, Pepper. I blow up, but it blows over." He waved his free hand in the air, the burn scar inside his right wrist a ragged ribbon. "We agreed it would be best for her to leave right away, to focus on her new venture."

She agreed? That surprised me. The new place was weeks from needing her full-time—and giving her a paycheck. Tamara hadn't seemed ready to cut the cord.

But he might have used the opportunity to corral the rest of his crew, to squelch any ideas they might have about leaving. To prevent poaching.

"So who'll take her spot? Tariq?"

Alex snorted. "He's not ready. An exec from another joint will step in until I decide who should do what."

"Alex, you've got to give your full attention to your defense. You can't be thinking about pots and pans while you're in here."

Prison jumpsuits aren't designed for restless men. The buttons strained their holes as Alex's chest swelled in anger spiked with frustration and anxiety, his face pinched in humiliation over the loss of control.

"I am still Alex Howard."

And that was the gist of the problem. No matter how much he begged me to be his eyes and ears on the streets of Seattle, he would never fully trust me—or anyone else. I sympathized with his lawyers.

"Who were her friends? She have enemies? Where did she live, with whom?"

"We were her family."

"Who else?"

He didn't know. Or wouldn't say. Alex was the kind of boss who managed to learn everything he wanted to know, in and out of the restaurant, one way or another. One more reason Tamara's plans pissed him off: His intelligence network had failed him.

"Ops can tell you where she lived. Fremont or Wallingford?"

"I found her right after six. Tell me where you were all afternoon."

He tried to lean back in the plastic chair, but the intercom's metal phone cord jerked him up short. "Got to the restaurant early afternoon. Can't say exactly when."

"And before that?"

He glared. I glared. He deflated, dignity melting like butter in a hot pan, then glanced over his shoulder to make sure no one heard. He leaned forward and spoke in a low simmer.

"Okay, I admit, I followed her. But Pepper, you can't tell them that. They'll think for sure I did it."

I wanted to strangle him. I strangled the receiver instead. "To her new restaurant? Why? To try to stop her from leaving?"

"No." His eyebrows narrowed and his mouth opened in protest. "Danielle turns everything into gold. If I'm going to stay a major player, and compete with my own trainees, I need the details of every new joint."

"You check up on every rumor you hear?"

"If it's somebody doing something interesting, or that might cut into our business, yeah."

"What time?"

"Two o'clock? Two thirty? Last thing I did before I went to the restaurant."

Where scads of people had seen him. People who depend on him for their paycheck and might not tell me if they'd seen him step out. I needed to confirm his whereabouts and find out when Tamara had spoken to Danielle. That call narrowed the window for time of death.

"How—how did she die?" he asked, his voice breaking.

"I'd be guessing," I said, fudging a pinch, "so I don't think I should tell you."

"Tell me she didn't suffer."

I'd read somewhere that death is rarely truly instantaneous. My face betrayed me. He bent over, head to his knees, his hands in fists.

"Alex," I said a few moments later. "Time's nearly up. Do you know when you're scheduled for a bail hearing?"

He raised his head slowly, eyes red and wet. "They say sometime next week, but I told them to light a fire under the judge. They can take my passport. I've got people to feed."

"You honestly think people will come to your restaurant, once they hear?"

"You watch. They'll be lined up down the block. Hey, I know it sounds callous, but if I don't get back to work soon, I'll go nuts." He stretched out his hand. "Pepper, thanks. I knew I could count on you to be my friend."

Friends. A little word that covers a lot of ground.

THE morning mist had turned to drizzle while I was inside. I pulled up my collar and slipped the hood over my spiky hair. One more advantage to the do: It's practically waterproof.

The hood—and the rain—put me in a monkish mood. What would Cadfael do? Retreat to his workshop where he'd light a brazier to warm his thick hands and a cup of mulled wine, and then he'd ponder.

Too early for wine, but not for the modern substitute, a nonfat, double-shot latte. I ducked into a coffee shop overflowing with old-world ambiance: wood counters mellowed by time and elbows, a vintage chandelier, and coffee-themed clutter. And a mural of a half-robed goddess gifting humanity with that blessed bounty, *Coffea*.

Go forth and multiply.

The hiss and hum of espresso and steamed milk made good background music for contemplation. Fascinating to see a powerful, sexy man out of his element, deprived of the command and control that define him.

No matter what, we were not getting involved romantically. His longing look, the outstretched hand—they were natural reactions to stress, to confinement in a place so lacking in the human touch.

He'd promised to be straight with me. I wasn't convinced he knew how. I'd have to stay alert, keep all my wits about me.

Besides, I had a spoon in this pot of stew. If Tamara had been killed with chiles, they could have been mine. The sample I'd given her was too small to cause harm, but Alex had bought them from me for ages. So had dozens of other chefs and commercial food producers. I'd scanned the sales records we'd compiled for the detectives, but no names jumped out at me. I'd need to cross-reference the list with Tamara's own contacts.

Or I could leave that task to Spencer and Tracy, who had resources I lacked.

One thing I knew for sure: If my shop and I had any involvement, no matter how inadvertent, no one would work harder to absolve and protect us than I. Detective Tracy had assured me last fall that the cops don't want to blame innocent people—and I believe him; I was married to one for thirteen years—but they don't always mind if we get knocked over and stomped on in the chase.

And I owed it to my employees to keep the shop alive and well. Except for Kristen, they needed these jobs, and they loved the place as much as I did. It had been my saving grace after the year from hell—when my marriage fell apart and my job disappeared, collateral damage when the law firm where I'd worked for more than a decade dissolved in a scandal of embezzlement, court-ordered sanctions, and criminal charges.

I owed it to the shop itself, and to the Market. Jane had seized the opportunity to create the shop when the Market was in crisis. More than a few businesses started back then had since disappeared, victims of changing times and a changing city. The Spice Shop had hung on, despite growing competition. Unlike the few bad apples at the law firm who'd taken the rest of us down with them, I believe a thriving business is a trust. We owe its success to our customers and employees, and to the community that embraces us.

People who meet me for the first time assume I'm named for my job. My grandfather gave me the nickname nearly forty years ago, but I take the coincidence as proof that I was meant to run the place. That it was entrusted to me.

So I would take the case, such as it was. For Alex and Tamara, for myself and the shop. In the spirit of Cadfael and Sister Frevisse.

I opened the door, paper cup in hand, and instantly stepped back. But sometimes even an instant is too long.

Street cops are like grade school teachers. Eyes in the back of their heads. Olerud, Tag's partner, braked his bike on the corner of First and Cherry, while Tag circled round in the street and stopped. The drizzle didn't seem to faze him.

No point standing inside pretending I wasn't about to leave or that I hadn't seen him spot me. The sooner I talked to him, the sooner I could get on with—whatever.

"Thanks for the Mariners tickets," I said. "They had a great time, despite the loss."

"Damn Yankees," he said.

Also like your third grade teacher, cops can make you squirm by their presence. Like you have to 'fess up, even if you weren't about to throw a spitball. If kids still throw spitballs.

"Needed a warm-up on my way to the mystery bookshop. Slow morning, so I snuck out."

He eyed me skeptically. "Thought you had a big project—records to compile for that warrant."

"Don't you treat me like a suspect, Thomas Allen Buhner." I am one of the few people who know his real name. But then, he knows mine.

He had the grace—or sense—to color. That was confession enough for me. I did my best to stay steady on the slick, steep sidewalk as I sashayed twenty feet downhill to the bookshop.

"Give me the next in the series," I told Jen. "And tell me when he's gone."

She shot a glance out the window, grinned, and headed for the historicals, talking as she went. "Ever notice how many deaths in the Middle Ages were by poison? Glad that's out of favor. These days, our criminals just shoot each other." She stepped behind the counter to ring up my purchase. "I sent you a job prospect, by the way."

"Thanks. I'd rather hire you."

"No dice." The phone started ringing. She handed me the book and spoke before picking up the receiver. "Coast is clear."

The Outlaw's Tale tucked in my tote, I scooted across the street to Fabiola's building, a solid redbrick and limestone structure built after the Great Fire of 1889 destroyed twenty-nine square city blocks of wooden buildings. When disaster struck again, in the form of the 2001 Nisqually earthquake that damaged dozens of downtown buildings beyond repair, she and a squadron of other dislocated artists had settled here.

And though I hadn't planned on popping in to see her, we had a sign issue to work out.

Some women wear their mood on their faces. Fabiola's outfit gave her away. Her dark hair, threaded with glitter extensions that looked like Christmas tinsel, hung loose, and if it had been combed today, she'd tugged away all evidence. Her white menswear shirt was misbuttoned, and one leg of her boyfriend jeans had come uncuffed.

Worse, no heels in sight and her flamingo pink toenail polish was chipped.

"I've lost clients before," she said, staring at me from her wheeled metal stool, "but not like this."

Sketches for a logo, a draft menu, even a mock-up of a cocktail coaster for Tamarack lay scattered across her white worktable. "Oh, Fabe. I didn't know you knew her."

Her hands flew to her cheeks as if of their own accord. "Pepper, I'm an idiot. Whining to you, when you found her."

"It's okay," I said. Not the discovery—that would always haunt me—but that Fabiola's emotions were so raw that she hadn't considered mine.

"I do Danielle's graphics, so she sent Tamara to me." Her long fingers fanned out over the designs. "She wanted a tree—not exactly hip, but I came up with this great leaf shape. Then I discovered tamaracks have light green needles. I remembered that found object artist you introduced me to last fall, and tried a tree made of forks. We were refining it when . . ."

I hooked a foot around the leg of an empty stool, rolled it toward me, and sat. "Wonder why she didn't take her idea to Alex and suggest a new restaurant within his empire."

"You said it: his empire. Any restaurant he had a piece of would always be his."

"Tell me about her."

"Gutsy. Determined. Incredibly passionate about food. She'd been planning her own place for a long time, and she knew what she wanted, but not how to bring it to life on paper. Working with her was kinda like working with you—lots of trial and error until it clicked, and then watch out." She threw her hands in the air like a geyser.

"Commission said no to my sign. No saltshaker shapes, no lights."

"Oh geez." The Fabiola geyser sank back into the earth. "I'm about out of ideas."

And in a week of strange things, that was the strangest of all.

Ten

L'arzento va dove e il piper. (*Silver goes where the pepper is.*)

—Piero Zen, Venetian ambassador to Constantinople,
1530, quoted in Charles Corn,
The Scents of Eden: A History of the Spice Trade

I STROLLED UP FIRST AVE, DRINKING IN THE RAIN-RINSED air and midmorning calm. Fabiola had gleaned few details about Tamara's personal life. Their friendship had been too new. But the pain of loss does not run a logical course, and the effect of the murder on Fabiola made me more determined to find the killer. Not just to save my good name, but for Tamara. For justice.

How did one kill with ghost peppers? Who would ever conjure up such a thing? I mean, I sell them, I pack them—I know the pain. Intentionally inflict it on someone else? Never.

I wrapped my arms around myself. Poor Tamara, dead so young. Her dream so close, destroyed.

Is there anything more inspiring than a passionate woman? A woman who throws heart, mind, and body into everything she does, whether it's Fabiola with her brilliant designs and crazy outfits, or the contemplative and fictional Sister Frevisse cocooned in her woolens and wimple. Seems to me the world needs more women like that. Too often, it squelches them.

Or outright kills them.

Half a block from the Market entrance at Pike, inspiration struck, and I stayed the course on First.

Even in my brief time in the spice biz, I'd witnessed fads and trends. Medicinal queries and purchases had exploded. While I don't mind selling turmeric in bulk to a woman I suspect is using it for her blood pressure and not her curry, I send customers seeking medical advice to Ron Locke or the herb-and-incense shop in the Economy Market.

Another trend: more African and Indian spices. It's gratifying when immigrant customers believe we've got the freshest, highest quality ingredients for their ethnic dishes, like the Lebanese chef at the Middle Eastern restaurant on the Hillclimb who buys his sumac and Aleppo pepper from me. (After the incident last fall, he offered me free falafel for life. It's a sin to refuse generosity, so I begged him for the recipe instead.)

On one of her recent forays into Seattle, Jane had eyed the jars we'd added since my takeover. "Used to be I sold more cinnamon, vanilla, and oregano than anything else. Kosher salt was exotic. Now it's pink salt, truffle salt, flake salt. And all the peppers—the hotter, the better." She was right about that. Foodies talk about Scoville units like they get what that means. Heck, even I barely know.

But I know ghost peppers burn up the charts. So who had mustered the creative cruelty needed to kill with them?

"Five minutes. I promise." I held up my hand, fingers extended. Dr. Ron Locke's clinic manager rolled her eyes and pointed toward his office. When my employee Reed's dad, a veteran acupuncturist and font of arcane medical knowledge, gets going, five minutes easily becomes ten or twenty, leaving his staff to placate impatient patients.

Across the book-and-paper-strewn desk, Ron raised his

eyebrows at my questions, but his expression quickly turned serious. "This is about the customer you found. So sorry, Pepper."

I described what I'd seen at the building site. Ron swiveled his chair toward a bookcase and hooked one brown forefinger on the gold-lettered spine of a fat blue volume. *Flip, flip, flip.* "Could make a powder into an aerosol for ease of delivery," he mused.

"Like bear spray."

"Exactly. That would cause temporary blinding, or chemical burns. You said no visible injuries, but her eyes were swollen and she'd been reaching out."

Or clawing for air.

Flip, flip, flip. "There's a kind of mushroom that expands when ground," he said. "Maybe the peppers emit a toxic substance when they're cut."

"No. Alex and I chopped a few dried peppers and extracted the capsicum in oil. The pieces softened as they rehydrated—or re-oiledrated—but nothing happened when we chopped them."

He held one finger in the air, putting me on pause, while the other raced down the page. Then he snapped the book shut. "My best guess is the autopsy revealed an inflammatory response in the lungs, sending the ME searching for other evidence that a hostile substance had entered the lungs. They may have found residue in her throat and lungs. Or particles trapped in the nose hairs—their function is to filter the air we breathe. Then they examined those particles by microscope and determined they were capsicum of some sort."

"How could they tell it's the ghost pepper?"

"I doubt they'd have a plant DNA analysis completed already, so it may be an educated guess. They'd ask what kind of capsicum would trigger an immediate immune response, severe enough to kill. Fluid fills up the lungs. It's essentially asphyxiation."

Uggh. Maybe I wouldn't replenish my stock after all.

And I certainly wasn't going to eat hot Thai curry anytime soon.

At the sound of my footsteps entering the shop, Arf barked once—a rare sound, the canine equivalent of "Where have you been? I missed you." I crouched behind the counter, giving him a good rub and an air-kiss. The employees take charge of him in my absence, and he's as fond of them as they are of him, but he clearly considers me his best bud. Besides, dogs have their needy moments, too.

"I could never work here." A chubby black woman with flawless skin pointed to the HIRING sign. "Just walking in makes me hungry."

"Occupational hazard," I admitted. One more reason to run around chasing a killer—exercise.

"But my sister would love it. And she's looking."

I handed her my card.

Kristen emerged from the back room, her nose turned up in distaste. "I've called everywhere. No replacement samovar."

"So we buy a big stainless coffee urn and fake it."

She fixed me a determined glare. "I am not giving up."

I sent Reed off to make a copy of the sales records we'd compiled, and retreated to the office to review the payroll and sign checks. Slipped Lynette's into an envelope. Hesitated, then added a note card sporting the shop's saltshaker logo. *Thank you for your work. Wishing you all the best in your future endeavors.* Better a boring cliché than a glowing fib—you never know what a disgruntled ex-employee will tell the unemployment office.

Losing Zak, on the other hand, set off a good pout. No one else on staff is tall enough to dust the chandeliers, even with the rolling ladder.

Time for a task I'd put off long enough. Over a day-old croissant and a bruised banana lunch—easy on the tummy, a little unsettled after Ron's hypothesis of death by *bhut C*—I studied the shop's tax return. Decent numbers. No room for emergencies—or for a staffing screwup. Your average employee doesn't have a clue about the costs of hiring. Hard costs like advertising, fees to headhunters and job services, expenses for uniforms and equipment. But the biggie is the cost of time and stress. All those hours recruiting, interviewing, and training. The time the rest of your staff spends picking up the slack and helping the newbie get up to speed.

And in my shop, wasted product when she measures out blue poppy seed instead of white or fenugreek when the customer wanted fennel. Staff take mistakes home, but it's money lost.

I still steam at the memory of the legal secretary who accepted the law firm opening I'd offered her only to quit a week later when the local FBI office made her the offer she'd been waiting for. When the personnel specialist called for a reference a week after she'd left me in the lurch, I answered the standard question "Would you rehire?" honestly.

Or as honestly as I could without swearing.

After a string of support staff mishaps, the law firm administrator had brought in a consultant to help us improve hiring and retention. One presentation focused on first impressions, teaching "Seven Ways to Make Those Seven Seconds Count." So at one fifty-seven that afternoon, when I was cleaning up a spill by the tea cart and Jen's applicant walked in for our two o'clock interview, I adjusted my attitude, straightened my posture, smiled, practiced my eyebrow flash, and leaned forward, extending my hand.

That's six, I know. You can't accomplish the seventh step—making eye contact—alone.

And she wasn't having it. We'd been taught to improve our eye contact by making a habit of noticing the eye color of everyone we meet. Eyelids lowered, she touched my fingers lightly, as though my hygiene wasn't up to snuff. Mud brown, I finally decided as we finished our brief tour of the shop and settled into the nook for a chat.

You can't just say, "I don't think this is the job for you." It's bad karma. Plus they might surprise you.

Not this woman. She brushed sugar—or spice—off the bench before smoothing her pencil skirt and sitting, her spine not touching the seat back. Unusual posture for a woman not yet thirty. She ignored the tea Reed placed in front of her and trained her eyes on the table, barely moving a facial muscle as she answered my questions. She asked none of her own. An interview ought to be a conversation—about the business, the job duties, the applicant's experience and her goals. There's a certain degree of puffing involved, both interviewer and interviewee emphasizing the upside. If you've developed a reasonable amount of emotional intuition, though, you'll learn what you need to know. You may not find out that she's a single mother with dicey childcare—the law says you don't get to ask. She may not discover that you've had a revolving door the last few months; it's none of her business. But you get a feeling.

"So, tell me what you like to cook," I said. "Your favorite recipes."

"Is that—a *dog*?"

I followed her shell-shocked gaze to the front counter, where a furry brown snout poked out.

She grabbed her bag—black patent leather in a style the Queen might carry; it matched her low-heeled sling-backs—and slid out of the booth like a greased pig.

"She might be allergic," Reed said as she disappeared out the front door.

"Or going on an interview to prove she's job hunting so she can keep her unemployment benefits." I sighed and sent the Universe a silent prayer. *One great candidate and I'll be happy. Two would be ideal, but I'll count my blessings if you'll please pretty please send me one perfect employee.*

Hey, how will the Powers That Be know what you want if you don't tell them?

LIKE most Seattleites, I'd had little reason to explore the halls of the new SPD HQ. Tag worked patrol most of our time together, based in the West Precinct that runs from SoDo and the International District north to Queen Anne Hill. Not that HQ is all that new anymore—ten years maybe, a super-eco-green building, both modern sleek and a good fit with its historic neighbors.

I passed through security and reclaimed my bag, pleased that the computer system Reed and I had worked hard to implement had made the shop records so easy to compile.

But I am the daughter of activists—a Vietnam vet turned dove and a hippie chick who'd been arrested a dozen times or more at marches, protests, and sit-ins. Our house mantra had been "Question authority."

My folks had raised their eyebrows when I married a cop. But they'd accepted Tag, who was a bit of an anomaly in his own well-heeled, suburban family. And they'd been quietly relieved when I left him.

Their voices murmured in my head. Should I be so quick to hand over my records?

Yes, I decided. The cops had a warrant. I had no legal grounds to withhold my customers' identities from the police. And if it helped flush out a killer . . .

But I could at least insist on getting something in exchange.

"This is everything?" Tracy said a few minutes later in the homicide detectives' office. He flipped through the half-inch stack of records like a ten-cent garage sale paperback that might give him cooties.

"I brought you everything that warrant asks for. Look, I know you and Tag don't like each other. But I've never given you any reason to distrust me."

Tracy's eyes, so dark the pupils nearly merged with the irises, bore into me. Wherever Spencer was, I missed her.

"Is that true now, Mrs. Buhner? Oh, that's right, you prefer Ms. Reece."

My cheeks burned. I hadn't told him everything I knew last fall as soon as I knew it. But eventually, I'd spilled it all—including a few details he should have rooted out for himself without an amateur's help. Apparently the insult still rankled.

"And of course," he said, as if about to pronounce a truth universally acknowledged, "there is the matter of your judgment. A food expert with such questionable taste . . ."

His words trailed off but left no doubt that he was referring not to my taste in food but to my taste in men. To Tag, and Alex.

"I've given you all the information you asked for. And if you think I sold the murder weapon"—using the term loosely—"don't you think you should tell me more about what happened? Who might have wanted to kill Tamara?"

"Besides your ex-boyfriend? No, I don't think we need to tell you anything, Ms. Reece. You didn't kill her. You don't have any stake in this."

How did they know that? Police aren't fans of the obvious conclusions the rest of us draw every day. (Arguing with a cop or a lawyer can be so frustrating. They cross-examine you and demand your "evidence.") Then it dawned on me. "You've already investigated me."

He smiled, eyelids lowered partway, deciding what I deserved to know. "Your employees confirm you were in your shop all afternoon. Surveillance cameras from the ATM up the block show you park your Mustang and start down the street. Barely a minute later, you called 911. Killers don't normally call us."

The temperature in the room seemed to plummet. "You saw the killer? On the video?"

His expression turned bitter, one of the five primary tastes. But he wasn't going to tell me what the video showed. He thwacked my sales records with his fingers. "We'll go over these with a fine-tooth comb."

As I walked back to the front entry, the chill seeped deeper into my bones. Had the killer been hiding in Tamarack while I was up front? Had I barely escaped being his next victim, before he—or she—escaped out the back?

You don't have any stake in this, Tracy had said. Maybe he believed that. But to me, it looked like someone was doing his—or her—best to make this crime very personal.

Eleven

❧

Though early European spice traders faced scurvy and dysentery, head hunters and cannibals, dervish winds and razor-sharp reefs, the rewards were so enticing that they often exaggerated the perils to deter interlopers flying the flags of rival nations.

IF HE ANSWERED HIS PHONE, THE STORY WAS HIS.

No such luck. I hung up before Mr. Ben Reporter's voice mail finished telling me to leave a message. I believe in the right to change my mind.

I stopped for the light at Fourth and Marion, where my old office building faces off with the city library. The tall black box from 1969 still looks elegant, if no longer modern, and *Vertebrae*, the giant Henry Moore bronze out front, is one of my favorite outdoor sculptures. Across the street sits the library. Some days, I adore its angled glass and steel mesh; other days, it looks like a cross between a mushroom and a UFO built out of Legos.

Today was a Lego day. Though the problem might be my own skewed perspective. Going to jail messes with the mind.

Aack—why didn't I think of her first? The brainstorm sent

me digging for the phone I'd already tossed back into my tote. A minute later, somewhere on the forty-second floor, the best legal researcher I knew answered.

"Got a project for you, about Alex Howard and the body I found."

A sixtyish woman in a pale gray raincoat shot me a nervous glance and edged away. I gave her the sweetest smile I could manage while talking murder. The light changed, and I let her race ahead of me before crossing the street and angling up the wide plaza steps to Ripe.

Callie joined me quicker than you could say, "Fig and prosciutto panino, please."

Laurel serves a coffee blend so rich and creamy it nearly makes me swoon. We carried our mugs to a corner table for a good huddle.

"Alex Howard," Callie said with a note of skepticism. "I thought you guys broke up."

"He's a son of a gumbo. But I don't believe he killed her. And I'm not doing this to save his neck." I took a sip, letting the hot liquid cool on my tongue. "They won't confirm the manner of death, but it's obvious they suspect death by *bhut capsicum*. Ghost chile. That puts me right in the thick of this—because he bought his supply from me."

Callie stared, one blunt-fingered hand flat against her chest. "Who else had access to—what did you call it, boot cap—?"

"*Bhut capsicum* is the botanical name. Less commonly called *bhut jolokia*. *Bhut C*, for short."

"So who else with access might have wanted her dead?"

"That's the question. Dig up everything you can on Tamara." The secret to investigation, I'd learned, is to start with the victim. Callie knew all the public databases and had subscriptions to a few private services. Everything she did would be legal and aboveboard. No hacking, no misrepresentation.

"You two can't be up to any good." Laurel slid our plates

onto the table and pulled up a chair. My sandwich came with her popular arugula, fennel, and cucumber salad. Nestled alongside the lovely spring greens and sliced fennel drizzled in a lemony mustard vinaigrette lay a single hot pepper.

I picked it up by the tip of the tail, like a dead mouse, and set it on the edge of Callie's plate. She burst out laughing and so did I. Before Laurel could demand an explanation, an employee called her name. She scooted back her chair and left, shaking her head.

I wiped the corner of my eye with a knuckle—even mild peppers can set those tender tissues on fire—and picked up my sandwich, blessedly still warm. The contrast between salt and sweet, creamy cheese and crunchy grilled bread sang in my mouth like a heavenly choir.

After the law firm fiasco had left us both temporarily unemployed, Callie signed on with a few good lawyers who'd been as shocked as the rest of us but quickly formed their own partnership. The part-time job left her more time to spend with her five-year-old, an adventuresome little guy—I'd helped her out once when he fed gravel through an antique nutmeg grinder in an attempt to make sand.

"What a bizarre way to kill," she said. "Do you think he planned it? He whoever—not necessarily Alex."

"That's been bothering me. I gave her a tiny sample, too small to do lasting harm. I can't think why she would have had it with her—the space was weeks from ready to stock. And no one walks around with a big bag of hot chile powder without a reason."

Ever the librarian, Callie made a few notes. "So you're looking for—?"

I sat back, licking a drop of cheese from my thumb before ticking items off on my fingers. "Addresses, employment history. Friends, relatives."

"Litigation," she added. "Collections actions, criminal history." Callie had taught the firm's legal assistants how to research, and they spent hours compiling dossiers from online and paper records for plaintiffs, defendants, witnesses, even potential jurors.

"Business licenses, building permit apps, health department records," I said. "The restaurant name is Tamarack, but I don't know the corporate name."

Would Danielle find a new chef and move forward, or drop the plans and leave the building, partially finished, for the next tenant? It already had a bad rep. Who would have enough ice in their veins to open a restaurant in a space where a woman had been killed?

"And property records," I continued. "Though I doubt she owned much—most young single chefs don't."

"Are we sure she's single?"

"No. No wedding ring, but in her line of work that's no proof. Stick with Washington for now. If we find a trail leading her here from another state, we can expand the search. And this time, I'm paying you, so track your hours. No arguments." I grabbed the check.

"No dice. But you can comp me a new pepper mill."

We gazed lovingly at the pastry case on our way out, and I vowed to give her a baking book she drooled over on every visit to the shop, aptly titled *Sugar Rush*.

Because we all need an extra dose of sweetness now and then.

ON my way into the Market, I paused at the corner newsstand to scan the headlines.

The daily paper led with the same image the TV cameras had used last night. CHEF ARRESTED IN EMPLOYEE MURDER. It wouldn't be long before the more tabloidal rags sprouted the puns: CHOPPED CHEF; MURDER ON THE MENU; ALEX IN CHAINS, a play on the name of one of Seattle's most popular grunge bands. I'd seen them in the early '90s in the Belltown club now home to Café Frida and Diego's Lounge, where Zak's band regularly takes the stage.

I bought a copy and headed down Pike, reading as I walked. Two paragraphs in, I stopped in my tracks.

"Sorry," I muttered to the man who'd bumped into me.

"Hello, Miz Pepper. How are you this fine day?"

No hint of the South in Jim's rusty voice, but he'd adopted Sam's habitual name for me. Jim and his sidekick, Hot Dog, a fortyish former boxer with a dicky heart, flanked me now. Since Sam's return to Memphis, they'd stopped by the shop regularly. To check on Arf, they said, but I had an idea Sam had extracted a promise to keep an eye on me. Two of the three-hundred-plus Market residents, they spend as much time outside as in. *What do I want with walls?* Jim had once asked, though he'd been without often enough to appreciate them.

Jim stood on my right, giving me the unscarred left side of his face and his good eye, a deep, clear blue.

"Gentlemen. Good to see you." I stuffed the newspaper into my tote. "Nice of the rain to stop so I could read while walking."

"You look worried." Half of Jim's face mirrored my expression, the other half immobile.

"I fired Lynette." She had not treated the men any better than she'd treated customers.

He grinned, or half his face did. "So why aren't you jumping for joy?"

"Zak's moving on. Landed his dream job, in a music studio."

"No! Well, good for him. He's a good kid," Jim said. On my left, Hot Dog groaned in sympathy. They knew what a help Zak had been to me, and to Tory.

"Either of you fellows ever want a job, say the word."

They each muttered a polite "no, thank you," then with a wave and a "you take care," they moseyed on.

Friday afternoons get busy, but this early, foot traffic was light. I zipped up Pike Place, exchanging friendly greetings and waves along the way.

Ben stood outside my building, his sage green shirt a nice complement to the ancient pink stucco.

"Saw your number on my screen and took a chance on catching you at the shop." His eyes were full of concern, giving me a warm, pleasant feeling.

Warmth, mixed with unease. If we were going to be mutual sources, pushing each other for info, that probably closed the door on anything deeper than friendship.

Not that romance was ever a serious prospect anywhere but in my employees' overactive imaginations.

I needed details that would help me prove I hadn't armed a killer, unwittingly or not. And, when you find a dead body, you feel a connection that drives you to seek answers.

At least, I do.

"What I want to know," I said, hitching my tote higher on my shoulder and crossing my arms, "is why half the reporters in town are calling me to talk about Alex Howard and Tamara Langston. And why are you so interested in a crime story? Aren't you the 'what's going on around town' reporter?"

"The food and fun guy," he said, his tone light, his expression stopping shy of a wink. "Yeah, but I did crime and general catastrophe for a few years. This has a food angle, so when I heard your name . . ." He had the grace to pink up a shade or two.

"And how did you hear my name?" I hadn't been identified on TV last night or in the paper.

"My source at SPD," he said.

Right. I knew a little about those "sources" from my thirteen years as a police wife. On TV cop shows, reporters say "my source" as if hinting at some super-secret, deep, dark, carefully cultivated, borderline backroom relationship. Sometimes that is the case. More often, it's a dance between the reporters and the Public Relations officers. One side wants news; the other wants to control it, managing what gets out when and how it sounds.

Ben followed me inside. Kristen waggled her eyebrows suggestively. I ignored her, bending down to pet my dog and buy myself a moment to think. *Find out what he knows, and go from there.*

Tracy's wisecrack about my judgment and my taste in men floated through my frontal cortex. It had stung, because it wasn't entirely wrong. In both my careers—HR and retail—I lived and died, and kept my staff employed, by my judgment. But in other arenas . . .

I gave Arf's ear a playful tug and stood, taking in a deep breath and letting it out slowly.

You're a story to him, Pepper. Don't go thinking it's anything more than that.

So I did the hospitable thing. I poured two cups of tea and handed Ben one, gesturing toward the nook.

"So what's the scuttle on me?" I slid into the booth, my back to the wall for a view of the shop, my tone airy.

"That you're smart, gutsy, and very attractive. All of which I knew. That you've made the Spice Shop cool again, rescuing it from financial near-ruin." He set his phone on the table and opened his notebook. "And that you have a knack for finding dead bodies."

Apparently two could play the smart-aleck game. I felt the heat rise in my cheeks. "Says your source?"

"My source," he repeated, his tone self-conscious, "says you found Ms. Langston's body, and that you had a professional relationship with her, supplying herbs and spices to her employer, Alex Howard. Who has been arrested, as you've heard."

"And you think I can help?"

"Well, you did know him. And, I saw you leaving the jail this morning."

So he saw you. Call him on his own bluff. "Right," I said.

"After you left the morning press briefing. With your source." He colored a second time, and I felt a twinge of regret for my snarky tone.

"They wouldn't have arrested Howard if they didn't think they had probable cause," he said.

A magic phrase in the legal world. As I'd often heard Tag explain the term, it means reasonable grounds to believe, based on facts, that evidence of a particular crime will be found in a particular place or that a particular person is guilty of a particular crime. Suspicion alone is never enough. The facts are key.

"So what facts did they reveal?"

Ben consulted his notes. "The victim worked as a sous chef in Howard's First Avenue Café. Snazzy joint. Named one of the country's hottest new restaurants when it opened. Makes all the 'Best of' lists. He's got a knack for getting great publicity, and I hear the food is that good."

Yep. It is.

"He lives the good life. Fast cars, fast crowd." He showed me a photo on his phone. Alex in chef's whites, king of the dining room. He scrolled to the next shot, Alex standing at the edge of a vineyard, clinking glasses with a gorgeous blonde. "A modern playboy."

I raised the tea to my face, hiding my blushing cheeks. I knew the woman, from a distance. She drove a classic Mustang similar to mine and owned an award-winning winery. And a good portion of Alex's affections.

"The victim—" Ben continued.

"Tamara," I said, tired of maintaining a professional distance. News might be Ben's profession, but this was more than a story to me. "Her name was Tamara."

Surprise and concern mingled on his face. *How young is he?*

"Sure," he said softly. "This must be rough. I haven't interviewed anybody she—Tamara—worked with yet, so no dirt on her," he continued. "Sorry—I mean no details. They must have the preliminary autopsy results or they wouldn't be charging him, but they're keeping their lips zipped on the murder weapon."

Except that I knew. Or rather, I had extracted an educated guess from Ron Locke. *Asphyxiation, caused by sudden inhalation of an extreme irritant, very possibly a spice known as* bhut C.

From across the table, his notes looked like personal shorthand mixed with a heavy dose of Greek and a dash of Morse code.

"They say they've served warrants and hope to have more evidence soon. But the clincher is, apparently Howard was overheard threatening her. Even after he fired her."

"What?" My shout alarmed staff and customers. I lowered my voice to a conspiratorial whisper. "What kind of threats? Who heard them?"

Silence from Tracy was to be expected, but Alex? *The slimy little rat.*

Alex had admitted going to Tamarack, but insisted it was hours before her death. Had the camera showed anyone else? If not, had the killer scouted out the surveillance system, or known there would be none on the alley, far from the prying eyes that keep watch on every bank branch and ATM?

Or gone in the back door for some other reason? I'd gone in on a whim. Had the killer?

That brought me back to my earlier question: Who, besides a spice girl on delivery duty, walks around carrying industrial-sized bags of spices?

"Don't know." Ben shook his head. "We asked, but they wouldn't tell us. Pepper—"

What else had Alex not told me? Why had I ever imagined I could trust him? I turned to Ben. "Haven't we all said 'I could kill her' when we're irked? A figure of speech is not a threat. But if you overhear half a conversation, or the context is lost in the heat and noise of a kitchen in full service, how could you tell the difference? We need to know who heard what, when, and where."

We. I'd said it. *Oops.* I broke eye contact and leaned back, the booth hard and unforgiving. I would not break my promise to help Alex, not because I felt any great loyalty to him but because I'd made the promise. Pure, old-fashioned honor, the watchword of my fictional mentor Brother Cadfael. When people put their trust in you, it's a sin to betray them, no matter what they do. A sin against all that matters. All that is holy, as the phrase goes.

I'd promised to poke around, making sure Alex understood that I wouldn't lie and I wouldn't withhold the truth. I'd meant from the police—I hadn't imagined a reporter knocking on my door.

And I'd agreed to help Alex as much for myself as for him.

"Pepper." Ben broke into my pointless reverie, his hand reaching toward mine on the table. "I'm asking too much of you, aren't I? You're emotionally involved in this. With Howard, I mean." He searched my face briefly, then tucked his phone and notebook away. His Adam's apple bobbed, and he slapped the table lightly with one hand, the hand that hadn't quite touched mine. He slid out of the booth and left the shop without a backward glance.

Oh parsley poop.

Twelve

✺

If Peter Piper picked a peck of pickled peppers,
How many pickled peppers did Peter Piper pick?

—19th-century nursery rhyme

UGGH. I'D BLOWN IT, WHATEVER "IT" WAS.

Kristen held a wicker basket brimming with boxes of tea. Zak had already left for his Friday night gig, so she'd stayed late to fill in. With my mind on Tamara's murder and Alex's arrest, I hadn't done a thing today to replace either Zak or Lynette.

"The Made in Seattle shop on First needs tea bags. I thought you could use the fresh air."

Gratitude for small gestures chased away my self-doubt. I took the basket and she hurried to the side of a customer baffled by our assortment of tea strainers.

What next? Sister Frevisse would pray. Me, I'd take the dog for a walk.

No substitute for footwork.

I grabbed my jacket and the leash. Arf wagged his tail in approval. Tea in hand, off we went.

Like Rome, Seattle is a city of hills. The Market is tucked smack into one of them. From the lower boundary on Western, where my loft is, up to First, the Market's eastern edge, is a steep rise. Happily, my shop is on Pike Place, a curious cobbled warren sandwiched between the two, so I rarely have to make the whole climb at once. I shortened the trek by heading out the side door and up to First.

"Tea, oh, tea!" the shop owner called as I walked in. "Where would we be without tea?"

Nothing boosts the ego like a happy customer, especially one who pays the invoice on the spot and gives my dog a handmade peanut butter and molasses treat.

Check in my pocket and empty basket in my hand, Arf and I stood outside and raised our faces to the odd, yellowish-white orb in the sky. The sun, celebrating the approaching end of Rain Season.

You said you were going to ask questions, Pep. No time like the present. With my dog as my excuse and shield, I took a deep breath and turned north.

Surprises me every time I see a cluster of smokers near the back door of a restaurant. Servers, dishwashers, okay—but cooks? Folks whose livelihood depends on their palates? Chalk it up to stress relief.

Three white-clad smokers stood in the puffer zone in the cobbled alley, FIRST AVENUE CAFÉ stitched in navy blue on their shirts.

Dogs are great ambassadors. Arf has a head that invites touch. Only those with serious canine phobia can keep their fingers from reaching out for his floppy ears or his fuzzy jaw.

"Hey, Pepper," the assistant sous chef said. "Hey, boy." He held his cigarette behind his back and extended his other hand at knee level. Arf immediately sat to be petted, and the man obliged.

"You must have been prepping the meat line," I said.

"I gotta go," the woman in the bunch said. She stubbed out her cigarette in a sand-filled flowerpot and shoved her phone deep in her apron pocket. "Chef wants to try that pound cake before service starts."

"Lemon pound cake with brandied cherries, fresh mint, and clotted cream," the sous said to me. "Orgasmic."

I returned his smile. Alex used the word so often, his staff had made it into a joke. "Must be weird, getting ready for a Friday night without Alex."

He pursed his lips and nodded, one hand stroking Arf's ear. Talk about orgasmic.

"Exec is a good hand. We'll do all right."

Kitchen hierarchy rivals law firm structure for its politics and strange bedfellows. In each of Alex's four or five restaurants, an executive chef oversees the menu, under Alex's hawkeyed scrutiny. "Exec" or "Chef" also orders food, manages staff, and handles the expediting—plating each order just so before the server whisks them away to the diners. He—or she—touches everything, assisted by the lead sous.

Except in this kitchen, where Alex handled the exec duties himself. His flagship, his baby.

And his lead sous had been Tamara. No wonder Alex, or Ops, had summoned help.

"Full house?"

"Friday nights always rock, but we could cram Safeco Field tonight."

"Might be easier. Only four plates on a baseball field." I winked, and his face twitched at the lame joke. "You know, I sorta feel responsible. It was my employee who told Alex that Tamara planned to leave, and he got all hot. Understandably. Now she's dead and he's—"

"In the slammer." He crushed his cigarette into the pot. "We were going through the freezer for leftover fish when he got that call. He had this seafood mousse in mind—well, it don't matter. He was furious. Marched out to the prep area— I'll never forget; she was trimming baby bok choy—and fired her on the spot."

Not what Alex had told me. I tightened my grip on Arf's leash. "What did he say?"

"Nothing. I had a hunk of halibut in one hand and snapper in the other, and he just stomped off. I thought he was pissed at me, so I'm trailing after saying, 'Chef, Chef,' and he's spitting and foaming. Wasn't till he started yelling at her that I had a clue."

"Must be awful to know someone you worked with every day is dead and your boss is accused."

His gaze on the dog, he went on as if I hadn't spoken. "She had a dream, and it got her killed, damn it."

He blamed Alex. After a long silence, while his grief filled the alley, he jerked his thumb toward the Café. "I got some good dog bones in the freezer."

"Thanks." We trotted after him. "When Alex lit into Tamara, who else was there?"

"Everybody. All the kitchen staff. We were too stunned to say a thing. Even Tariq, who can't usually stand still."

"I guess you're both in line for a promotion now."

He scowled and reached for the side door. "That kid. Seems like every week, I gotta put somebody else to work helping him prep."

Inside the tiny back entry, I looped Arf's leash around the doorknob and promised I wouldn't be long. The cook bounded through the shiny kitchen, already beginning to thrum, and disappeared down the steep stairs.

To the left, the dining room glimmered, ready for its close-up. Behind the zinc-topped bar loomed Scotty Glass, large as ever, his catcher's mitt hands busy with ice and bottles.

"Well, if it isn't Posh Spice. Sit."

I sat. The beveled mirror in the mahogany back bar reflected a casually elegant space, the dark tables set with heavy wineglasses, water tumblers, and white napkins, the parchment-colored plaster walls giving the room old-world atmosphere in a city that constantly teeters between its heritage and modern aspirations.

A dishwasher staggered out of the kitchen, half hidden by a tower of plastic trays of steaming glassware. The kitchen clatter stopped and started as the doors swung back and forth.

Down the bar from Glassy, a young woman wearing a crisp white shirt and the navy apron took a sip of a Bloody Mary. Her eyes widened, and she sucked in her breath as if to cool it down. "Hot. Good. It's a keeper." She plucked a lemon from a crate and used a mezzaluna, the half-moon knives the Inuit call *ulu*, to cut it in half, sending a sharp citrus scent into the air.

Glassy set a cranberry red Cosmo in front of me with all the grace of a dancer on point. "It's five o'clock somewhere."

"A good bartender always remembers." I took a sip. Crisp and tangy with a touch of sweetness. "Perfect. And so pretty."

"Like you," he said.

"Practicing your BS for the busy evening?" It's not a stretch to call me cute, especially with my hair in full spike mode, but my features are not delicate enough to be called pretty or classic enough for beauty. Not that I mind a compliment, but an exaggerated one makes me nervous. Like I'm about to be hit up. Or hit on.

I sensed a movement next to me. Ops. A moniker reminiscent of a Bond movie, though with her compact build, short platinum hair, and perpetual motion, she looked more like Judi Dench as M than a Bond girl.

"Glassy's sharpest tool," she said. To him, one manicured hand on the edge of the counter: "We've got the sidewalk tables set for bar seating. I've called in extra servers." Outside the front windows, two young men unstacked tables and chairs. A shade too cool for open-air dining, but warm enough for a preprandial cocktail outdoors.

"We'll be ready." He tilted his big head toward the growing pile of lemon wedges. On the floor stood a box of limes and another of oranges. Ops waved and headed for the kitchen.

"How do you stay focused, with all the gossip swirling?"

He wiped an invisible drip off the counter. "We are professionals."

And that was the answer. The chefly ego and sense of responsibility extended from kitchen to bar to dining room. In attitude as well as management, Alex, Scotty Glass, and Ops were all on the same page.

"Heard you made a visit to the jail. Thanks." His voice was low and gravelly.

"What's your theory, Glassy?" I fingered the stem of my drink.

He flipped the white bar towel over his broad shoulder. "Alex has a temper. He says things."

"Would he strike back if he felt betrayed?" A few feet away, the lemon cutter glanced from her boss's wide back to me, then refocused on her cutting board, the blade snicking sharply, a little louder, a little faster.

His blue eyes met mine. Beneath his bushy red beard, his jaw twitched. "You know better than that."

I pushed my half-empty glass toward him. My favorite drink had lost its appeal. "His hurt feelings don't mean she should be dead. I told him I'd dig around, and you know I keep my promises." Unlike Alex, who seemed to be more selective in that department.

He took my glass and dumped it out, his face momentarily hidden. The kitchen door opened, and the sous emerged, carrying a brown paper shopping bag.

"Dog bones," he said.

As the door swung back and forth, I caught a glimpse of the kitchen. Tariq peered out, a steely chef's knife in hand.

I thanked my benefactor, and the door swung shut behind him.

When I looked back at Glassy, his features were blank, composed.

"Alex didn't kill Tamara," he said. "I'd stake my life on it. Dig if you have to, but dig carefully. You never know what secrets people have got buried."

Thirteen

❧

Many people swear ants will not cross a line of cinnamon. Urban legend or fact? Next time you're unlucky enough to be invaded by the family Formicidae, test it for yourself!

"IT'S QUIET NOW, BUT TWO BRIDES ENROLLED IN THE registry this afternoon." Sandra's eyes sparkled. "One is a cookbook fiend with a monster guest list."

Her enthusiasm lit me up, too. We were juggling a lot of new projects, each with its own demands and payoffs. Too bad I couldn't clone her.

I'd just flipped the red-and-white sign in the shop's front door to CLOSED when Callie called. "Hey, that was fast. What did you find out about Tamara?"

"Pepper, I am so sorry. I'd planned to spend the afternoon on your project, but one of the partners dumped a rush on me. A huge business deal that's supposed to close next week could go south if they don't iron this out. I've got to spend the entire weekend helping research software patents for fax machines."

"They still make those?"

"The patents still have value. Give me till Monday or Tuesday?"

"Sure." What else could I say? Even the smartest and most prepared lawyers—including Callie's bosses—couldn't foresee everything, leading to late nights solving last-minute emergencies.

I am not without research skills. I know how to source spices, check quality, and negotiate prices and delivery terms. But tracking people and searching for bad blood? I didn't know where to start.

So I ran the till and counted the cash drawer while Sandra dumped out the tea and scrubbed the pots and Reed swept the floor.

At half past six, Arf and I trudged up the steps to my loft. Well, I trudged, deflated and uncertain. He, being a dog, does not know the meaning of trudge.

I gave him fresh water and a small bone from the restaurant's supply. "Thanks for being such a great sidekick, Arf." I poured a glass of Chianti, opened my laptop, and settled on the couch. Googled Tamara's name. Though I'd been mildly successful once before finding a key detail online that led to more info—and more unanswered questions—I quickly realized this was going nowhere.

It's a basic HR principle: Follow your strengths. Instead of floundering around in cyberspace looking for details that might not matter and connections that might not exist, why not start with a woman who knew Tamara?

But I needed help. Kristen had rushed home to help the girls get ready for a Daddy-daughter dinner at their school. Some mothers might covet that evening alone, but my pal would be as antsy as I was.

"It's ten minutes from your house. Meet me in half an hour." One of the great things about having two wildly different best friends: different partners for different challenges.

Half an hour later, I strolled into Magenta, in the heart

of Madison Park, and settled at a tall table in the bar that overlooked the entire establishment. Since Kristen is always late, I counted on a good fifteen minutes before she arrived. I hooked my heel on the chair rung and scanned the place.

Danielle Bordeaux's newest joint embodied casual neighborhood elegance—what Tamara wanted to achieve at Tamarack. Here, the buzzword meant tables close enough for cozy but not for clusterphobia. Free-form chandeliers of the style made famous by Chihuly and his Pilchuck Glass School hung from the ceilings, their colors and shapes evoking flowers, seashells, and otherworldly creatures. The space blended light and dark, soft and hard, shadow and shine. It made you want to drink and share secrets, eat, and share more secrets.

A few women had dressed up for the evening, but others appeared to have come straight from work. I did not feel out of place in my soft caramel jeans, brown ankle boots, and an open-weave paprika sweater.

"What may I bring you from the bar?" The server, in black pants, shirt, and tie, did not look old enough to drink.

I hesitated, my usual Cosmopolitan holding no appeal. He stepped into the void. "The bar is featuring Washington gins tonight. We're mixing a special martini with any of these." He drew a card from the tabletop stand and showed me a list of temptations. "Or if you prefer more flavor, may I suggest a Negroni? Campari, sweet vermouth, and gin, with an orange twist, on the rocks."

"Sold." The waiter slipped away, leaving me to relax and drink in the atmosphere. Around me, conversations ebbed and flowed, punctuated by the clink of glasses and silver on plates, by the sound of corks popping and laughter rising.

"Pepper. What a nice surprise." Danielle appeared at my table, like a genie I'd summoned. She wore a simple charcoal gray tunic over black pants, a black-and-white scarf looped around her long neck. I felt like an awkward freshman awed by an older student's senior project.

The server delivered my cocktail. An unspoken message passed between them, and he left us. She sat across from me.

"My first time here," I said. "No wonder Tamara wanted to work with you."

She closed her eyes, as if to fight off a wave of emotion. "Hard to believe it's only been two days. Feels like a lifetime."

I knew the feeling. We sat in silence as I tried to decide which of the hundred questions swirling in my mind to ask first. Danielle solved my dilemma.

"A few weeks after we opened, Tamara came to me with a proposal. Told me I'd prompted her to pursue her dream. I thought that was flattery at first, but the more we talked, the more I liked her. Her passion inspired confidence—as a chef should." The server set a glass of ice and a bottle of Perrier in front of her. She reached out a trembling hand, fingers quieting when they tightened around her glass.

"What does it take to start a successful restaurant?"

"The Big Three—concept, chef, location. If one is weak, the venture will fail. Look around here." She gestured with open hands. "I knew I wanted this place to be different from my others. Urban but inviting. A place where you might meet a friend for a drink and stay for dinner on the spur of the moment. Food that's interesting, but not too weird."

"Foodie, without being precious," I said.

"Exactly. You want a team leader, not a one-man show, if you want the place to last."

"So you were open to developing her idea?"

"In partnership, yes. She had the fire. I like a heat seeker."

"What about location? Don't you worry about competition?" I could eat my way down Magenta's block for a week and be happy.

She shook her head, revealing dark streaks in her blond bob—not roots in need of touch-up, but a carefully planned look that said, "I'm so artfully not planning anything."

"No. Put two or three compatible restaurants close together

and they all prosper. You create a hub, a magnet. Just don't pair two Italian joints, or French sit-down and a pizza parlor. You want to attract the same crowd, then offer a choice." She sipped her mineral water.

"Would opening Tamarack next to Tamarind have given you a similar advantage? Ethnic paired with what—modern American?"

Her well-defined brows darted toward each other. "I'll admit, I wasn't crazy about the location. Near the Center, people are focused on events, not food. They're rushing to get to the opera or the Dylan concert, so they're not going to have that second drink or stay for dessert. But more and more companies are locating nearby—"

"South Lake Union's hot," I said, mentally ticking off a few big names headquartered there.

"—and her plan looked solid. I wasn't sure Tamarind would give us that synchronistic boost, but Tamara made a good case. She'd done the due diligence—talked to the neighbors, counted foot traffic, even worked out parking validation."

"But you still weren't convinced."

One corner of her mouth curved up in a question mark. "It was nothing, really. That part of the block has an iffy reputation."

"Ghosts?" I said, remembering Tamara's comment, though it was hard to imagine this sophisticated businesswoman quelling at the specter of a specter.

"Maybe. It had a strange—what? Aura? I think I mentioned at the scene, we had questions about the wiring. She wanted to dig around before we spent a ton of money."

"Right. She mentioned electrical problems."

At precisely that moment, Kristen arrived. "Lemondrop, up," she told the server and introduced herself to Danielle. Then, to me, "More problems at the shop?"

"Tamarack," Danielle said. "Power outages, practically

every visit. Odd noises. A smell. Like—and this is weird—like cinnamon."

My rib cage froze. When I'd walked into the empty space, I'd found myself remembering a trip my family took to Mexico when I was a kid and the cinnamon-chile cocoa we drank. Still one of my comfort foods. Olfactory memory is like that: You're back in your great-grandmother's tiny, dark house or dreaming of your college boyfriend before you notice that you're smelling rosewater or Geoffrey Beene's Grey Flannel. I had thought I smelled cinnamon and chile but dismissed it.

Now I knew the chiles were real. What about the cinnamon?

The hostess whispered in Danielle's ear. "Excuse me," she said and followed the woman to the far corner of the dining room.

"What did you find out?" Kristen asked. "Isn't this drink gorgeous?"

"The building was giving them fits, but that's par for the course. Let's eat." I was suddenly starving. We picked a few small plates to share, and I ordered another Negroni. The sweet vermouth balanced the bitter liqueur perfectly, and nothing refreshes a Friday-night brain better than citrus.

"Sorry for the interruption." Danielle slid into her chair. "Problem solved—the AC started blasting a table for no reason. A restaurateur has to be a Jack—or Jill—of all trades."

"And a casting director," I said. "Lots of parts to fill. I seem to remember a review, right after you opened here, saying expansion had improved the quality of your food. How did you manage that?"

"If you're good at what you do—if you cast the right people in the right roles—then expansion gives you opportunities to do more things. And not one egg drops where it shouldn't. There are chefs who are great cooks, and chefs who are great restaurateurs."

"What would you call Alex Howard?" Kristen beat me to the question.

Our server brought our food and a champagne Negroni for Danielle. "Great chefs are not always easy to work for. Getting fired upset Tamara, but didn't surprise her. Still, to kill her . . ."

"Say it wasn't him." I watched reluctance cross her face. "Who else knew about her plans? Who would have been angry with her?"

"A few of my people knew. My business partner, our accountant, my office assistant." She sipped her drink. "I can't blame the police for sniffing around us."

What could Danielle gain from Tamara's death? A way out of the deal? But while she'd had her hesitations about the location, she'd given it the go-ahead.

"I didn't know Tamara well," I said, "but her enthusiasm was contagious. I'd been looking forward to working with her."

Beneath the glamourous hair and makeup, a shadow crossed Danielle's face. Sadness, or guilt?

I scooped up a bite of the wilted kale salad. "What is this cheese?"

"Cambozola. Similar to Gorgonzola, but creamier. Not so sharp and blue-y."

"You start staffing yet?" Kristen said. "Big job."

Danielle snapped a seeded breadstick in two. "She had a cook she wanted me to interview, and a couple of servers. Somehow, I doubt any of Howard's employees will be applying for a job here anytime soon."

"Dweek?" I swallowed my bite of salad and repeated myself. "Tariq?"

"No. She approached me with him in tow, but he didn't pass the test." She waved half a breadstick toward the kitchen. "I asked them each to cook a meal for me—standard request. She was terrific—efficient, curious, hardworking. Top-notch food. She'd already begun planning her menu. Every meeting, she brought me sample dishes. Her pastries and desserts were superb."

"What about him?"

"He's watched too many TV cooking shows. Lots of talent, no focus. Easily upset. Dishes weren't ready at the same time. If he can't handle a three-course for a four-top by himself, he's not ready for full service."

Made sense to me. But to Tariq?

The glorious Negroni triggered another thought.

"What about a bartender? Cocktails were key to the concept. A guy like Glassy could make the place."

Danielle froze, breadstick in hand. Under the table, I touched Kristen's knee, a signal to keep quiet.

"Glassy," she finally said, "is Alex's man. There are lines you don't cross."

I cast my mind back to our conversation this afternoon. Had he been hiding something? Or sending me signals I hadn't quite grasped?

She slid off her seat, professional smile back in place. "I'm so glad you came in tonight. The drinks are on the house."

"Danielle." I reached out a hand. "Wednesday, at the scene, you said you came down because Tamara called you. What time was that? I—I need to know if I could have saved her, if I'd only gotten there a few minutes earlier."

The smile wavered. She pulled her phone out of her tunic pocket and swiped her finger over the screen. Held it out for me to see the call. Received almost exactly an hour before I'd arrived.

That icy grip on my abdomen tightened. I reached for the last bit of gin.

She tapped the screen, and we heard Tamara, speaking from the grave. "I think I know what's going on." Her voice rose and sharpened, with an edge that could have been excitement or terror. "There's nothing wrong with—"

A sound in the background broke up her words.

"But I won't know for sure until—"

Though the ice in my drink had long melted, my blood froze. *Until what?*

Fourteen

If you can't stand the heat, get out of the kitchen.

—Harry S. Truman

AN EERIE QUIET GREETED ME BACK HOME. THOUGH I SEE my neighbors mostly in passing, knowing they were away made the building feel a little empty and me a little lonely.

I knew it was all in my head, a reaction to the revelation from Danielle's phone. The police had copied the recording, she assured us, so lab techs could analyze it. Had Tamara's last words been a clue? Had she been trying to give Danielle a message—or a name?

The lights on Arf's collar shone a dull blue-white, the loft light dim but not dark enough for a full glow. We'd reached the time of year when, even though you can't see the sun, you know it's coming back. The ultimate act of faith.

I slipped into my rain jacket and swapped my boots for running shoes. "Where to, boy?"

He indicated no preference, so I made for Second Ave. A crowd surged out the front doors of Benaroya Hall.

"The Symphony?" I asked a woman in a shiny red raincoat.

"Portland Cello Project," she replied. "Cello like you never imagined."

In truth, I don't imagine cello much. "Thanks."

We merged into the foot traffic going north, Arf trotting along happily. And if he's happy, I'm happy. Some people say dogs know who they can trust and who's out to hurt you. Others say they're picking up on cues their humans give off. I don't know.

At the moment, I didn't care. He made me feel safe.

A fine mist caressed my skin. It didn't exactly fall—it seemed to emerge from the air itself. The foot traffic thinned, and Arf tugged me toward the water.

"Hold on, boy. I'm in charge here." Clearly not in agreement, Arf stuck his tail in the air, and I realized where we were. "Ha. You want more bones."

I understood. Like a moth to a lightbulb, I was drawn to the scene not of a crime but of a confrontation that may have led to a crime. A confrontation I had inadvertently triggered.

The sidewalk tables stood empty, but at half past ten on a Friday night, the First Avenue Café buzzed. Were it any other night, were Alex on duty, I might have stopped in for a hello, a quick drink, a casual chat. Not that I'd done that recently, but it was tempting to polish the memory, to forget what a schmuck he'd been.

Still is, I corrected myself.

I glanced inside once more. If that wasn't Ben standing at the bar, next to a woman with a cap of shiny black hair, it was his twin brother.

My rib cage tightened. He had every right to be there, and yet, I felt like it should have been me with him, spying in tandem. This was my case as much as his. But I hadn't been willing to commit to working together, and he'd walked away.

"Heel, boy." I headed downhill past the Café's side door, glad for soles that gripped the wet pavement. Voices poured out of the alley, and I stopped. Angry voices. One big and booming, barely controlled, the other low and hard to hear.

"I don't give a rat's ass what you want, you skinny pip-squeak. You got nothing. She's dead, and everything she told you is hearsay."

A slender man rushed past me, his dark skin a sharp contrast to the white jacket, open at the throat and marred by end-of-shift spatters. If Tariq noticed me, he gave no sign.

Why was the bar manager in the alley chewing out a line cook? And what did Glassy mean?

I pivoted, praying Arf would not whine for a bone as we passed the side door a second time. We dashed back up to First and rounded the corner just shy of a run. The mist felt thicker now, the soft yellow light of the Café barely spilling onto the sidewalk as we hurried past. I didn't look for Ben.

I didn't care what Cadfael would do. I only knew I needed to get away.

We passed Café Frida, the piquant aromas of the most creative south-of-the-border cuisine in Seattle merging with the street smells and the brine that clings to everything this close to the water. Outside Diego's Lounge, clusters of the young and hip threaded their way in while others tumbled out, music trailing them. I recognized the strains of the Zak Davis Band, but did not dare linger to listen.

Slow down, Pepper. Breathe. Beside me, Arf showed no signs of fear or hyperalertness. The sounds and shadows I feared were little more than the rhythms of the city at night.

The mist grew heavier as we fled Belltown.

Two blocks later we neared the Market and cut down Post Alley. Irish music drifted out of the pub. A couple emerged from the Pink Door and dashed toward the parking garage. We wove down Pike Place past the shop. A few papers—job applications, I hoped, and the usual flyers and junk mail—had been stuffed in the door. I left them there.

Ahead on the sidewalk, a slight figure glanced back at

me. The Market is a magnet for eccentrics, but this one caught my eye. Neither clearly male nor clearly female, dressed in shades of gray, a long red scarf, and a large, shapeless black hat. The figure took a left and disappeared.

I pulled up my hood. A trio of women descended from a second-floor restaurant, laughing as they all tried to fit under one umbrella.

My brother and sister Seattleites, out for the evening in pairs, trios, and crowds. Winding up and winding down.

And me, alone with my dog, hustling through the rain to our empty home, driven by the fear of imaginary things, invisible threats nipping at our heels.

"WHY is it," I said Saturday morning as I flipped through a stack of job applications, "that every woman named Ginger or Rosemary thinks she's destined to work here?"

Sandra lowered her dark head and peered over the top of her glasses, today's frames red with black stripes. They made me dizzy. "A woman named Pepper has to ask?"

There are certain things you never tell certain people. I have never told Kristen what songs take a crowbar to get unstuck in my head, knowing she would take the least opportune moment to whistle a few notes of the theme to *The Brady Bunch* or "O Canada." And I have never told Sandra my real name.

"One Sage," I said. "Weren't there three the last time we hired?"

"Some names mature better than others. Grandma Sage has a good ring. But can you imagine Grandma Bambi or Nana Tiffani?"

"Point. But if a Harissa or an Epazote walks in, the job is hers."

"Fenugreek," Sandra said in a musing tone. "Ooh. Angelica."

I'd stopped listening, my attention captured by a plain white piece of paper, the same size as the job apps.

"Boss?" Sandra said. "You're white as a sheet."

Wordlessly, I crooked a finger. She stepped closer and gazed down at the note. Blocky lettering, handwritten with your standard black marker.

Do you believe in ghosts?

They believe in you.

She sucked in her breath, and her hand flew to her mouth. Reed peered over her shoulder. "There were a couple of applications stuck in the door this morning. I tossed them on your stack. It must have been mixed in." He sounded anxious.

"Don't worry about it," I said. "It's not your fault." But was it a joke or a threat? I started to smooth the page out, then stopped, my hand freezing midair. It might be evidence.

Or a warning.

I don't believe in ghosts. I don't disbelieve in ghosts. Most of the Market legends—and they are legion—have just enough basis in fact to seem real. Visitors often report seeing a man in a black suit and top hat dancing in the Atrium, near the original Market offices. Arthur Goodwin, who designed the building's interior, had an office there—and was known to wear a top hat when he assigned the vendors their spaces. And he loved to dance.

Every Market merchant knows the story of Jacob, the name the owners of a bead shop Down Under gave to a youthful specter who regularly jumbled beads or dropped the perfect necklace in front of a customer. When the owners unsealed the wall to a small room behind their shop, they discovered piles of beads, notes they'd written, and coins. Speculation is that Jacob may have been one of the stable boys, young orphans who worked in the Market in its early days in exchange for blankets and a place to sleep.

The ghosts of Butterworth Mortuary get the blame for a

series of failed restaurants in the space. After a while, flying bottles and shot glasses that jump off the shelves by themselves cross the line from "atmospheric" to "creepy." They seem to have declared a truce with the owners of the Irish pub that thrives there now, on the Post Alley side. I guess even spooks enjoy the occasional draft of Guinness or sip of Scotch.

Far as I knew, my building—the historic Garden Center—had never had any ghosts.

Had we just acquired one? A chill racked my chest, and for a moment, I couldn't breathe. Was Tamara sending me a message?

I picked the note up by one corner and carried it to my office. Slipped it into a clean file folder. "It's a prank," I muttered, my teeth clenched. "Don't give it another thought." I was overreacting, unnerved by Tamara's death and Alex's arrest. Like I'd let my mind spook me last night, with crazy visions of someone stalking us in the rain. I'd gotten a little unhinged by my own proximity to murder, and a feeling of responsibility I couldn't shake.

And a touch of exhaustion. When I'd talked with my parents in Costa Rica this morning—we check in every Saturday—my mother had called it leftover Catholic guilt.

Life—and sleuthing—were simpler in the Middle Ages. Not easier—not by a long shot. Just simpler. If anyone had slipped an anonymous note to Cadfael or Frevisse, I didn't recall. With parchment and literacy in short supply, the odds were slim and the suspects numbered.

Anybody could have stuck that note in our door.

I swiveled my chair back and forth, staring at it.

They believe in you.

What if it wasn't a prank? I shivered. The message didn't make much grammatical sense, but the gist was that Tamara wanted me to keep investigating. That I could help find her killer.

How? And why me?

I tucked the file and note in the only locked drawer, next to the personnel files. No one but me had access.

But then, that never stops a ghost.

I let out a deep breath before reading over the applications and choosing four likely prospects. Two calls went to voice mail. A robotic voice told me the third number was not in service. I double-checked—not a misdial. We all make mistakes occasionally, but if an applicant isn't careful enough to check her phone number, she probably isn't my ideal candidate. The next call got a live human. We chatted briefly and scheduled an interview for Monday.

Back out front, the witching hour had struck, and the door had opened for business. Saturdays are great fun. From open to close, thousands of people crowd the Market streets. Weekends are the best time to load up on the freshest of the fresh, discover new and unusual taste treats, prowl the artists' tables, and pay homage to an essential part of the region's history.

When a gaggle of women in their early twenties burst in, Sandra showed them the new wedding registry. We passed out our spice and herb checklists, organized by type of cuisine. "So you want to cook Italian" starts with anise and ends with thyme, while the Middle Eastern list runs all the way to za'atar, a great blend to mix with olive oil and spread on flatbread. I've heard that Lebanese children eat it before exams, to focus the mind.

Food always focuses my mind. I plucked a raspberry rugelach off the tray Kristen had brought in and took a bite while surveying our boxed sets. Our box of four jars of popcorn seasoning had sold well over the winter, as had our "Coco-nuts" set of flavored cocoa mixes and our four- and eight-jar baking assortments. For spring, we'd put together salad seasonings. For summer, the theme was obviously grilling. And, of course, wedding and shower gifts.

Soon it would be time to plan the fall blends. When we began the Spice Club mailings, we'd underestimated how long a new project takes. I breathe better when my ducks are swimming straight well before they reach the starting line.

I filled a vintage pressed aluminum tray with cups of tea and stood outside the shop, offering samples and chatting with passersby. Last night's rain had cleaned the air and the streets, and the Market bustled.

Much as I love our product, I couldn't do this job if I didn't enjoy the people. Even the rude ones, who act like I'm passing out poison or refuse to make eye contact because they're so afraid I want something from them. That's okay. As a former supervisor of mine used to say, it's a good thing it takes all kinds, because there are all kinds.

"Founded in 1907," I told a tourist wondering about the Market's origins, "as a true farmers' market. The idea was to cut out the middleman and let consumers buy directly from the producers." Still the idea, although we now have a few permanent produce merchants who buy for resale.

"I'll take a cup of that," a familiar voice said. I hadn't heard the whir of wheels, hadn't had time to brace myself for the constant battle of wits and emotion that my relationship with Tag had become. His partner was nowhere in sight. Probably chatting up the orchard girls, the cutest fruit sellers on the daystall side. Since Zak married Tory, Officer Olerud had taken over the unofficial role of Market Flirt.

In a momentary lull—and lapse of judgment—I let down my guard. "What did you find in the search?"

Tag kept his sunglasses on, a habit he knows irritates me. If the eyes are the windows to the soul, Tag prefers to keep his shut tight. "Last time we had dinner, you gushed about all your plans for the spice business. The new bridal—what is it?"

"Registry." I bit off the word.

"Right. And the new products and gearing up for summer. And now you're busy hiring. Stick to business, Pepper."

"Tag, I found her. I—" I stopped myself. If he wasn't going to share any confidences, neither would I. Pushing him would get me nowhere, but the sympathy card might work. "At least tell me how she died."

He'd kept one foot on a pedal, the other on the curb, and now he switched feet, shifting the bike. "I think you've already worked that out."

A wave of horror rippled through me, and I smacked the empty tray against my leg. As satisfying as it is to be right, I'd really, really wanted to be wrong. "So it was the ghost chiles. I sold them to him. You know that—you've got the records." The all-inclusive "you." How much info detectives share with patrol officers varies case to case and officer to officer. Tag and Tracy don't always act like they play for the same team. "It's part of their regular order, every two weeks. But isn't it a weird murder weapon? I mean, you don't go around carrying hot peppers in case you find food you want to torch—they're like powdered butane—or someone you want to kill. Who would even think of that?"

Had I remembered to tell Tracy I'd given Tamara a sample? The records wouldn't show it. But that had been Tuesday morning. No reason to leave it in her bag, more than twenty-four hours later. And it had been small, an ounce or two.

How much was too much?

Tracy and Spencer would be furious. My prints wouldn't be on the plastic bag—I always handle *bhut C* with gloves. But the label . . . I couldn't remember seeing the bag at the scene. Terror has a way of focusing and filtering the mind at the same time. Certain details are indelible; others barely register.

I slumped against the corner of the building, ignoring the rough stucco poking through my thin T-shirt. Maybe it was time to give up this tug-of-war. To tell him about the sample and Lynette's role in triggering Alex's anger.

And the prankish note.

Tag beat me to the punch. "Stay away from this case, Pepper. Stay away from Alex Howard. I thought you'd dodged that bullet, but here you are again." The sunglasses didn't hide the throbbing cords on his neck or disguise his patronizing tone.

I straightened as if the wall itself had shoved me, had told me to take a stand. Weight balanced evenly on my feet, spine straight, I stood as tall as I could—half a foot shorter than Tag's six-one, but at the moment, I had a rare height advantage.

And I had the advantage of a woman scorned. As trump cards go, it was old and worn, but it worked.

"So. After all this time, you still care more about keeping me from finding happiness with another man than you care about finding Tamara's killer."

My happiness did not lie with Alex Howard. But there was enough truth to the accusation to strike Tag squarely in the chest. His foot slipped off the bike pedal, his cleated shoe scrabbling for purchase on the cobbled street. Despite his natural athleticism, it took him a moment to recover.

"Pepper, there's more going on here than you know." His voice wavered between a plea and that dictatorial tone that sets my cells on edge. "With—Howard. Let Detective Tracy handle it. Don't put yourself in the middle. You'll only screw it uh—" He interrupted himself. "You'll only get hurt."

And he knew all about hurting me.

I resisted the temptation to bring my tea tray down on his head. "Back off, Buhner. You have no right to tell me what to do or who to spend my time with. If there's something I need to know, then tell me and let me make my own decisions. I am done letting you make them for me."

I can screw up perfectly well on my own, thank you.

Fifteen

True love is like the appearance of ghosts: everyone talks about it but few have seen it.

—François de La Rochefoucauld,
17th-century French writer and nobleman

WITH EVERYTHING ON MY PLATE, THE LAST THING I should do was leave the shop. But what's the point in hiring capable people if you can't trust them to get along without you from time to time?

And the spat with Tag had made me antsy.

Arf and I wove our way through the Market and down Western to the parking garage under my building. That sounds grander than it is. The original three-story structure dates back nearly a century, with a loading dock trackside and warehouse space on the upper floors. Pittman Automotive operated streetside for decades, two stories up, servicing downtown delivery trucks. In the 1930s, another three stories were added. In the 1970s—that bleak era when Boeing went bust, urban removal threatened the Market, and a billboard blared WILL THE LAST PERSON LEAVING SEATTLE TURN OUT THE LIGHTS—the mechanic relocated and the warehouse emptied. Eventually, an antique shop—a favorite haunt of mine—opened below, and the upper floors were converted into lofts.

I put the Mustang's top down, hoping to clear my head as we followed the trail. Before leaving the shop, I'd made a quick call. As Alex had promised, Ops gave me Tamara's address, in Wallingford.

Time to give this the Pepper touch. Or the canine touch.

I wound my way through Belltown to Aurora and drove north. On the right, Lake Union glistened. A small sailboat with a rainbow jib sped through the waters. *Eyes on the road, Pepper girl.*

Tag's comments nagged at me. Last night, after Danielle returned to work and the conversation turned personal, Kristen had said we were too stubborn to admit we were still in love with each other. "Neither of you has been able to make a relationship last longer than three months in the nearly three years since you split up. Why do you think that is?"

I'd chalked her question up to the vodka, but in the sober light of day, I knew she had a point.

I frowned. When Tag told me not to get involved, he'd mentioned both Alex Howard and Detective Tracy. Was there some link between them, besides chief suspect and chief investigator? A history?

On the bridge over the canal, I switched lanes and signaled my exit. *No.* It had been another ploy to control my life—mainly my social life. If putting up with Tag's interference was the payback for letting him treat me to dinner now and then, no thanks.

Wallingford is a crowded slice of the city, sandwiched between Highway 99 and I-5, running roughly from Gas Works Park on the shore of Lake Union north to Green Lake and the Woodland Park Zoo. It's a mix of Craftsman cottages, compact condos, and a smattering of eccentric homes with edible yards and roundabouts crammed with drought-resistant wildflowers. As in other neighborhoods, the industrial has given way to the sophisticated, and in recent years, the bar and restaurant scene has spilled from North 45th down Stone Way.

I turned up Woodlawn and slowed, searching for the number Ops had given me. Parking, predictably, sucked. Two blocks up, I squeezed the Mustang into a spot, and we strolled back, Arf lifting his leg on trees and fire hydrants alike.

We halted in front of a redbrick bungalow in need of TLC. Ops had thought Tamara had a roommate, but the wilted white geranium on the front porch and the mail overflowing the black wall-mounted box suggested she—or he—was away.

I rang the bell anyway. No sound—disconnected? I knocked on the door. No answer. I knocked a second time, glancing up at the windows.

Nothing.

A greige stucco apartment building dwarfed the bungalow on one side. I marched up to the entrance and pushed the buzzer marked MANAGER. No reply. Pushed again; same result. The third try woke a woman—elderly, by the sound of her, and cranky.

I looked at Arf. "You can't work your charms if no one will talk to us."

On the other side stood a two-story house with a new roof and half of a new paint job. I skirted the scaffolding, took a deep breath, and knocked on the door.

Tell the truth. You knew Tamara—don't need to say you found her—and you wanted to check up on things. Offer your sympathies to her roommate. Make sure the mail's taken in and the family is on top of things.

And I accused Tag of BS.

But it wasn't entirely that. The door opened in the middle of my self-rationalization for snooping.

A barefoot thirtyish man in paint-spattered jeans gave me a quizzical look. I stumbled through my introduction. "And the mail's starting to pile up."

"Zu must be away. I'll grab it." He shoved his feet into flip-flops, and Arf and I followed him back to the redbrick.

"Quite a project you've got going on," I said, making conversation. Deep in my tote, my phone buzzed. I ignored it. "You mentioned Sue. Tamara's roommate?"

"Zu," the neighbor clarified. "Z-U. Wong? Wing? Little bitty Chinese girl. From China, I mean. Plays viola with the Symphony."

"Do you know how to reach her? She may not know about Tamara's death."

"I don't. We rarely saw either of them. Like I told the cops—what were their names? Not Cagney and Lacey . . ."

"Spencer and Tracy," I said.

"That's it. Tamara worked late—we rarely saw her. Zu moved in a few weeks ago. They're both gone a lot, and quiet when they're home. Ideal neighbors."

"Thanks. Any chance you know Tamara's friends? Previous roommates? The landlord?"

"Sorry. We just bought our house last fall, and with the remodel and a new baby, we've been keeping to ourselves. It's a shame about Tamara, but . . ." The words trailed off.

"Thanks. One last question. Did the cops conduct a search?"

"I presume so. They went inside, but I was painting out back and didn't see when they left."

A galvanized tin watering can stood on his porch. "Mind if I borrow that?"

I may not have been able to prevent Tamara's death or dig any dirt in the neighborhood, but there was no excuse for letting her flowers die.

IF Tamara had worked out parking validation for the new restaurant, she'd scored big-time. I circled a several-block radius around Tamarack's space and was half a second from ditching my plan to canvass the neighborhood when a white smart car with the distinctive Car2Go blue stripe pulled out of a spot. I squeaked in.

"Time to make a plan," I muttered as I stepped on to the sidewalk, Arf's leash in hand. Down in tote-landia, my phone buzzed again; I groped and found it. Caller—M. Tracy. Scrolled back to the previous caller—Tag. I swore softly and stuffed the phone back in the bag.

The shell of a restaurant midblock drew me like honey draws bears. A strip of yellow crime scene tape stretched across the bleak facade.

I let out a long, hot breath and straightened my spine. "Let's go, boy. We have work to do."

Arf did his best, but no one we talked to recalled seeing anyone suspicious near the once-and-future restaurant Wednesday afternoon. "People came and went. Construction guys, mostly," said a fortyish woman reorganizing the nail polish display at the salon down the block. She turned to her coworker, a woman of about twenty-five with a lavender streak in her pale blond hair. "Your chair's got the best view."

Lavender picked up a comb and her blow-dryer. Her customer flipped to a new page in her magazine, unruffled by her stylist's inattention. "The day the chef was killed. When she showed up—early afternoon? I'm not sure of the time— this guy darted out of nowhere. Grabbed her arm and started yelling. I wondered if maybe I should call somebody. But then he threw up his hands and left, and she went inside."

"What did he look like?" I said.

"Older. White guy. Tall, dark hair starting to gray." Lavender gestured with her comb. "Bit of a swagger."

A flush of recognition zipped through my brain. *Alex.*

"Tell her about the younger guy," the other stylist said.

A cotton candy flush crawled up Lavender's fair cheeks, a sweet complement to her hair. "Black. Cute. He said he was hoping to catch someone at the new restaurant so he could apply for a job, and wondered if we'd seen anybody."

Tariq? But Danielle had turned him down. So what had he hoped to gain by pestering Tamara?

"Any idea what time?"

"'Scuse me a sec," she told her customer. At the front desk, she ran a short finger with a purple nail down a column. "I was doing a color on one gal and highlights on another. Between two and—no, she rescheduled." Her face scrunched as she tried to puzzle out the times. "That whole afternoon got all messed up, with changes and lates and a drop-in. I want to say between three and four, but it coulda been sooner or later. I'm sorry."

Me, too. "Do you know if he went in the building, if he talked to her?"

"By that point, a parade coulda passed by without me noticing."

"For the dog," the other stylist said, coming around the counter and holding out a small bone-shaped cookie. "If that's okay."

Like anyone could ever look in Arf's eyes and say no.

MY stomach rumbled. I hadn't eaten since the rugelach this morning. And Laurel and I had missed our chance earlier in the week for Indian.

You'd think that, working with spices all day, I'd be immune to the smell. But the aroma in Tamarind, Ashwani Patel's restaurant, evoked India, at least in my imagination. Indian spicery is so much more than curry, itself a blend of half a dozen spices or more. I detected ginger, mustard, cardamom, chile, and a hint of cinnamon.

Purple velvet chairs lined the entry, and a nubby deep orange silk covered the walls. The hostess stand was unattended. A glass-front case held desserts for those who wanted to take a sweet bite home, for after the concert or ballet.

I peered behind an ornate screen, gold scrollwork painted on a deep red ground, into the empty dining room. Heavy curtains lined the walls in rich colors that conjured a bygone era. I pictured women in elegant saris and men in Nehru jackets. But this being Seattle, a man in a tie would be considered dressed up. And the clientele would cross all cultures.

"Get that dog out of here."

The command cracked the air and startled me. I'd been too caught up in fantasies of East meets West to notice the man in white limping rapidly toward me.

I held out my hand. "Ashwani Patel? Pepper Reece. We met the other night, when—when the tragedy occurred next door. I was hoping you'd have a moment to chat."

"No dogs." Fever spread across his high forehead, his skin the color of toasted cumin seeds, rich brown with a saffron undertone. (I just can't help describing colors in spice terms.) He came to a halt, six feet away. "I don't care who you are or why you're here. This is a restaurant. No dogs."

Though he had no accent—American born, or at least American raised—he shoved the words out, one after the other, as if hurrying me along.

Arf resisted my initial tug, looking over his shoulder at the man who'd barked at us. I led him to the door, glancing at Patel. "Can you pop outside for a chat?"

Patel's eyes narrowed in answer.

I tied Arf's leash to the bench where I could keep an eye on him through the glass of the wood-frame door. Inside, Patel stood behind the hostess stand, his features stern.

"Sorry," I said. "In the Market, half the shops have dogs, and I forget sometimes he can't go everywhere with me. I'm the woman who found Tamara Langston. She was a customer and a friend. I just feel involved, you know? And I wanted to extend my sympathy." Babbling isn't my usual style, but it seemed like good cover.

"So sad," he said, shaking his head slightly. "Very sad. Young woman, so promising. I only wish we'd heard or seen something, but we were hustling, getting ready for the evening."

"Lovely decor. Judging from the front of the building, I'm guessing your restaurant and the space next door were one big space, divided at some point."

Before he could reply, the door opened and a sixtyish man with a bulging belly walked in. Patel's eyebrows rose, and his lips parted slightly. I turned my attention to the desserts, recognizing *gulab jamun*, the fried balls served in a saffron-infused syrup, creamy rice puddings studded with pistachios and raisins, a dusting of cardamom on top, and sweet, milky dumplings stuffed with coconut and spices.

The new arrival picked a menu out of the basket on the counter. "We like the heat. You serve any dishes with those ghost chiles we've been hearing about?"

So much for secrecy.

"Nothing right now." Patel took the menu from the man's hand. I couldn't blame him—I'd felt no rush to replenish after the police seized my stock. But they were a staple of much Indian cuisine, and as popular as they were wicked.

"What do you recommend instead?" The persistent diner gestured toward the menu in Patel's hand, and the two began conversing about various dishes.

A tiny woman in a deep red sari, her black hair pulled back tightly and a bright red bindi on her forehead, peered at me from behind the display case. I started—I hadn't noticed her, sitting on a stool in the corner. Patel's mother or grandmother?

"There's been a *bhut* hanging around," she said, her accent strong and rhythmic, her eyes intent on mine.

I leaned closer to hear her better. "A boot?" Images of cowboy boots, ski boots, and knee-high black leather boots with stiletto heels sashayed into my mind's eye.

"You can tell it isn't alive," she continued, her voice laden with awe. "Their feet face backward. They float. They always wear white."

Her meaning dawned on me. "Where did you see it?"

"Oh, around." The stack of gold bangles on her arm tinkled as she waved one hand. "Here and there."

Her hand stopped midair, palm up, fingers pointing toward the north wall. Toward Tamarack.

The two men stared at me, wide-eyed. Impossible to tell how much they had heard. I looked back at the woman on her corner stool, a satisfied expression on her face. "Thank you," I said to her, and to Patel, "and you. I'll be back for dinner soon."

The door opened, and Ben Bradley walked in.

"Hey." I took his arm. "You found me."

He gave me a goofy grin and let me lead him out. I glanced over my shoulder to the woman in the sari. She flopped her hand from one side to the other and mouthed the words "here—and there."

Sixteen

🌿

Meet me at the Needle, Nellie. Meet me at the Fair.
The Monorail will take you, Nellie, and I'll meet you there.

—parody of "Meet Me in St. Louis," sung by John Raitt
at the opening ceremonies of the Seattle World's Fair,
April 21, 1962

BLESS THE MAN. HE WAITED UNTIL WE'D CROSSED THE
street and gotten lost in the Saturday throng headed to Seattle
Center before dropping his arm—keeping hold of the hand
not looped through the leash—and turning to me, eyebrows
raised.

"Thanks for the save," I said. "After yesterday . . ."

"Don't give it another thought," he said. "I hope you and
your sidekick got more out of the neighbors than I did. Running into you's the best luck I've had all day."

I let my tote slip off my shoulder as an excuse to drop his
hand and hitched the bag back into place. "Did you hear the
man in the restaurant quizzing Patel about his hottest dishes?
From his reaction, I'm guessing it wasn't the first time today.
The ghost chile genie must be out of the bag."

Ben pulled me out of foot traffic and handed me the

morning paper. Below the fold, small head shots of Tamara and Alex marked the latest account:

INVESTIGATION CONTINUES
IN MURDER OF CHEF

Below that,

INDIAN SPICE SUSPECTED

The headlines sucked me in. "According to a source close to the suspect," I read, "the victim is believed to have died after ingesting a dangerous, exotic pepper." The words scorched my eyeballs, and flames licked my throat as I tried to speak. "That—that's what those messages were about. They—they think *I'm* the source."

I'd been too busy following my nose—and too annoyed with Seattle's Finest—to respond to Tracy's message telling me we had an urgent matter to discuss or to Tag's text saying, *What do you think you're doing?*

There's a certain kind of silence that gets your attention. "You thought so, too," I said. "Why would I do that? I'd be implicating my own product."

The corners of his lips twitched downward, and it took him a moment to look me in the eye. "To make it look like you had nothing to hide? Or to get out in front of the gossip."

"That's crazy. Tracy said he knows I didn't kill her."

"So whoever leaked it either wanted to cast blame on you, or didn't know the cops had ruled you out," he said. "Who does that leave?"

"No idea. Obviously, Alex had access to *bhut C*, but so did other people. And it's kind of a ridiculous murder weapon." Not something you carry around. And not something you plan to use. That made this a crime of opportunity.

A crime of anger. Rage. Fury.

Since we were obviously following the same path, maybe it did make sense to join forces. "I don't know the official working theory, but one good guess is that the killer forced her to breathe in the peppers. The throat and lungs become inflamed, and the person can't breathe."

"Holy cow," Ben said.

Crowds surged past us. Ben pointed toward the Center entrance. "Let's go in, take our minds off murder for a while."

We wound around the north side of Key Arena and through a corridor of lush, fragrant shrubbery, then paused at the stone rim of the International Fountain.

"Wow. Coolest wading pool ever," Ben said as we watched streams of water spike from a silver dome to the rhythms of Duke Ellington.

"It used to be filled with sharp, white rocks—you couldn't play in it like kids do now." I gestured toward the shallow, paver-lined bowl that held the fountain. On the first warm weekend of spring, the water beckoned, and dozens of kids, toddlers to teenagers, had responded. They edged close to the dome, then shrieked and darted back as the water erupted. The music changed to Beethoven's Ninth. I swizzled my hands in the air. "My dad likes to stand here and pretend he's conducting."

"Kane!" A few feet away from us, a woman called to a boy of about six kicking a shiny blue ball through the water. Beside her, a man pushed a stroller back and forth, a pink stuffed animal strung on a white ribbon signaling a girl on board.

Beside me, Arf barked loudly, once.

"Kane, be careful! You're splashing people!"

Arf barked a second time.

"Arf! Hush!" His bright eyes focused on the child, hips forward, one front paw raised, ready to break into a run. I tugged at his leash. "What is wrong with you? You don't bark at children."

He poked my knee with his nose, then rubbed his muzzle on my leg, stopped, and looked up at me.

"That was weird." I looped the leash through my hand, shortening it. Arf turned his big head as we moved on, watching Kane whirl his arms, trying to catch the falling water. "He's never done anything like that. He hardly ever barks."

Over beer and fish tacos in the enclosed area outside the food court, Ben asked me about the Center. "Seems like there's always something going on."

"Concerts, art fairs, international festivals, you name it. Built for the World's Fair in '62. You can see the Space Age theme in the architecture. Key Arena's a flying saucer, the Science Center's got those futuristic white arches, and, of course, the Space Needle. The newest addition is the Chihuly Glass House—that will blow your mind." From our table, we could see the crowds surge past. Kane and his parents headed into the Armory, the boy carrying the blue ball, his sister's pink-shod foot sticking out of the stroller.

Ben listened as I shared memories of events at the Center: My first trip to the ballet—*The Nutcracker*. High school graduation in the old Mercer Arena, damaged by the earthquake and still closed. Folklife and Bumbershoot, the sprawling art and music festivals that bookend the summer. I even confessed my first kiss, on the roller coaster in the long-vanished Fun Forest.

The man was surprisingly good company, lacking the self-absorbed arrogance of other recent male companions. Plus, my dog liked him.

Ben brought up the murder first. "Can't blame Patel for being hypersensitive after what happened. Especially when people get all bloodthirsty over ghost chiles and people like you and me come snooping around."

"I wasn't snoop—" Heat rose in my face, and not from the midday beer. "I found her. I know what it's like to deal with all the looky-loos when a dead body shows up. At least he doesn't have crime scene tape blocking his front door." Ben tilted his head, questioning, and I told him about my prior brush with murder.

"Then there's Howard," Ben said. "I stopped in for a drink last night with my editor. Howard's in jail, on murder charges, and the place was jammed."

So that had been him. And his boss. I hoped my cheeks didn't betray me.

"Charges haven't been filed yet. But it seems inevitable." Even I, no defender of Alex Howard but a defender of truth, justice, and the American way, had started to think he might be guilty.

I fed Arf the tail end of my taco. Kane and his family emerged from the Armory, each working on an ice cream cone. Regret is a waste of time, but I couldn't deny feeling a teeny bit left out. By the time Tag pronounced himself ready for kids, the batteries on my biological clock had run down. Then he'd decided to recharge himself elsewhere.

After our divorce, my mother had confessed surprise that Tag and I lasted as long as we had. Not, she'd hastened to add, that she'd foreseen infidelity. "You two never seemed to fit."

And yet, Kristen had a point. We couldn't seem to stay away from each other—or move on. When I discovered his affair—he swore there had been just the one—I'd briefly considered leaving Seattle. But where would I have gone?

Besides, when our marriage ended, I'd had a job I loved. So I stayed and bought the loft. Poured everything I had into building it out and jazzing it up.

Then lost the job.

But Seattle is my home. I hadn't felt restless. I hadn't heard the siren call of other lands.

"Do you believe in ghosts?" I asked as we scooted back our chairs.

"I don't know. There's a lot going on that we can't see."

The Ninth was reaching the finale as we neared the fountain, and the "Ode to Joy" sent plumes of water gushing into the air, soaking anyone not quick enough to dash out of reach.

When the music and the cheering stopped, he was the first to speak. "Pepper, you're smart, and you know the people involved. I'd like your help with this investigation, without feeling like we're sources or rivals for information. I'm serious about that feature story and—well, I want to see more of you. Personally, I mean. We can go bowling, or come back here to the Glass House."

"Bowling?" I laughed.

Few features in a man are more attractive than a willingness to admit he's interested.

Too young? Too soon to tell.

"Yes," I said. "To all of it." We circled back toward the entrance, making plans for an interview and photographs next week at the shop. And maybe bowling.

"Kane!" Ahead of us, out of sight, the mother shouted, shrill, terrified. "Kane!"

"KANE, NO!" The father, his shout louder, deeper, just as frightened.

The leash ripped through my fingers as Arf shot toward the commotion, weaving through the crowd. I tore off after him, not seeing him, not knowing what he was running to. Ben surged past me, both of us shoving our way forward, yelling Arf's name. Pounding footsteps, more shouts, a bark, a screech.

Silence.

Ben flung out an arm to stop me from tumbling off the curb onto First Avenue North. Not five feet away, in the middle of the asphalt, Kane's father threw his arms around the boy, snatching him up, the small feet windmilling as the driver of the Volvo got out of his car, eyes wild, hands clutching the top of his head.

"Where did he come from?" the driver said, adrenaline thinning his voice. "What was he doing?"

Across the street, the blue ball hit the far curb, bounced twice, and came to rest.

Amid the chaos stood my dog. He barked again.

"The dog ran after the boy," someone said. "He pushed the boy aside and saved him." A few feet away in her stroller, Kane's sister cried.

My knees gave way, and I sank to the sidewalk. Arf bounded into my outstretched arms. "Good dog. Bad dog. I just got you." I blubbered into a furry ear damp with my tears. "I can't lose you." He touched his nose to mine, and we embraced, my dog and I, my brave, panting, slobbery dog.

THAT after-the-fact fear had me rattled. The what-ifs—what if Arf hadn't been there, what if he and the boy had been hit—kicked in and kicked my butt. I drove home still shaking.

Still wondering why my dog had gone racing after a child he did not know to protect the boy from a danger he could not see. Where had he learned that?

I parked the car, and my dog and I trekked up Western. I needed to wash the adrenaline sting out of my mouth. And Arf needed serious treats.

Definitely an elevator day. I punched the button and glanced up the Hillclimb steps, the steps we weren't taking. Seven metal figures, each sculpture holding a white globe light, climb the walls, dance on the stair rails, and otherwise challenge our sense of up, down, sky, and ground.

Mine had been challenged enough today, thank you.

The elevator creaked its way up, and I replayed what I'd learned that morning. I'd struck out with Tamara's neighbors. Even if I knew the names of her former employers, I couldn't call up and say, "So sorry, she's dead—tell me about her." The police had the advantage there. So did Brother Cadfael and Sister Frevisse. They didn't always know the victim or suspects, but cloaked in credibility by their vows, they had little trouble getting people to talk. My job in HR had given me a similar semblance of safety.

In the outside world, such trust is harder to come by.

The stylists had seen Alex arguing with Tamara. They'd also seen him leave while she was still alive.

And they'd seen a man I assumed was Tariq.

I bought a raspberry smoothie at the bakery and walked slowly up the street, sipping and mulling. According to Danielle, Tamara had wanted to bring Tariq with her on the new venture, but he hadn't passed the test.

That had been weeks ago. If he'd been unhappy—and who wouldn't be—he'd have told Tamara so back then. No reason to follow her, camp out across the street from the new space, and wait for an opening.

Unless he hadn't known he was out of the picture until Alex's tirade. If she'd left him dangling, only to discover unexpectedly that he was being left behind, that might have fired him up. Spurred a confrontation. Prompted an impromptu assault with a deadly pepper.

I shivered. Tariq had sat in my car. Petted my dog. Hadn't mentioned that he'd hoped to be part of Tamarack.

If he'd expected Alex to fire him at any hint of treachery, no wonder he kept his lips zipped. I'd obviously acquired a reputation for being closer to Alex than I actually was—a pipeline of info to and from the chef himself.

I tucked that thought away. Investigating Tariq would have to wait.

I paused to let a delivery truck pass. Took another sip and noticed the note written on my cup:

Watch for the changeable lady.

I stared at the words. *What on earth—?*

In the shop, Arf munched a dog biscuit, and I relayed his adventures to my staff. The vet had guesstimated Arf's age at roughly five, and he'd belonged to Sam for about a year. Before that, who knew.

"Have any of you seen a character dressed all in gray, except for a red scarf and a black hat? I saw him—her—whatever—last night when I walked by, and something seemed odd. But I was too far away to tell."

"Odd is the middle name down here," Sandra said.

"Truth to that," I said. "If you don't mind, I've got another wild hare to chase."

"Investigating?" Reed's face lit up at the hint of intrigue. Sandra rolled her eyes and waved one hand in the air as if to say, "Bosses—what can you do?"

I hopped a bus and zipped down to the jail, hoping visiting hours hadn't ended. On the way, I read the newspaper article again, more carefully. The only new piece of information was the cause of death. *Bhut C* hadn't been named specifically, but figuring that out didn't take a rocket surgeon. Any serious cook could make the link.

Any serious cook . . . That knocked the suspect pool flat open.

"I almost didn't come here," I told Alex through the Plexiglas and the plastic phone. My nose twitched—the jail staff did not stint on disinfectant. "Because everywhere I go, every question I ask, I discover that you haven't been telling me the truth."

On the other side of the clear wall, Alex shifted in his seat. Energy radiated off of him, as always, but this time, the vibes had nowhere to go.

"I didn't kill her, Pepper. You have to believe me."

A spasm stabbed my neck. *I don't have to believe anything.* "So who did?"

His eyelids fluttered shut. Did he not know, or not want to say?

"I struck out at Tamara's house," I said. "But I talked to a few restaurant neighbors—retail clerks, a couple of hair stylists, and the guy who runs the Indian place next door—"

"Ashwani Patel?" Alert now. A crease cut across his forehead. "Don't believe a thing he tells you."

"You know him?" I shouldn't have been surprised. Everyone in the restaurant biz seemed to know each other.

Alex tried to fold his arms, but the short metal phone cord stopped him. "We—crossed paths. He and his wife had a series of restaurants. None really took off. Probably why they split up."

My brow furrowed. If Tamarind wasn't a success, why had Tamara so badly wanted to open next door? "Where is she now?"

His left knee bounced like a drummer's hand. "Gone, I guess. You know cooks."

I was learning. They skip around like drops of oil on a hot griddle.

"Alex, you promised to tell me the truth. You admitted you went to see Tamara Wednesday, but you didn't tell me you argued on the sidewalk. Yelled and threatened her."

He blew out a noisy breath. After a long moment, he wriggled in his chair, half turning from me, then glared through the scratched plexi.

"I needed to know why." He was the chef, demanding cooperation. "After all I had done for her, why?"

His changing moods and tones were giving me whiplash. "Seriously? Her plans surprised you? Did you honestly expect her to stick around forever?"

When he finally answered, head tilted back, eyes hooded and unfocused, his voice was tired and thick, like a dough that's been overworked. "Maybe not. But she was different. Lot of flakes in this business. Talented cooks who do their work and go home—or get stoned or high or drunk. You try to hold on to the good ones. You push 'em to do better, better,

better." His hand tightened on the phone. "To meet your standards, night after night after night. But you ride 'em too hard, and one day, they don't show up. Or they walk out in the middle of service and you got nobody to take their station and orders piling up and you're disappointing people. You're messing with the rest of your crew. Your diners are goners and everybody suffers and it stinks."

He stared at failures I couldn't see—the server impatient for a missing meal, the too-rare filet sent back for refire that throws off all the intricate timing, the night's special that sparks no palates. "You get a sense for who's gonna last. And you hope to hell you're right. Sometimes, though, you fool yourself. You don't wanta know what you know, so you shove it aside. But you know."

I'd been in enough kitchens to understand what Alex was telling me: Every image of the confident chef in sparkling whites waiting, *just waiting*, for you to walk in and feel the love, teeters on a tightrope. He—or she—dare not for one second admit that he might fall, might fail, might tumble to the floor and crack like a raw egg or a crystal goblet.

I let the silence sit between us as long as I dared. Jail guards watch the clock the way a fish cook watches a pan of butter browning for the halibut.

"Who else, Alex? You were watching for signs. Who else did you think might leave?"

He didn't answer.

"Promise me you won't fire anyone," I said. "But what about Tariq?"

His eyes snapped to attention. "Tariq? What do you know that I don't?"

"Promise me." He nodded reluctantly, and I continued. "He thought Tamara was taking him with her, but Danielle had other ideas. I don't think Tariq knew until you canned her in front of the full staff."

A cranberry flush covered his face. He leaned back as far

as the phone cord let him. "Kid's a hothead. That's part of his problem in the kitchen. Thinks he's special because he's heard that all his life. Doesn't realize out in the real world, everybody's special and you have to work your tail off."

In other words, Tariq wanted to be Alex. "But would he kill her?"

"Apparently so." He gave me one of those believe-it-because-I-said-so looks. I hate those looks.

And I didn't buy it. Alex had had another suspect in mind before I mentioned Tariq. Who?

"You said you should have known Tamara would leave eventually. But tell me the truth here, if you can." I leaned forward, my hazel eyes boring into his browns. "Before Lynette dropped the dime, did you know—did you even suspect—that Tamara had other plans?"

His lips tightened. "I'd like to say I did. But she blindsided me."

And in Alex Howard's world, that was a fate worse than rubbery calamari.

Seventeen

❧

The hills are so steep in downtown Seattle that some
of the sidewalks have cleats.

—Murray Morgan,
Skid Road: An Informal Portrait of Seattle

I HOPPED BACK ON THE BUS AND, ONCE AGAIN, FOUND
myself at the First Avenue Café in the pause between prep
and service.

"Alex is hanging in there. He asked me to give you a message," I told the staff gathered at the big table in the basement.
Familiar faces, mostly, except the borrowed Exec, who'd
greeted me warmly. I deleted the expletives and rephrased the
rest, giving the boss's words a kinder, gentler tone: "I'm so
sorry I'm not there with you to mourn and remember Tamara.
The best way to honor her is to keep the faith. To keep on
cooking. I'll be back before you know it"—or as he'd put it, *as
soon as these dickheads cut me loose.* "In the meantime, I'm
counting on all of you to help the police find the real killer, and
to keep our customers satisfied."

Then I settled into the chef's office off the basement
kitchen—roomy by Spice Shop standards, but dwarfed by the

executive office Alex keeps upstairs in the corporate suite—for interviews. Or as I'd told the staff, "conversations."

"Thought you might need a little liquid courage." Scotty Glass tossed a thick paper coaster sporting the Café logo on the desk and topped it with a stunningly beautiful drink, the orange twist stretching up the side of the glass like a ballerina's curved arm. "I hear you been talking to a lot of people. Everybody who knew Tamara."

I stared at the drink, a perfect Negroni.

Coincidence? Or a message that he knew I'd talked with Danielle Bordeaux? She'd called him Alex's man, in a tone that implied she and Scotty were not the best of friends.

Why would he care?

"Nothing you say goes beyond me. You have my word," I repeated to each employee. By the end of the interviews, and the end of the Negroni, the sounds drifting down from the main kitchen told me Saturday night promised to be as crazy busy as Friday. One prep cook, one hostess, and two servers confessed they'd known about Tamara's plans and had hoped to join her staff. Reasons ranged from wanting to work with Tamara to being part of something new to escaping the strictures of Alex Howard's domain. As the prep cook put it, "Every good chef is tough. I wouldn't want to work for one who isn't. But I don't need my head bashed in every night."

Figuratively speaking. While they all mourned for Tamara, no one wanted to accuse anyone else of murder.

I felt Tariq's eyes follow me as I passed through the kitchen. Hard to imagine that sweet face belonging to a killer.

No doubt what Eve said to Adam when one son killed the other.

The prep cook put a hand on my arm. "You wanted to know how much ghost pepper we had left. Three ounces, ground. Two eight-ounce bottles of oil—boss used all the whole chiles making the oil."

"Thanks." That pretty much accounted for their standing order. In other words, no *bhut C* had gone AWOL. "Hey, do you all clock in? Who keeps the time records?"

"They're in the office," she said. "Behind the door."

I trotted back down the stairs. Pushed aside the apron that had been tossed haphazardly over the wall-mounted machine. Half modern, half 1950s, an electronic recorder flashed the current time, a rack of paper cards next to it. The cards, marked for each day of the week, fit into a slot for stamping. The bookkeeper would then manually calculate each employee's hours.

"Tariq Rose," I muttered, scanning the cards, and sure enough, it was right where it ought to be. But Alex Howard Enterprises apparently paid on Fridays. The only time records were for yesterday and today.

Parsley poop.

Back upstairs, the energy in the kitchen had risen to medium boil. Knives flew, sauces simmered. No one could be interrupted, even to ask if Tariq had been on time last Wednesday.

"Hey, Glassy." I perched on a barstool.

He took my glass and raised it, asking if I wanted another.

"No, thanks. Why didn't you tell Alex that Tamara intended to leave the Café? And that she invited you to go with her?" That last part was a guess, drawn from the undertones of Danielle's comments, but it made sense.

For an instant, all motion stopped. Then he picked up where he'd left off, the mirror behind the bar showing his hands shaking as he reached for a bottle and a corkscrew. A muscle in front of his ear twitched.

"Who says I didn't?" He set two glasses of white wine on the bar, the wine just cold enough to fog the outside of the glass with a thin veil of condensation.

"Because I know who told him." Though I doubted Glassy knew Lynette or her role, his nervousness told me I'd guessed right. Her name had not made the news accounts, and Alex had sworn he hadn't told anyone but the lawyers and detectives. "And if he imagined for one half second that you'd considered going with her, the explosion would have rocked this building off its foundation."

A server grabbed the wine. Glassy waited until she'd stepped away. "Alex and me go way back. Sometimes a good friend's job is to save you from yourself. Self-made men don't always understand that other people just want the same chances they had. My way of thinking, if an employee doesn't want to stay, why would you want 'em to?"

"Wouldn't you want to talk, see if you can salvage the relationship?"

"Sure. But if they're determined, I say go, be happy."

"So you helped her make the break, but you didn't tell him. Because you thought he'd try to stop her."

The big man leaned forward. When he spoke, his voice left no room for doubt. "Not by killing her. You know him better than that."

Truth be told, I thought I did. What made Alex an SOB at times was that he drew lines and expected other people to honor them, no questions asked. And despite what some may think, there is a clear line between being a hard-nosed businessman and being a killer.

"Thanks for the drink, Glassy. Your Negroni is almost as good as Danielle's."

His thin smile held no joy as he reached for a bottle of gin.

I rescued my dog from the darkened shop. He'd been alone less than ten minutes, but I felt guilty anyway. We took the long way home, circling through the park so we could stretch our legs and peek at the sky.

Though I try hard to see the metaphorical blue sky, nothing beats the real thing.

With encouragement—and compost—from my neighbors, I'd nursed a few perennial herbs through the winter and now had a lush deck garden. I snipped a few sprigs of parsley and mint, a variety called Mojito, and despite feeling fed up with Alex Howard and his troubles, I flicked on the TV news to check for updates. If there were any, they'd been pushed aside by news of road project cost overruns and the search for a missing child on Bainbridge Island, which ended happily when the boy was found asleep in a neighbor's camper.

That reminded me of young Kane. I whirred the ingredients for lemon-tahini sauce with my immersion blender, nicknamed the whizzy-uppy thing, my pulse matching the motor's vibrations. My heart, alas, did not stop racing when I unplugged the blender.

In the corner, Arf gnawed another bone from the friendly sous. Bones serve many uses in kitchens, but what better use than rewarding the hero of the afternoon? I still wondered what had prompted him to take off after the child, but he wasn't telling.

"Even dogs deserve their secrets, eh, boy?" Canned garbanzo beans drained in the sink. I chopped red onion and dumped it into the big food processor, adding the beans, fresh herbs, cumin and other spices, and more lemon. My Lebanese chef customer deep-fries his falafel, but while I don't mind cleaning out the food processor, I hate washing up a grease-spattered stove, so I pan fry them instead. Healthier, too. Plus the leftovers would be yummy on salad next week.

Scoop, pat, pat, pat. Eight falafel burgers lined up on the butcher-block counter. I warmed the pan and talked to my hero, working his bone. I told him everything I knew. It wasn't much. It wasn't enough to acquit Alex, or to accuse anyone else.

"Here's the problem." I lifted the first batch of hot burgers out of the pan. "The two people we know who had motive to kill Tamara are Alex and Tariq. But Alex . . ." The next batch hit the heat with a sizzle.

Alex was too rational, too self-controlled, too—I waved the spatula like a wand, hoping to conjure up the right word. "Scheming" sounded too harsh. The man simply expected people to fall in line. It never occurred to him that he wasn't king of the world.

By all accounts, the kitchen tirade when he fired Tamara had been theater, conducted as a warning to the rest of the staff. They'd all agreed on that.

Tariq, on the other hand, was a loose cannon. He had the cheffy temper tantrum down, but hadn't yet grasped that it only works when paired with commitment and discipline. If Tamara's public firing had been his first hint that she'd ditched him, he could easily have lost it and attacked her. I could see him tending that anger, feeding it like a sourdough starter until it bubbled up and boiled over. I could see him following her to the new space the next day to confront her.

And then, carried away by rage, kill her? That wouldn't get him the job he wanted, but young firebrands don't think that far ahead. He'd choke her, hit her with a hammer or a two-by-four, shove her so hard she fell and hit her head on a sharp corner.

But force her to breathe a lethal dose of *bhut C*? The killer had to either fling it in her face, leaving traces on her clothing and in the space around her, or stick her head in a bag.

Uhhhh. My shoulders rose and my whole body shuddered.

I cut a pita in half, split it, and slipped it in the toaster oven. Popped the cork on a light Pinot Noir from Oregon. Took a sip—suh-weet. Set my glass on the dining table, a round, slightly battered cedar table my former mother-in-law had given me when I set up solo housekeeping. She knows my love of timeworn furniture, my passion for pairing the mismatched.

All that reminded me of Tag. I hadn't returned his text or Tracy's call, using *It's Saturday* as my mental excuse. And, *I didn't do anything wrong.*

Not that either of them would care.

Tag couldn't understand why finding Tamara's body meant I had to get involved. And he wouldn't understand why I'd feel guilty if she'd been killed with my chiles. Does a gun dealer feel responsible when a customer shoots and kills, or turns the gun on himself? Does a car salesman feel guilty when a buyer crashes?

Maybe I didn't need to be involved. Maybe I should back off.

I stuffed veggies and a hot falafel into half a pita and spooned in the lemon-tahini sauce. Carried my dinner to the table and curled up on a pale pink wrought iron chair topped with a floral print pillow.

Laurel would say I think too much, and on that, she and Tag would be in rare agreement. But if those were my chiles, then I knew the killer. And I needed to help bring him to justice.

After I worked out who he—or she—was.

My tote sat on the other chair. I dug out my copy of the ghost chile customer list. *Sip, eat, read, repeat.* The list ran the gamut of restaurants and food producers, and covered five counties. The incestuous nature of the restaurant biz meant Tamara could have known any of them.

I sat back, swirling the wine. A fruity aroma—it comes from grapes, after all—but I tasted cherry and blackberry, with earthy undertones and spice notes. This variety reminded me of visits to the tobacco shop. And cinnamon.

After more than a year and a half owning Seattle Spice, I knew most of my customers personally. I'd made a point of calling on the commercial accounts, so they could put a face to my name and I could identify their needs, figure out how to help them. When they call to place an order, I always take a moment to chat.

None of them seemed like a killer. And none had any connection that I knew to Tamara, Alex, or Tariq. But then, I hadn't known that Alex and Glassy knew Patel. Or that they had worked with Danielle, as I surmised from her comments—and that she had apparently called Glassy after our Friday night conversation.

While I consider myself a major player in the innovative spice market, I'm hardly alone. Either Alex or Tariq could have bought *bhut C* from one of my competitors.

I took my plate to the kitchen and refilled my wine. Turned off the TV and turned on the CD player. Set the shuffle mode—randomness fit my mood. Sat in the red corner chair, sipping and staring out the tall windows as night crept in. I had been assuming Tamara's killer was connected to her through food, because I was—and because she was killed with a spice. I'd assumed that the motive was tied to her leaving one restaurant to start another.

Logical enough, but murder isn't logical.

People kill for a million reasons. To get something. To stop something. To keep someone else from getting something. To protect someone. To cover up a past crime, or prevent a future one.

To keep secrets hidden.

Tamara's coworkers had given me no clues. Time to try her roommate again. Or I could call my customers and dig—say I was checking in, and wanted to reassure them that I would have ghost chiles available soon, when the furor died down. (Better not say "died.") And if they mentioned Tamara, then follow up.

Chancy, but investigation—like business—takes risk. And it would have to wait till Monday.

Getting nowhere can be exhausting.

But I had one other motive I would never admit to Tag. The mysterious note slipped in with the job applications had pricked my conscience. *Do you believe in ghosts? They believe in you.*

Foolish as it might sound, I felt Tamara reaching out, asking me to find her killer.

I only wished she'd given me a little more to work with.

Eighteen

❧

A yawn is a silent scream for coffee.

—Author unknown, on the Internet

"I NEVER WORKED WITH ALEX," LAUREL SAID. "BUT I wouldn't be surprised if Danielle did."

My ever-changing cast of employees had wreaked havoc on the Spice Shop's schedule the past few months. Sandra and I had settled on alternating Sundays, and she took Mondays off. That gave me one day to myself every other week, a day to start with Laurel, drinking too much coffee over brunch, then walking it off.

Today, we sat in her kitchen. The alder interior glowed warmly in the shy sunlight, doubled by the reflective water outside. The roar of a big powerboat surged through the open window. We rocked gently on the wake.

Laurel stirred cream and honey into her mug. "She has a phenomenal palate and a dead-on sense of what makes diners keep coming back. Plenty of ego, but she keeps it in check."

"Tamara's phone call to Danielle clears her of suspicion," I said, cradling my mug and letting the heavenly steam soften my skin. "Besides, she had nothing to gain from killing

Tamara, and a lot to lose. If she'd changed her mind about Tamarack, there were easier ways to pull the plug."

I plucked a warm date bran muffin from a basket on the table, split it open with my thumbs, and reached for the butter. "There's something she's not telling me. She seems so friendly and frank that you think she's wide open, but when you replay the conversation later, you realize she keeps her cards close to her chest. Or is it vest?"

Laurel dragged one hand through her hair, an amethyst drop earring peeking through the wild gray-brown curls. "Necessary self-protection when you're both a woman and the boss." She slid out of the booth and bent to peer into the oven. Satisfied, she drew out a porcelain baking dish of sausage patties. Fennel and oregano scented the air. She tossed green onions and red bell pepper into a hot, buttery pan.

Friends who cook well are gifts from the gods. Or goddesses.

Upstairs, feet hit the floor. Laurel smiled. "The smell of coffee means nothing to that boy, but sausage? Better than any alarm clock."

She cracked eggs into a bowl, stirred the vegetables, plucked a whisk out of a crock. "A busy kitchen doesn't have to be a difficult place to work. Some chefs enjoy the stress. They make a kind of cult out of the craziness. That never worked for me."

"Male-female thing?"

She slid the vegetables onto a plate and added more butter to the pan. "Don't know. It's easier for women to create a different working atmosphere because we don't face the same expectations. You walk into a female chef's domain, you already know things are going to be different."

"I'm almost positive she told Scott Glass she'd talked with me. But why? Do you know him?"

Laurel shook her head. "Only by reputation. One of the best bar guys in the business. He and Alex are thick as thieves."

"Nobody I talked to, including Danielle, thought Tariq up to the challenge of running a kitchen. I wonder why Tamara suggested him."

"Maybe she didn't. Maybe he tumbled to her plans and insisted she take him, too." Laurel topped off my coffee, then turned back to the stove to scramble the eggs.

"Oh. Blackmail that backfired. Hadn't thought of that. Hello, Snowball." A giant white fur ball jumped on to the bench beside me, and I scratched behind her ear.

In bare feet and striped pajama pants, Gabe kissed his mother and me, then poured himself juice and dropped to the floor beside Arf. The cat ignored them both.

By unspoken agreement, Laurel and I left all talk of murder behind, reveling in the joy of cat, dog, sleepy teenager, and delicious food.

We picked the topic up as we left the weathered dock and climbed the wooden steps. Young leaves danced on branches, and the morning air carried the lively smell of early spring.

At the corner of Eastlake and Louisa, Laurel stopped. Two water bugs had been carved into a concrete marker, labeled LEPTODORA on one side and TRANSPARENT CARNIVORES on another. Thick teal and cobalt glass rectangles bore the street names, a green compass star in the corner. Like their live counterparts, the carved water bugs have a prehistoric, creepy-cartoonish look. Gabe had told me all about them, one afternoon on the dock. They eat other bugs.

"Sounds like you've eliminated Tariq," Laurel said.

"Not sure. He makes a great suspect. He's impulsive, he's arrogant, and he tracked her to the construction site to confront her. But the time of death's clearly fixed by her phone call to Danielle and my discovery of the body. And by then, he should have been at work, but I haven't confirmed that yet."

She clucked her tongue. "If he'd been that late, you'd have heard about it from the staff."

When I'd mentioned Tariq, they'd all just shaken their heads. *In his own world*, one had said. *Surprised they've put up with him this long*, another told me. *But he cooks great*.

We strolled down Eastlake. "The women in the salon couldn't pinpoint when they saw him. Safe to assume he wanted to confront her about not telling him the plan had changed."

"I hate to say this, Pepper, but if you're trying to eliminate Alex, you're not succeeding."

"I'm not trying to eliminate him. I'm trying—oh pooh." I threw up my hands, accidentally thwacking Laurel's shoulder. "Sorry. I don't know what I'm trying to do. I thought it was important to discover where the killer got the chiles, to eliminate any suspicion that I had a part in the killing. A conspiracy. But much as he hated to admit it, even Tracy said they didn't suspect me of direct involvement—killers don't call the cops."

"Neither do accomplices." We paused in front of our favorite home decor shop, where Laurel and I had found the antique metal lawn chairs that sit outside her front door and my favorite reading lamp. Closed—my credit card was safe. "So you're worried that you facilitated the crime. Unwittingly. But it's no crime to sell peppers, even if someone does use them to kill. You could never have predicted that."

"When everything happened last fall, I expected the customers to run for the hills. Instead, foot traffic increased and the curious browsers actually bought stuff. But this—"

"Except the tea."

"Yeah, though tea sales bounced back pretty quickly. And not one of my commercial accounts ever mentioned it. But this is the second time the Spice Shop's been linked to homicide in less than a year. If someone commits murder with my spices, it taints me. The police are contacting everybody who bought *bhut C* from me. Treating them like suspects." We reached the next corner and another bug in the pavement.

"And you found her."

"And I found her." Alone among my friends, Laurel

seemed to grasp that finding a dead person links you to them. It's as though you owe them justice in this world so they can rest more easily in the next. "Plus I can't help feeling Tamara would still be alive if I hadn't chided Lynette for mistreating a customer."

She snorted. "That woman. Don't waste one more half second thinking about her. You are absolutely not responsible for her ratting to Alex or for his reaction."

My head knew she was right, but my gut disagreed. "Then there's the note left in the door. It's like I'm waiting for something else to happen."

"The note was a prank." Laurel tempers her woo-woo side with a heavy dose of cook's practicality. "A Market jokester."

"No shortage of those."

"Humans," Laurel said. "They drive you buggy."

No arguing with that.

Nineteen

Rainy days and Mondays always get me down.

        —Roger Nichols and Paul Williams,
                    "Rainy Days and Mondays"

YOU CAN'T KEEP A DOG DRY ON A RAINY DAY. THE uneven cobbles on Pike Place had become a watery eco-system, a map of a thousand tiny rivers.

Most mornings, I love being here alone. When I first started working in the law firm, it surprised me that so many lawyers came in super early. No phones, they said. No interruptions. Just fresh coffee and a fresh mind. Less true now that smartphones have taken over the world.

I reached for the light switch behind the front counter. Frowned. Jiggled the switch.

Nothing. My frown deepened. No lights on the electronic scale or the cash register. I crossed the shop to the tea corner and switched on the red lamp.

It did not light up.

I opened the front door and stepped outside. Across the street, the big green enameled lights under the North Arcade roof glowed brightly. Lights shone through the windows in the Triangle Building. I peered up Pine. Both the kitchen shop and the inn had power.

I swore softly and dug in my tote for my cell phone. Called the PDA office—the Public Development Authority, aka the landlord—and was informed that no one else had reported a problem and that a maintenance staffer would be over "as soon as I can find one."

Somewhere in the back rooms of my mind, the other shoe hit the floor.

Nothing so frustrating as a routine interrupted. I couldn't turn on the lights, and I couldn't start the tea. I could grumble, and I did, muttering as I straightened jars on shelves, aligned displays, and let my fingers do the worrying. Old buildings—things go wrong. I'd been lucky so far.

"You're SOL," the Market electrician told me half an hour later. We were due to open in ten minutes. The maintenance man held a large yellow-and-white umbrella over us as the electrician crouched and pointed to a power connection box on the exterior wall. "That wire is fried. We're gonna have to open up your wall and run a new line."

"How long will that take? What do I do for power in the meantime? And how did it happen?"

He held up both hands. "Won't know how long till I get in there. As for how, somebody did this on purpose."

A jolt shot through me.

"Show me what you've got," another voice said.

The rain and bad news had kept me from hearing Tag approach. On the bike, rain or shine, but wearing a waterproof jacket and long pants. And the sunglasses. As the electrician explained, I realized that he'd called the police when he found the burnt wiring. Tag nodded, clicked on his radio, and barked into it.

He clicked off and our eyes met. "You're calling the fire

marshal? Isn't that overkill?" I was cold and wet and angry, and taking it out on him.

He followed me inside, leaving his partner, Olerud, to watch over the scene. "Pepper, this is serious business. Someone tampered with your building."

"I get that." I wasn't pacing; I was stomping. "Believe me, I get that. But you heard the man. It's an inconvenience, not a fire danger. Somebody wants to mess with my business, and maybe my head. But they aren't out to hurt me physically."

"Not yet." His cold, flat voice echoed my unspoken thoughts. "What did you do over the weekend to trigger this?"

"What did I do? What makes you think—?"

A knock on the door caught my attention. Zak, visibly surprised to find it locked. I opened the door and fished a twenty out of my pocket. "Minor electrical problem. They'll have it fixed in no time. Will you run and get coffee for all of us?"

"Sure." He raised a hand to greet Tag, then loped down Pike Place. His last week. Whatever would I do without him?

Focus, Pepper. One problem at a time.

The trouble-ache in my gut worsened when the CSU van arrived. Spencer and Tracy pulled up behind the van, she bounding up Pike in a stylish black raincoat, he trudging behind, tugging an old beige trench over his rumpled sport coat. They disappeared from view, no doubt conferring with Olerud and the CSU crew.

Inside, Tag and I alternated glaring at and ignoring each other. Yesterday, when I'd left Laurel and gone home to clean the loft, do laundry, and think too much, I had thought oh-so-briefly that maybe Tag was right and I should leave the investigation alone. Trust the system. He was part of that system, and I trust him to do his job well. Spencer, too, and Tracy, mostly kinda sorta. But I couldn't shake the sensation of a hand drawing me deeper in.

Tamara's hand, or my imagination?

I fumbled my way through the semidarkness to my office and extracted the note from the locked drawer. When I returned to the shop floor, Spencer and Tracy were waiting for me.

"Why is it," Tracy said, "that you can't stay away from trouble?"

Before I could ask whether he really wanted my answer, the scrape of Tag's bicycle cleats on the wood floor snagged my attention. He folded his arms and shot Tracy an irritated look. Tracy glared back, contempt on his face.

"Pepper, so sorry for the disruption of your business." Spencer stepped forward, blocking the two men from each other's view. "Our folks will wrap things up quickly so the electrician can get to work."

"Okay. But why are you here? Since when does tampering with electrical service bring out the homicide squad?"

"Attempted arson, Pepper. Like I was trying to explain when you wouldn't listen." Tag trotted out his photographic memory of the Washington criminal code. "Knowingly or maliciously causing a fire or explosion that endangers human life or a building where people are."

"But we just lost power. We weren't in any danger."

"That's not so clear," Spencer said. "And anytime a potential felony remotely touches a witness to another felony, we're on it."

For the nano-est of seconds, I wondered how close the nearest defibrillator was.

The shock reminded me of the folder in my hand. I laid it open on my front counter. "We found this stuffed in our front door Saturday morning. At first, I thought it was a prank, but now . . ."

Tag trained his flashlight on the note, and the three cops read over my shoulder.

"Whoever left it knew I found the body. You gave out my name at your press briefing Friday, but it didn't make the papers until Saturday. So maybe the culprit's an early riser who reads the newspaper." As if that narrowed it down.

"Who knew you found the body?" Spencer said.

"My staff. A few friends." I ticked off names. "Danielle Bordeaux and whoever she told. Anyone who saw me at the scene. But doesn't this prove Alex isn't the killer? He's in jail. And why would he ask me for help, then threaten me?"

Tag snorted. "You don't get it about him, do you?"

I longed to wear glasses so I could give him a withering, teacher-glaring-over-the-tops-of-the-lenses look. I gave him my best substitute. "I get that you and Alex despise each other. What you don't get is that I am not flattered and I don't care."

Tracy cleared his throat. "He is still in custody, but he has people."

Oh-kay. So someone in his circle had leaked word about the chiles. But the rest? If one of his cronies wanted to make sure I stayed on the case, surely I'd proven my commitment when I went digging at Danielle's, then quizzed folks at the Café. "You think whoever messed with the electricity also left the note?"

"A possibility," Spencer said. She unfolded an evidence bag and slipped the note inside. "Who handled this?"

"Reed and me. It spooked me enough to put it in the file as soon as I found it with the job applications."

"But not enough to report it," Tag said.

"You'd have told me you weren't the ghostbuster squad." He glowered. Tracy snickered, and Spencer stifled a laugh. "And just so you know, I'm not the one who leaked word about the ghost chiles to the press."

Tag and Tracy looked skeptical. I was debating whether to out Alex as the informer-by-proxy when the maintenance man knocked at the door.

"Sorry, Pepper. I tried to find you a generator, but they're all being used—we're pumping water like mad. And in this rain, I can't say when one will be free."

My face felt like someone had tied weights to my jaw and cheekbones. The officers departed. Outside, CSU took photos and prints and did other detective stuff. I dug around in the back room and scored one flashlight, sans batteries, and one headlight on an elastic band, perfect for crawling around plugging in printers and other gadgetry.

Zak returned with coffee and pastry, and I sent him out for batteries and more flashlights. Dang, I was going to miss him.

Monday mornings may be quiet, but we were not going to close.

"Better whip up a sign," I told Kristen a little while later. It was Sandra's day off, and Kristen had managed to get here earlier than usual. "'Lights out—but we're open!'"

I folded one arm across my chest, my other hand cupping my chin. Ever since Tamara had come into the shop last week, things had been going wrong. Minor at first, the strange incidents seemed to be escalating. *Who, and why?*

And what next?

"Pepper, you see a black Sharpie anywhere?" Behind the front counter, Kristen's flashlight beam zigged and zagged.

"In the drawer next to the box cutter and price labels."

"Not there. I'll have to write big and go over and over my lines."

Zak got the old-fashioned manual scale down from its display shelf. "Good thing you kept this."

The first shopper arrived, her expression puzzled. I handed her a flashlight. "Power outage. Imagine you're camping."

Her face lit up, and she prowled the aisles, filling her basket with teas and spice blends. I took her credit card number and promised to run the transaction as soon as the system was up and running.

Midmorning, I took a quick stretch break and walked out the side door to check on the repairs. The rain had stopped, and the CSU crew had gone, but the electrician was nowhere in sight.

I sighed and stepped back inside. Luckily, the phones worked and I could make calls in my windowless office, sipping the last of my cold coffee. First up, Ops, who answered her line, "This is Barbara."

She was loyalty and efficiency personified. I told her what I needed, but not why.

"Sure, I can pull up those time cards," she said. Clicking and clacking followed. "Oh, ri-i-ight. Wednesday. Tariq called around noon, saying he had an emergency and would be in late. But the sous got someone else to help him prep, so it didn't throw us off."

Red flags waved. "What kind of emergency?"

"Car? Apartment? He said, but I don't remember."

"Alex didn't mention it."

"He came in late, too. Midafternoon sometime. I don't know why—he's usually in the restaurant, or the office, well before noon. Oh. You don't think he—Alex—Tariq . . ."

"I don't know what to think. When did Tariq clock in?"

"Five fifteen. Prep should be done by then, and everyone ready for service. I think he and I need to have a talk."

The chill I got did not come from the power outage. "Thanks. Hey, heard anything yet about a memorial service for Tamara?"

No word yet, but we promised to keep in touch and rang off.

I sat back, hand to my mouth. If Tariq had gone straight to work from Tamarack, he could have been at the site as late as five o'clock. When Tamara called Danielle.

His anger, I could understand. But had he killed her?

"Pepper, your interview's here," Kristen said. "He's—interesting."

Code word for "not likely"?

I yanked off the headlight, ran a hand over my spikes, and put on my confident HR smile. Not easy when the chandeliers are dark and you're operating in the weak, shadowy light that managed to push through the gray skies, find the windows, and filter down to the shop floor.

The applicant's most striking feature was his hair—shoulder-length red dreadlocks. We shook hands. Nice grip. I appreciated the effort to dress up—a shiny brown fake leather jacket over a white shirt, a vintage skinny tie, black pants, and those big boots the young guys wear that look like they're about to fall off.

We talked about the shop, then sat in the nook to review his application. "Taking a break," he said, from a local culinary arts program. "Out of money, and I'm not sure I'm cut out for restaurant life. So when you called the career center, they called me."

Limited retail experience, but his interest in food and his outgoing personality were pluses.

Applicants know what interviewers want to hear. They always assure us they're serious about the job. I had my doubts. But if I found a full-timer with long-term prospects, he'd make a good second hire.

What about the hair? Zak hadn't fit my image of a retail clerk, either, with his tattoos and shaved skull, and he'd been a model employee, so I banished the temptation to dismiss Red Dreads on appearance alone. After all, the Market isn't a law firm. Plus the black-and-white dress code and shop aprons make the staff readily identifiable.

Not to mention, my own spiky locks raise eyebrows from time to time.

"I'll get back to you midweek."

I walked him to the door, then peeked around the corner to our exterior wall. A cluster of men in uniforms studied the damaged power supply. I crossed my fingers. The electrician gave me a thumbs-up. "Twenty minutes, tops."

Despite the threatening skies, I felt bathed in sunshine.

Back inside, I returned a call from an herb grower on Whidbey Island about a new variety of chamomile and a culinary lavender I'd been searching for. She promised to send samples. I checked our inventory of packaging and mailing supplies and made an order list. Called Red Dreads's former employers and his culinary school advisor, leaving messages.

Stared at my customer list, summoning up the guts to make calls—a fishing expedition disguised as a client update.

Decided to put that off until it felt less deceptive. No new job applications had come in. I had not found The One, so I tried the disconnected number again. No luck. I was about to feed the app to the shredder when a teeny little light went on—figuratively speaking.

Out front, Reed had arrived for his afternoon shift. "Just who I needed to see. Any chance you know whether this app was tucked in the door with the ghost note?"

He took a quick look. "Yeah, I think that was the one."

Spencer answered on the first ring. I explained my thinking.

"So, basically, you're saying the app is bogus and it was slipped into your door with the note so that if you picked them up right away, you'd see the app first."

"Right. Whoever left it wants to stay in the shadows."

"I'll send someone down to bag and tag it." Another pause. "Be careful, Pepper. This is getting a little creepy."

Took the words right out of my mouth.

Twenty

Enjoy Seattle weather. 10 million slugs can't be wrong.

                —T-shirt popular in the Pacific Northwest

THE RAIN HAD STOPPED. OR PAUSED—WE HAD A COUPLE of weeks to go in the semi-official rain season. I grabbed a slicker and a leash, and Arf and I sauntered out to clear our heads. Mine, anyway.

One of the orchard girls—Angie, slightly taller than Sylvie—waved from the other side of Pike Place.

"What's going on?" she said after we crossed the street, gesturing toward my building. Arf nosed her leg, and she caressed his ear.

"Electrical problems. Someone messed with the wires."

Her dark eyes widened. "Pepper, no. Are you okay?"

"Rattled, but yeah. You get here early. See anyone hanging around?"

Her shiny dark ponytail wagged back and forth. "Be careful."

I turned to Herb the Herb Man and asked the same question. Same answer. Then another thought occurred to me. "Herb, you sell fresh herbs to Alex Howard's restaurants, don't you?

Any chance Tamara Langston talked to you about supplying her new place?"

Tall and gangly, his hairline long receded, Herb reminded me of a clown minus the makeup. Nothing funny about him now, as his chin rose, his lips tight. "She talk to you?"

Herb and Jane had come to the Market at about the same time, and stayed close. He never treats me as a competitor, nor I him. We send each other customers all the time. If he was eyeing me warily, it must be because he had planned to sell fresh herbs to Tamara, and my relationship with Alex gave him pause.

"Yes." I faced him straight on. "And I admit I'm partially to blame for Alex finding out. My employee told him."

"Behind your back!" Angie said from her adjacent space. "And you fired her."

Herb's features softened. "I should have known you wouldn't break a promise to keep quiet until it was time. Danielle sent her to me—I've been her supplier since she first opened her doors. It's a shame, is what it is."

I reached out and squeezed his hand. "Change of subject. You ever hear about a ghost in the Garden Center Building?"

He scratched one of the remaining reddish tufts stuck onto the side of his oblong head. "Not that I recall. Some people think ghost stories add to the Market's mystique, but I'm a see-it-to-believe-it guy myself."

"Thanks, Herb." I wove my way through the crowd, lost in thought. Clearly, Herb had had no beef with Tamara. Who did—and knew about her plans?

"Pepper, watch out!"

I turned toward the shout, instinctively jumping aside. A towering stack of produce crates tumbled down, crashing to the Arcade floor where I'd just stood. The crates splintered and spinach flew. Radishes and potatoes became miniature bowling balls, and carrots and tomatoes bounced and rolled across the floor. They struck shoppers' feet and caromed off their legs, creating a clattery, splattery, goopy mess.

"Holy rigatoni," I said, gaping at the chaos.

"Pepper, are you okay?" That was Angie, Herb towering behind her. "What happened?"

"I must have brushed too close to the boxes."

"A clumsy shopper, not watching where he was going," Herb speculated.

"Not you," a flower seller said, a Hmong woman not five feet tall. She made a shoving motion with both hands, then pointed toward the Desimone Bridge, which led to stairs down to the waterfront. "That person. Gone already."

I followed her gaze but saw no one.

"Long gone." The produce man glowered. "Some people."

"You mean, on purpose?" The light fixtures seemed to sway, and I steadied myself on the nearest pillar.

The flower seller nodded. Vendors and shoppers were already picking up veggies and mopping up the damage. The produce man waved off my offer of help, saying, "Thank God you're okay."

What was going on? Unsettled but grateful that no one had been hurt, I sought out a few more Marketeers who regularly supply the restaurant trade. Tamara had quizzed the butcher about the origins and availability of numerous cuts of beef, lamb, and more. She'd hinted to the cheese maker that she might want to do business, and talked serious bread with Misty the Baker.

No one had noticed anyone unusual near my building. But they're busy, and it takes a lot to stand out around here.

And none of them had heard boo about a Garden Center ghost.

So much for that theory.

I'd picked up a few groceries on my rounds and decided to add one more item.

"Funny you ask," Vinny the wine merchant said. "She came in, musta been last Tuesday? Said she didn't know much about wine and alcohol distribution and could I give her the nickel version. Now, why does a sous chef need that kind of detail? So I put two and two together and asked if she had a partner or were going out solo. Partner, she says, but she wanted to find her people herself. I respect that."

I waited patiently. There is absolutely no percentage in rushing Vinny.

"So I tell her, Tamara, I says, you need a bar manager. A guy with experience. And she says she thought she had one but he turned her down. And did I maybe know someone." He set a wineglass on the counter and showed me a chilled bottle of rosé. "From southern France, the Languedoc. Tastes like spring."

My French is as rusty as Bill W.'s corkscrew, but I'm pretty sure that region is not called the Leaky Duck. I perched on a stool. A tad early for wine tasting, but Vinny knows his stuff. Even if he can't always pronounce it.

Vinny also knows a lot about the Market ghosts, in part because the old Butterworth Mortuary, the most famously haunted building in the city, is a few doors away. "Vinny, you ever heard any ghost stories about my building?"

He slid the glass toward me, the wine blushing deeply as if embarrassed to overhear gossip about other spirits.

"Not as I recall. Now some folks think ghosts, the spirits of the dead, are electrical phenomena. So it makes sense to think one of them might be behind your troubles." Vinny knew all about my troubles before I walked in. Like something in the air had whispered to him.

"But do ghosts mangle power lines? This is terrific." Bright, almost sparkly. Like a grape kissed a strawberry. I had a sudden urge to go on a picnic.

"And affordable, 'specially after your discount." He set an unopened bottle on the counter. "No reason why not."

"They don't have bodies." I swirled the glass to release more flavor and aroma. "How could they use tools?"

"They got powers we can't fathom. Your computers been working okay? Your watch?"

"Now that you mention it, the cash register's been a bit wonky lately. And we had a problem with the overhead lights last week. Tuesday." The day I fired Lynette. Big day, as it turned out. I glanced at my bubble gum pink watch. When had I last looked at it? Not since eight fifteen, apparently, because that's what time it said. I took another sip and reset my watch. "But why would we all of a sudden have a ghost, when we've never had one before?"

"They like to show up on anniversaries," Vinny said. "Big deal days, to remind the living of their presence."

I scrunched up my face. "If we don't know who the ghost is, how would we know its birthday? And by your theory, it wouldn't be Tamara—the glitchy stuff started before she was killed." It started while she stood in my shop, very much alive.

Didn't that make it more likely that the ghost had some connection to her?

Ridiculous. All this ghost talk was nothing more than someone trying to drive me crazy, and I was not going to let them succeed.

WHAT'S ridiculous, I told myself a few minutes later, is how much I love my shop. It may be, if it's not melodramatic to say so, the love of my life.

The thought of losing it, of not selling spice, purveying adventure and flavor to cooks of all stripes, of this marvelous, maddening old building turning to ash, of not spending my days working amid all these amazing, crazy, wild, woolly people—the kaleidoscope that is the Market—made me sick to my stomach.

I sniffed back tears. "No one is going to take this away from me."

"Nobody will, Pepper. We're all behind you." I didn't realize I'd spoken out loud until Kristen replied and wrapped an arm around me. We were standing on the sidewalk, under the ancient awning, waiting for the all clear from the electrician.

Moments later, we began to gingerly plug in lights, the electronics, the teakettle. Kristen had relocated the cracked samovar to the mixing table, where it shone with pride of place, despite having been doomed to an ornamental existence.

"You're sure it was deliberate?" I asked the electrician.

"No question. Your wiring was redone in the big redo forty years ago, and it's been upgraded over time. But all these old buildings got some funky wires that don't go anywhere. You got some in that wall. Your vandal cut the new wires and spliced 'em onto the old so it all looked right but nothing worked."

"Sounds dangerous," Zak said.

"You bet. To the building and everyone in it, and to the person who did it. He knows just enough to do some real damage. Nursing a serious grudge, if you know what I mean."

My whole body burned. How dare he—they—whoever? "You said you found old wires in that wall. Where did they lead?"

He pointed vaguely to the corner of the building. "Don't know. Might justa been a junction box or your standard outlet."

"Any chance they led to a lighted sign outside?"

He gave a quick shake of his head. He couldn't tell. But it gave me an idea.

I called Fabiola and told her my latest brainstorm.

"I'll let my sign guy know you're coming," she promised.

"Great. I'll swing by his shop this afternoon and talk

design. Better to take a full-sized sketch to the Historic Commission than an idea they can't visualize. Maybe we can get it approved and up before the spring festival." I switched gears. "Fabe, how you doin'? With Tamara's death, I mean."

"Funny how hard it's hit me," she said. "We were just getting to be friends, but I adored her passion. She was jazzed about creating a new restaurant, but it was more than that. She was creating something for herself."

Now that, I understood.

LOVE my shop, love my dog, and here I was, leaving them again. But the staff do the real work anyway.

The industrial district south of downtown changes every time I go there. Some peeps call it SoDo, for South of the Dome—the old, gray Kingdome, long replaced by a sleek modern stadium with a retractable roof. Revisionists say it's short for South of Downtown. Dumb nickname either way, but it seems to be sticking.

I drove past the old Sears building, built by the railroad a century ago when catalogs ruled the day, to entice Sears to make Seattle its western shipping hub. We bought school clothes in the retail store eons ago. Now it's Starbucks's headquarters, the green mermaid peeping out over the clock tower. It's great to see the old buildings reclaimed, though some of the losses make me sad. My favorite sushi place on Capitol Hill is in an old plumbing supply building—beautifully redone, but where did the pipes and drains and valves go? I admit, I felt a little unanchored when I heard that the nuts and bolts company was moving to the suburbs.

Laurel's right: I think too much.

I turned off First Avenue South then made a right, creeping down the block while scanning for the sign maker's address. Two highways plus railroad tracks make the area a bit of a maze. I tried to circle the block and promptly found myself in a dead end. I was backing up when I spotted Ashwani Patel. He aimed his clicker at his car, then limped down the street. I wondered where he'd gotten that limp—he wasn't much older than I.

On the seat beside me, the phone rang. I glanced at the caller's name and frowned—why was Vinny calling me?

That quickly, Patel had disappeared.

"Oh, I know!" I parked the Mustang in the next block and scurried down the sidewalk. A well-known food broker—mainly dry goods, and some spices—occupied one of the old brick warehouses. If Patel wouldn't talk to me in his restaurant, maybe I could corner him there.

Score! There he was, opening the door to Big Al's Imports.

But what excuse could I give for being here that wouldn't sound completely idiotic?

I took a deep breath and opened the door. The man behind the counter, at least six-three and three hundred pounds, looked up.

"Hi. Pepper Reece from Seattle Spice." I held out my hand. "You must be Big Al. I was hoping we could chat about—oh, hi." I greeted Patel as if seeing him for the first time. "I know you, from the Indian restaurant by the Center, right?"

Patel didn't say a word.

I turned back to Al, donning my best look of wide-eyed innocence. "This may sound weird, Al. You heard what happened to Tamara Langston, the chef who was killed? Right next door to Mr. Patel."

"Sad business," Al said.

"Horrible. Anyway, the police took all my ghost chiles for chemical analysis. A couple of customers are begging for them, and my replacement stock hasn't come in yet." Of course not. I hadn't placed an order. "If you have any on hand, could you sell me a few ounces? Full markup—I don't expect any deals. That way, they get what they need without having to make an extra phone call or a trip down here . . ."

Not bad for a complete fabrication, made up on the spot.

"You mean, that way, you don't have to send your customers to me and risk losing their business." He gave me a knowing smile. "You're in luck. By chance, I'd sold out when the police came knocking, but I got a new shipment this morning. Barely opened the boxes. Hang on."

He disappeared into the warehouse behind him.

Leaving me alone with a glowering Ashwani Patel.

"This is all such a tragedy," I said. "Rest assured, I have no intention of interfering with your relationship with Al, but I know spice isn't his main gig. So if there's ever anything he can't get for you, I hope you'll give me a call."

His full lips pressed into a thin line. "Your predecessor closed that door."

News to me. "Things change. Hey, Saturday, I couldn't help overhear the customer quizzing you about dishes with ghost peppers in them. Pretty tacky if you ask me. You have to wonder about people sometimes."

The look on his face said he wondered about me.

I rattled on. "Must be rough, knowing a young woman lost her life right next door. Not to mention the impact on your business, after the ghouls lose interest. You know Alex Howard, don't you? Do you think he killed her?"

Patel fixed me with a disconcerting stare. "I have no idea what that man is capable of."

The door swung open, and Big Al tossed a sealed bag of innocent-looking peppers on the counter. "Sorry to take so long. Call from another damn reporter. They all want to talk about ghost chiles."

I laid cash on the counter. I didn't really need the peppers, but I needed to find out where the killer could have bought them. "Next thing you know, people will say that building is haunted." The little lady behind Patel's take-out counter already had.

For a dark-skinned man, Patel looked awfully pale.

Twenty-one

🌿

Some sources claim that herbs and spices were used in the Middle Ages to make rotten meat edible. Others note that no amount of doctoring makes rotten meat safe—and no one who could afford spices would eat rotten meat. More likely, they say, that spicery dressed up the taste of salts and vinegars used to preserve food.

I WAS STARING AT THE GROCERIES SPREAD OUT ON MY kitchen counter, trying to remember what I'd had in mind, when my phone rang.

"I'm out on bail, and I'm going nuts. Come over and let me make dinner."

Did I hate being summoned more than I loved letting one of the city's finest chefs cook for me?

Fifteen minutes later, Arf and I stepped off the elevator and into Alex Howard's penthouse. That's a word usually used for top floors of skyscrapers, but in this case, apartment and loft were too mundane. My first time here, I'd been seriously envious—effortless style, expensive taste, no detail spared. But then I realized it was the work of a chic and pricey decorator, and my envy vanished. Clearly, she'd understood what image he wanted to project. Alex wasn't a guy to trudge from one furniture store to another or spend hours studying flooring samples. He was a guy who wanted someone—preferably a good-looking woman—to scout out the options for him so he could say no, no, yes, yes, no, yes.

Alex greeted me with a peck on the cheek and a glass of bubbly that made me forget all about Vinny's rosé. The days inside had taken their toll—his cheeks had sunk, and underneath the beard stubble, his skin had gone ghostly.

But jail food hadn't ruined his taste buds—the aromas coming from his kitchen nearly made me swoon.

"What is that heavenly smell?"

"Pork loin. Hey, boy." Alex rubbed Arf's head and put a bowl of water and a plate of what looked like pâté on the entry's slate floor.

His kitchen couldn't have been less like Laurel's. Both photo-worthy, but in oh-so-different ways. This one was meant for show as much as for work. Cherry cabinets lined the back wall, uppers and lowers separated by a white marble work top veined in gray. Stainless steel everything, from the six-burner stove to the glass-front fridge and freezer and the built-in espresso maker.

Guests gravitate naturally, as I did now, to tall chairs set along a high cherry bar, Alex's work space on the other side. That way, he could show off his cooking skills without turning his back on his guests. His audience.

"Grilled asparagus with chopped eggs, olive oil, and your spring blend—the fennel, garlic, and coriander combo. Whidbey Island mussels in garlic-parsley broth." He pushed classic white dinnerware toward me. His voice teetered between frantic and exhausted, and beneath the short sleeves of his tight black T-shirt, the muscles in his upper arms quivered.

"So, you got bail." I speared a mussel and dropped the shells in a bowl. "Tell me what happened."

He paused, his stainless steel spoon frozen midair, his eyes shiny as black currant sauce. "It's bizarre. You're charged with the worst crime imaginable. Everything is surreal, like it's happening to someone else, but the someone else is you. It's all routine to the judge and the lawyers, and before you know it, it's over. They took me back to the cell while Barbara posted my bail. They rushed the paperwork to get me out by five. Either they needed my bed for somebody else, or a clerk didn't want to work overtime." He reached for a tumbler of water, gripped it tight. "I swear, going outside was such a shock, I nearly hugged the closest tree."

Chefly instincts intact, he plucked a tray out of the wall oven, then arranged his olive popovers with herbed sour cream on a plate and placed it before me. Our eyes met briefly, and I wasn't sure whether this dinner was my reward for helping him out or an attempt at seduction.

Not in the bedroom, a sleek black-and-silver enclave with deep rose accents, but in the court of public opinion.

Why was he trying so hard? To get me to tell him all I'd learned, or to promise to keep quiet?

I sipped the wine, reminding myself to keep my wits. The night was young. I plucked a popper off the plate and held it up, like a communion host, before taking a bite. "Why did you call me, Alex?"

He didn't look up, busy slicing and dicing. "I needed a friend."

"Glassy's your friend. And the Café's closed on Mondays, so he's free."

"You aren't sick of my cooking." His blade thwacked the cutting board, turning a large red shallot into teeny, tiny dice. But it wasn't the sulfuric gasses making his eyes water. "Why arrest me when the real killer is still out there? Why are they trying to ruin me?"

"Ruin you? Your restaurant is booming. And who are 'they'?" I shifted on the barstool, my skin a little hot and twitchy.

"Who do you think?" His eyes cleared, his voice sharp and honed. "Your pal Tracy."

"What? He's not my pal. He can't stand me."

"He and your ex, Officer Hot Wheels, would like nothing more than to put me behind bars and leave me there to rot."

I opened my mouth to ask what on earth he was talking about, but he'd turned his attention to the stove. Shallots flew into a hot pan. Butter popped and sizzled as the water and other compounds released in the heat and began the transformation into sauce. Alex was a picture of compact energy as he deglazed the pan and sprinkled in parsley and other magic ingredients. A part of me wanted to leave, to run away and have nothing more to do with this maddening, presumptuous genius. But my dog was happy and my mouth was watering.

We sat at a cozy table for two next to the floor-to-ceiling windows. A better view than mine—higher up the hill, unimpeded by the Viaduct. It was almost like a date, except for the conscious effort I had to make to keep from thinking of it that way.

"This is fabulous. Thank you."

Alex laid his fork down and gazed out the window. "I can't believe she was going to leave. I had plans for her."

"People get to make their own plans, Alex. Even employees. Zak's leaving for his dream job. I didn't see it coming, and I can't possibly replace him." I leaned forward. "Life—and business—is just one long series of transitions."

He cocked his head, not hearing me, still seeing the future he'd envisioned. "In a year, tops, she could have taken over the Café. She would have been ready for any kitchen in my company."

"You're missing the point, Alex. She wanted her own place. Like you did. Like Danielle Bordeaux and Laurel Halloran. Ashwani Patel and his wife. Bringing her vision to life."

He looked shocked, as if he hadn't thought of it that way. "A mistake. I could have made her a star."

The Pinot Noir he'd poured, a reserve from the Willamette Valley, sparkled in the light as I swirled the glass. I'd never eaten Tamara's cooking. When it came to food and fame, Alex might be right. But he still didn't get that people value what they create themselves far more than the boxes other people make for them.

I told him about Tariq hanging out near Tamarack on Wednesday afternoon. "It takes a good fifteen to twenty minutes to get downtown from there. If your time clock is right, he could have come and gone before she called Danielle. Or maybe he caught her moments later. Hard to see him as a killer, but I can't rule him out."

The moody dinner light picked out the pulsing in his temples. His nostrils flared. "The lying little creep. Ditches prep and waltzes in late, without a second thought." His words stabbed the air between us. "He is dead. The scrawny punk is—"

He spotted the horror on my face, my hands gripping the arms of the chair.

"I don't mean it, Pepper. You know I don't mean it."

Less than a week ago, he'd threatened a woman I'd found dead barely twenty-four hours later. And now he was threatening the chief suspect.

I'd told Ben we use phrases like that all the time, and they aren't threats. But now . . .

Tariq's lies bothered Alex more than the possibility that the young cook had killed Tamara.

And that bothered me way too much to stay for dessert.

HAD I just fled dinner with a killer? I stalked down the street, dog beside me, muttering unkind thoughts. Had I talked myself into believing Alex not guilty, despite the evidence to the contrary, because we had a history together, short and checkered as it was? Or because if Alex had killed Tamara with *bhut C*, I'd supplied the murder weapon?

More than I wanted to save my shop's reputation, more than I wanted to be a part of the Market, providing jobs and spices, more even than I wanted to prove to Tag and my parents and everyone else that I was capable of creating something that *mattered*, I wanted to believe myself a good judge of people.

And I had blown it.

I'd nearly been seduced by perfect asparagus and a good Pinot.

"Dang it, Pepper, you are an idiot sometimes. You think you've got life figured out, but you can't see when a guy you know is a big-time user is trying to use you. You aren't even able—"

Arf barked once, sharply. I tensed and looked around. Nothing. "What is it, boy?" I bent to see the world from his height, if not through his eyes. "You were hoping for more pâté? Sorry."

But rotten as I felt, we couldn't go home and sleep it off quite yet. We had an appointment.

"YOU brought the dog?" Vinny's friend Hal asked. Hal had a high forehead and a pointy chin, and in the blue-white rays of the streetlamp outside my shop, his head resembled a lightbulb.

"'Course she brought the dog," Vinny said. "They see things we don't."

"Some ghosts don't like dogs." Hal opened a hard black plastic case and withdrew a box, dials and gauges covering the top. "Gimme a minute to tune the equipment."

"If the ghost don't like dogs, then that's a clue to who he

is." Vinny sounded exasperated. "You oughtta know that. You wrote the book on ghosts."

I'd met Hal once before. My former employee Tory and some friends had opened an art studio and gallery in Pioneer Square, and when she and Zak invited me to a pre-Halloween ghost tour of the area, I'd gone along for fun. The author of several books on Seattle's ghosts, Hal was shorter than both Vinny and me, with frizzy white hair and wild eyes. But while he shared Vinny's enthusiasm for the unseen, he lacked the boy-out-of-Brooklyn accent.

"What is that thing, anyway?" I said.

"An electrospectrograph," Hal replied, and I could have sworn he said electrospooktrograph. "It detects the radiographic waves that ghosts emit."

"You should see this thing upstairs in Butterworth's. It goes ballistic," Vinny said.

I'm a relatively normal woman, so why am I standing outside my shop at midnight with two men who are so absolutely not normal? Vinny'd had me fooled for years. Give me a good spiel and deal on wine and I lose all good sense.

Convince me you can solve an unsolvable crime and the real trouble starts.

I unlocked the door to the shop.

"What's that red light?" Vinny's words tumbled out like ice cubes in an old freezer.

Weird. We always turn the apothecary lamp off when we close—it's a fire hazard—but the red silk shade glowed in the corner.

"Leave it on," Hal said. "If a ghost lives here, it's used to the lamp. 'Sides, we don't want to startle it."

Arf's cold nose poked my hand, and I stifled a yelp. "It's okay, boy," I said quietly. He trotted behind the counter, nails clicking on the plank floor, and settled on his bed, uninterested in the ghost hunt.

The instrument had a small, built-in light that illuminated the dials. "This is the one we gotta watch." Hal used a jade chopstick to point at the middle dial, the largest.

He traced the perimeter of the shop slowly, gripping the instrument with both hands, eyes on the gauges. Vinny hung on one shoulder. I stayed a step or two behind, close enough to keep an eye on the dials without running into either man. Or getting poked by a chopstick.

When we reached the side door, Hal spoke. "If there's anyone here, please speak up."

Vinny shifted his weight from one foot to the other, and for a moment, I thought he might open his mouth.

Hal raised his voice. "We come in peace. We only want to know who's here and if there's anything you need from us. From the living."

"And why they're messing with my electricity," I said under my breath.

The red hand on the left gauge jumped slightly, then dropped back into place. "What was that?" I said.

Hal took a step back. Nothing.

We detoured into the restroom and my office. I followed them back into the main space and glanced to my left. The red lamp flickered.

"Did you see that?" I said.

"See what?" Hal asked.

"I don't see nothing," Vinny said.

The gauges did not move. The two men moved on to the mixing booth. I stared at the lamp. It glowed steadily.

By the tea cart, the right hand dial popped to life briefly, but Hal said Vinny had brushed his elbow and dismissed it. Behind the front counter, he stepped carefully around my sleeping dog and I wondered if my seemingly intrepid ghost hunter wasn't a tad bit afraid of dogs.

Hal processed to the middle of the shop, the instrument in front of him like a crown to be placed on the royal head. "If there is anyone here—man, woman, or child, or dog—who rests uneasily in the afterlife, please signify your presence."

Vinny sneezed. "Sorry," he said in a stage whisper. "Rubbed up against the cinnamon display."

"Please signify your presence," Hal repeated, "so Pepper can know you're here. She doesn't expect you to leave, but she's been having some problems with the electricity. And somebody left her a note that was a little troubling."

I did expect them to leave, and the note was more than a little troubling.

"You don't need to leave," he said again, "but she needs to know that the building and everyone in it will be safe. That's a reasonable request. If you're here, let us know that no one will be harmed."

The red light in the tea corner flickered, and I nearly jumped out of my yoga pants.

A few minutes later, we were outside, huddled by the streetlamp.

"Nothing," Vinny said. "I for sure thought we'd see a shadow or detect some protoplasm or electro whatevers."

Hal tucked the instrument back in its case. "Five years of letting you tag along and you still don't know the terminology. But you know, with ghosts, it's hard to rule them out. They don't always appear when you ask them to. Sometimes they've got other places to go."

Neither man had seen the lamp flicker. My imagination, no doubt, after yet another long, stressful day. I tugged Arf's leash, pulling him a little closer, and huddled deep into the thick fleece jacket I'd grabbed from my office. It did nothing to ward off the chill no one but me seemed to feel.

"We can try again another night," Hal said, latching the case shut. "But as I told Vinny, I've never heard tales of hauntings in this building."

"What about someone who died recently," I said, "in another part of the city. But she'd just been in my shop. And she might have died because of something that happened here."

"Possible," he said. "Though in that case, we'd expect her to come talk to you when summoned."

I remembered what the woman in the Indian restaurant had told me about the floating ghosts in white. "What do you know about *bhuts*?" I said. "Indian ghosts. East India–Indian."

"Not much. Never encountered one in Seattle. I imagine they behave same as any other ghost—some nasty, some nice." Hal shook his head, and his Einsteinian white locks formed a spectral mist above his scalp. I shivered and glanced down, afraid of what I might see.

But his feet pointed forward.

"Thank you, gentlemen. Time to go home, Arf. We're overdue for a long nap."

Twenty-two

My head hurts, my feet stink, and I don't love Jesus.

—Jimmy Buffett's version of a bad day

"YOU DID WHAT?" SANDRA HOOTED AT MY TALE OF MID-night ghost hunting with Vinny and Hal.

I felt rather ghostly myself, dragging in late. The black pants and T-shirt did not improve my pale skin and baggy eyes. Didn't help that I'd run out of hair goo and had to wear a Mariners cap.

"They didn't find anything. Their meter gadget is pretty funky—I don't know what it was supposed to pick up." I sipped my latte. "There was one weird thing. The red lamp was on, and I.swear, it kept flickering. But nobody else saw it."

"I know I switched it off when we closed," Zak said. "After all the electrical problems, I made double sure."

My staff and I exchanged looks, and the creepy-crawly, pee-your-pants factor rose.

"Reminds me of the ghost next door when we were kids," Kristen said. I remembered the incident, but Sandra and Zak didn't know the story. "Big old fixer-upper. A single woman bought it and started restoring it. Then she got in a car accident and spent months on crutches. The living room fireplace had electric sconces with glass lanterns on either side. The lights would go out, and she'd look over and see that the lanterns were upside down. She'd drag herself over, flip the lanterns right side up, and the lights would go back on." Her hands made flipping motions as she talked. Like the little lady in the Indian restaurant.

"By the time she got back to her chair, the lanterns would be upside down again. This went on for days. Finally, she decided it was time for a talk. 'Look,' she said, 'I'm on crutches. You don't have to leave. Just stop messing with the lights.' She never did figure out who her ghost was. But the lights never went out again."

"Good story," Sandra said, "but I've worked here more than twenty years. We do not have a ghost. And no spook messed up that power line."

I wanted to believe her, but after last night, I wasn't so sure. Maybe the power problems were another message from Tamara's spirit, pestering me to find her killer.

Oh, Pepper. I shook my head at my own foolishness. *Shoulda got a triple shot.*

Sandra updated me on the wedding registry, and we whispered plans behind Zak's back for a going-away shindig. I helped two women spice up a spring dinner party, then spruced up the cinnamon display. Made new recipe cards and a poster: CINNAMON OR CASSIA—WHAT'S THE DIFFERENCE? Set out bowls of broken bark for taste testing.

"Forgot to tell you about yesterday's interview," I told Sandra in a momentary lull. "Red Dreads. Not perfect, but he'll do, if his references check out."

"No such thing as the perfect employee, boss."

"Except for you," I replied, and she cackled, a happy hen.

I tugged the ball cap tight over my misbehaving hair and set off for the PDA office to submit the drawing for the new sign.

Pooh. Next to Rachel the Brass Pig stood Officer Hot

Wheels, as Alex had called him, straddling his bike and chatting with the electrician.

"Gentlemen." I headed for the narrow, curving stairs Tag and his bike could not negotiate.

"Pepper, wait!" Tag called. The electrician waved and squeezed past me, forcing me to step to the side and face my nemesis. "I hear your friend is out of jail. I hope you take my advice to keep your distance."

I hated to admit his advice hit home. So I didn't. "Tag, I want to know who killed Tamara. If it had any connection to me and my shop, I will feel guilty for the rest of my life. But at least I'll know."

"Some people ought to feel guilty and don't."

"Like you?" He flushed, and I wished I could see his eyes behind the shades. "You mean Alex, and you might be right. But he wasn't the only person at the Café nursing a grudge against Tamara."

"We're looking into that," he said. "Into everything about her and her plans."

That didn't sound good. I wanted Danielle to be in the clear. "Don't let me keep you. You have criminals to chase. And meter maids."

"Like you're chasing college boys? And ghosts?"

I ignored the crack about Ben. And after pumping Vinny for gossip, I could hardly be ticked that he talked as freely to others as he did to me. Besides, Tag's job includes keeping his finger on the downtown pulse. "I admit, the note and the tampering have me rattled. Tag, tell me. Honestly." I resisted the temptation to say "if you can."

"Shoot." He leaned his bike against the wall and peeled off his gloves.

"Alex thinks Detective Tracy has it in for him. I'm not going to ask you to criticize another officer, but you know I've had my own run-ins with Tracy. He's . . ." I paused, searching for the word.

"Abrasive," Tag said. "But effective."

"Point is, is there some history I don't know about? Some bigger reason you and Tracy don't trust Alex? Besides him lying to me." Tracy had no reason to care about that.

Tag was slow to respond. "A lot goes on behind the scenes in the restaurant world."

"What, wage theft? Hiring illegal immigrants? Or are you saying Tamara's death is drug related, and Alex is involved?" It's not uncommon for young people who work long and late under high pressure to use drugs to come down, or to ramp back up after they've burned out. But nothing I'd heard linked Tamara or Alex to drugs. If Alex had used in the past, Tag wouldn't like it—aside from some youthful mischief, he'd always been clean and lawful—but it wouldn't explain his intense dislike of the man.

And flattering as it was to credit jealousy, I suspected there was more to it.

He nodded quickly. Too quickly. The thin white scar inside his wrist throbbed, a sign I had learned to read too late to save our marriage.

A flash of heat burst in my throat. "Dammit, Tag. Stop withholding the truth. Tell me what's really going on."

"I wish you'd let this go, Pepper. But I know you won't." His radio sputtered noises I couldn't decipher, and he told the noises he was on his way. He stared at me intently as he pulled on his gloves. "It's one of the things I love about you."

Leaving me to sputter.

Out of the corner of my eye, I spotted a movement. "Tag, see that person? Something strange—oh pooh." He followed my gaze but the figure had disappeared behind a crowd cheering on the fishmongers as they teased tourists and tossed salmon through the air.

He peered over the tops of his glasses, and I heard genuine concern as he said, "Be careful, Pepper. There's a lot of trouble out there."

* * *

CALLIE hadn't checked in on the research project—and no word from Ben, either. On my way out of the PDA office, I sent them each a text.

After last night, I finally believed that Alex was capable of killing Tamara. But as I'd told Tag, he wasn't the only one.

I called the shop and said I'd be back in an hour.

Midday, midweek, parking in Wallingford was a lot easier than on Saturday. I'd left my conversation starter napping in the shop—my own charms would have to suffice.

"Are you police?" Zu the viola player rubbed sleep out of her eyes and raked her fingers through her straight black hair.

"A friend of Tamara's. I was helping her with the new restaurant. Can we talk?"

She led the way to the kitchen. A top-of-the-line espresso machine and burr grinder sat next to the apron-front white farmhouse sink. Behind a small tiled table for two, a giant baker's rack contained a restaurant's worth of pots, pans, and ovenware. Wire hooks on the backsplash held spoons, ladles, and spatulas of every size.

And next to the stove stood a double-layered lazy Susan chock full of spices.

But it's bad manners to wake a woman up and scour her spice rack to hunt for deadly peppers.

Zu filled a kettle and turned on the gas. "Last night, when my taxi pulled up, my neighbor met me to tell me Tamara is dead."

"I'm so sorry," I said. "Were you two close?"

"She need a roommate. I need a house. I didn't see her much. But she would leave me dinner from the restaurant."

"Did the police tell you what happened?"

"They called, but I did not want to call them back. I did not do anything wrong. The Symphony manager told me it was fine, okay to talk, but . . ."

Even legal immigrants often fear the police. And while I knew better than to assume her accent meant a lack of understanding, she might worry that her English wasn't adequate for a difficult situation. "Is there someone from the Symphony who can sit with you when you're interviewed? I can call an immigration lawyer I know, to make sure you understand our legal system. I was married to a cop and . . ."

Her head shot up, her dark eyes wide and afraid. "Go now. You should go now."

I held up my hands. "I'm not connected to the police. Promise. I meant to say they'll want to ask what you know about Tamara's family. Her friends. Anyone who was upset with her, any strange occurrences. They won't harass you. They want to know what we all want to know: who killed her."

The whistle blew, reminding Zu of her obligation to hospitality, and she busied herself making tea.

"Mmm." I cradled the mug she handed me and breathed in the fragrance. "Jasmine blossoms. Lovely."

And at that, the waterfall began. I grabbed a box of tissues from the bathroom and led her to the table. When she stopped sniffling, I reached out a hand. "Your neighbor said the police were here. They should have left an inventory of what they took."

She scooted back her chair and scurried off, returning a moment later with a handwritten list. We bent over it together. Ordinary stuff: financial papers, files related to the restaurant venture, a calendar. Her laptop.

"Her notebook. She always carry a notebook."

Her notebook. She'd had it with her in my shop, making lists and drawings as we spoke. "It was probably in her bag when she died. The police would have it. Did Tamara tell you about anything unusual? Anything that upset her?"

She tore a tissue from the box and scrunched it between her palms. "The phone call."

"What happened? Who called?"

"A man. I answer. I told him Tamara's not home. He said, 'Tell her, keep quiet.'"

"When did this happen?"

"A week ago? More? I do not know. Before I left to New York, to see my teacher. He called a second time; she answered. She slammed the phone, walked here, there"— she pointed back and forth—"talking, very mad."

"Do you remember what she said?"

Zu thought a moment. "She said, 'It's time. I work, I wait, it's time.'"

My heart sank. It had to have been Alex, angry about her leaving. But if Zu was right about when the call came, he couldn't have known her plans.

Keep quiet, he'd said.

I thanked the musician for the tea and left my business card.

Keep quiet about what? I'd presumed Tamara's murder was related to her work because murder comes from passion. Except when it comes from pathology. And Tamara's passions all involved her work.

Unless she'd triggered someone else's misguided passion or pathology. But what, what, what?

Outside, I called Detective Spencer. "Tamara's roommate, Zu, is back. She mentioned something I should have remembered—Tamara's notebook. She showed me the inventory from your search, and it wasn't listed. Did you find it at the construction site?"

I heard Spencer clicking keys, consulting her notes. A long silence. "Thanks for the call, Pepper."

If I read her right, no. I pictured it. A hard green cover, bound with a black spiral, maybe six by nine. If the police hadn't found it in the apartment or the building site, then the killer must have taken it.

Find the notebook, find the killer.

* * *

I wanted Tariq's side of the story. But I could hardly stake out the bus stop where I'd run into him the day after Tamara's murder, waiting for him to show up.

Sometimes you just have to ask for what you need. I called Alex's office, and Ops—I still thought of her as Ops, though I remembered now that her name was Barbara—gave me the cook's address and phone number. And an update on his employment status that was more irritating than surprising.

Confronting a potential killer in his own home would be off-the-charts stupid. But Seattle isn't the most caffeinated city in the country for nothing.

"Don't know why I'm bothering to listen to you." Twenty minutes later, Tariq slid back the hood of his gray UW sweatshirt. He pulled a wooden chair from the square black table I'd claimed in Cappuchimpo's far back corner, swung it around, and straddled it, hands draped over the slatted back. The gesture said, "Talk fast, 'cause I'm not promising to stay." He said, "You got me fired."

"I did, and I'm sorry about that. Alex promised me—"

He snorted. "Yeah, Chef's full of promises. Everybody in this business is full of promises." His tone told me what he thought of those promises.

"I'll get right to the point. You went to the construction site to talk to Tamara last Wednesday afternoon. Why?"

The barista set his triple shot in front of him. He grunted in thanks and wrapped his hands around the small white cup, never taking his glower off me. "I wanted answers. Why did she let Danielle cut me out of our plan? Why didn't she have the balls to tell me?"

Because chefs are full of promises. Because she had her own plans and they mattered more to her than you did.

"So when you asked her, what did she say?" I watched him over the rim of my own double mocha.

Pain replaced the bluster. Relieved of kitchen duty, he hadn't shaved today, and a shadow softened his jawline. "That she realized when she watched me cook for Danielle that I didn't measure up after all. That I needed to decide whether to work harder or waste my talent."

A little blunt for my HR brain, but she'd gotten her point across.

He met my gaze. "I know what you're thinking. Yeah, I was pissed. But I didn't kill her. When I figured out she was planning to leave, I talked her into letting me go with her because I wanted to work with her. I still did. Swear to God, she was alive when I left."

I wanted to believe him. He was calm enough now, but everyone described him as a hothead. "Last Friday, out on the sidewalk, Glassy gave you a tongue-lashing. A warning."

He squinted, shaking his head slightly. "Beats me. It was like he thinks I know something, might try something. But what?"

His confusion seemed genuine, and it complicated the picture. "Any of the dishes you were responsible for use ghost chiles?"

"No. Heck, you got to be in Chef's inner circle to get access. He all but locks 'em up. Like we might grab the jar by mistake and turn the lobster bisque into fireball soup."

That's what everyone else said. Alas, it put me no closer to finding out who'd used my peppers to kill.

The monkey-in-a-coffee-cup logo grinned down at me. "So who did kill her, Tariq?"

"Chef," he said. "Who else?"

And that was the question.

"SHOOT. Were we meeting today? My watch has been acting up." I glanced at my wrist. Right. More like my brain was acting up, the result of interference by electrospooktro-graphic waves.

Ben gestured at the photographer crouched in front of the Chinese apothecary, snapping away. "We came downtown to shoot another story and took a chance that you'd be here."

"Give me a moment to freshen up." I dashed to the washroom. No fix for the bags under my eyes. While my uniform wasn't stylish, it was clean and spoke "Spice Shop." The Mariners cap? I'd sneak in a reference to being named for a famous ballplayer and my family's love for the game.

"Don't worry, you look great," Kristen said when I emerged. "Natural blush is always best."

Smarty-pants.

While Ben interviewed my staff, the photographer directed me to pose first in the nook, then beside the apothecary, assisting a customer. Next, I pretended to serve tea from the cracked samovar we'd left out for atmosphere. He got a sweet shot of Arf poking his nose out from behind the counter.

After the photographer left, Ben and I sat in the nook. I'd given interviews before, and nothing he asked was new—how I came to own the shop, what we offered, spice trends—but I always appreciate opportunities to expand our audience.

"What's your real name?" he said after I explained the origin of my nickname.

"That's for me to know, and you to never find out."

"I love a challenge." He closed his notebook. "So, we just came from a press conference Alex Howard held. He and his lawyers made statements and took a few questions. He's adamant about his innocence."

"Blaming the police for railroading him, wasting time they could be using to track the real killer?"

"You've talked to him, too." Ben's tone was wry.

"Maybe he's right. He's an easy target—the boss who fired the victim and threatened her. But what if someone's using that as cover? Someone else with reason to want her out of the way. Oh pooh." I frowned, squirming on the hard bench.

"This still makes you uncomfortable," he said. "Mixing work with pleasure."

I knew what he meant—I wouldn't deny feeling some chemistry between us. But it was more than that. Investigating Alex, being warned off by Tag, and now being charmed by Ben—it was all too confusing.

His blue eyes locked on mine. "Like I said Saturday, I'd like to spend a little time together."

Maybe we could. Maybe kindness makes a man more attractive. And maybe the only way to learn to trust my judgment again was to dive in.

Ben tucked his notebook in his pocket and started to slide out of the booth. I reached out and grabbed his wrist. Pulled him closer and kissed him.

Twenty-three

Job named a daughter Keziah, possibly after the Hebrew word for cassia, the cinnamon-like spice much valued in ancient times. One biblical scholar says the name came to symbolize female equality, since Job left all three daughters an inheritance in a time when that was rare.

—Paul J. Achtemeier, *HarperCollins Bible Dictionary*

"I'M NOT CALLING HIM STUPID OR DISHONEST, AND I'M not saying he's always late," the woman on the other end of the line said of Red Dreads. "But he can't make change, and he can't read a clock."

"Bummer. I appreciate your honesty."

"Hey, I know how frustrating it is when no one says anything more than 'yes, he worked here.' Good luck."

Hiring, along with almost everything else in my life, was becoming a lost cause. I blamed my bad attitude on the late-night ghost hunting, a pastime more akin to Don Quixote tilting at windmills than Jessica Fletcher digging up dirt.

Arf rested his chin on my knee. How do dogs always seem to know when their humans need comfort?

"Boss." Sandra stuck her head in the office. "TV news wants to interview you."

My hair might be hopeless, but the publicity might help with hiring.

"One measure of heat in food is Scoville heat units, which quantify the concentration of capsaicin—the compound that creates the sensation of heat. Another test measures pungency. Neither is precise," I told the reporter a few minutes later, camera rolling. "Seed lineage, climate, even the soil all make a difference. Ancho chiles score relatively low, at 3,000 units. In comparison, jalapeños clock in at 25,000. Ghost chiles can reach one million Scoville heat units."

The reporter blanched, and the customers clustered nearby gasped in unison.

"How do they kill?" The reporter stuck the microphone an inch from my nose.

"You'll need to talk to a toxicologist for that. We're strictly culinary here."

"Do you have samples we can try?" The camera panned the Spice of the Month display and the tea cart. The cracked samovar was getting an atmospheric workout.

"Sorry. I'm out." I did have the bag from Big Al's, but I sure as hemlock wasn't going to risk disaster with the cameras rolling. And I didn't want to give anyone ideas. No doubt the reporter had been at Alex Howard's press conference, too, and was working her way down a witness list similar to Ben's. Figures—I wear a ball cap and wind up in two photo shoots. "By the way, we are hiring. Must love food, retail, and the Market."

The Historical Commission rep came in, holding the door for the departing TV crew. I steeled myself for more hoop-te-doodle.

"No approval without historical evidence of a lighted sign. If it were up to me," he said, shaking his head to suggest he was on my side. I wasn't convinced.

Since none of the pictures I'd found so far showed a lighted sign, my last recourse was a dusty afternoon in the County Archives, poring over old photographs.

Thinking of lights made me think of the electrical danger we'd been in. Danielle had said Tamara was poking around in the new space because it had electrical problems. Now we had electrical problems.

Did that mean whoever left the note knew about our weird wiring and Tamara's discovery? What if both were the work not of the same ghost but of the same prankster?

Someone who wanted me to investigate and who wanted to scare me.

It was working.

THE Archives weren't as old and dusty as I'd expected, but they weren't exactly comfy, either. Nearly two hours later, after flipping through files stuffed with photos of the Market, enduring countless paper cuts, and going half blind over microfiche, I uncramped myself and let out a long sigh. Sore muscles and dry eyes don't matter if you find what you're looking for.

But I hadn't. Not one shot showed a lighted sign outside my building.

Halfway down the courthouse's wide, marble-tiled hallway, I paused to flex my cranky knee. A few feet away, a man in a navy suit sat on a long oak bench next to an elderly woman wearing a mint green coat dress and heels of a style I hadn't seen in decades. He cleared his throat, his tone too low to overhear, and pointed to her left hand. Her fingers shook as she slid off her wedding rings and handed them to him, their eyes not meeting. A debtor exam, where a lawyer representing a client with a judgment to collect literally takes the valuables off the borrower's hands.

I wanted to disappear, my only consolation the knowledge

that both of them were too focused, and too embarrassed, to notice me. But the sight gave me an idea.

In the Clerk's Office, I pulled up the civil litigation records. (I knew from experience that they weren't online.) No collections suits under Ashwani Patel's name or Tamarind's. Good—I wasn't sure I wanted to do business with him, but at least we could clear that hurdle.

As I made my way out of the building, it wasn't Cadfael's words that came to mind but those of another fictional sleuth. What about the dog in the nighttime, Mr. Holmes asked Dr. Watson. The dog who didn't bark.

Ashwani Patel, everyone said, had married another cook. They'd run the restaurant together until she left him.

But his name appeared nowhere in the court records. No petition for divorce and no decree.

I left the building, head down, thinking, and ran smack into Detective Spencer. She wore another of her stylish-but-sturdy black suits. Her sidekick was nowhere in sight.

She held out her hand. "Thanks for alerting me about Zu Wang. Union rep from the Symphony brought her in. She didn't know much, but every bit we can learn about the victim helps."

"I suppose you talked with all the restaurant staff, too."

"They're not so easy to run down. Some of them don't like the police." One corner of her lip turned up. "Doesn't help when Howard fires them."

"You mean Tariq Rose," I said. "He thought he and Tamara were starting the new place together. When Alex fired Tamara, Tariq realized she'd moved ahead without him. I spilled the beans, after getting Alex to promise he wouldn't let Tariq go. But he changed his mind."

Spencer cocked her head and gave a low whistle. I've always wished I could do that. "Kind of a hard case, isn't he?

Howard, I mean. But what you're saying about Rose complicates things . . ."

"Right. Makes him a suspect, too. Detective, I don't suppose you can tell me whether CSU linked any prints on the electrical stuff in my building to the ghost note and the mysterious job application?"

She eyed me closely before speaking. "I couldn't really say. But you know, sometimes they make a tentative match, but the prints aren't in the database."

We were standing outside the courthouse. There was no reason for me to feel out of breath. Except that she was telling me without telling me that I'd been right about a connection. And ghosts don't leave fingerprints. "So they can't put a name to them. Sometimes they find the same prints at two different scenes, right? Like maybe an attempted arson and . . ."

"And a murder scene. Yeah, that happens, too. Hey, I wanted to ask about that job opening. Part-time, full-time?"

"SPD not treating you right, Detective?"

She smiled. "My daughter, Tessa. Loves food, loves the Market. I wish she'd go back and finish that degree, but until then, she needs a job."

"Degree? You can't be old enough for a college-age daughter."

"She's twenty-four. I finished high school one week, had a baby the next. Applied to the department on her second birthday, the first day I was old enough. Needed a good job to support her on my own."

We were the same age but had led such different lives. "Not always easy for a woman to navigate a course through a sea of difficult men."

Her demeanor remained placid, but if my eyes didn't deceive me, a shadow crossed her face.

"I'll have Tessa get in touch. Thank you, Pepper." She turned and walked away, heels rapping on the sidewalk, leaving me wondering what chord I'd unwittingly struck.

* * *

I slipped into the next building lobby, sat on a bench, and brought up the County Recorder's website on my phone. If Patel had been married in Washington State, there ought to be a record, though I didn't know how far I'd get with his name alone.

Far enough. The "length of search" indicator on the website said it took 2.7 seconds to find that Ashwani Patel and Ashley Brown had been married five years ago this past February 14.

I sat and pondered. Married. Disappeared. Of course, she could have divorced him in another state.

Why did I think it mattered?

WWCD? What would Cadfael do?

GHOSTS aside, spaces can hold emotions, and I knew something was wrong the moment I walked into the Spice Shop. I swung behind the counter to pet Arf, then grabbed the first available employee.

"What now?"

"It's on your desk." Sandra's chin quivered. "Came right after you left. A customer said someone outside asked her to deliver it."

She followed me to the back room, clutching her elbows. Seeing her flustered worried me more than the note itself.

Murder most foul, as in the best it is. But this most foul, strange and unnatural.

I sank into my chair. Fragments flew around my brain, not quite connecting. "Send Reed in."

"Hamlet," he said a few minutes later. "It's from the scene where his father's ghost appears to tell him what looked like an accidental death was really murder."

"But we know Tamara's death was murder," I said. "Not even the police doubt it. So why is our ghost—our prankster, or note-ster—so insistent?"

But my History major, English minor employee had no idea. Neither did the others. "Maybe I should stick around another week or two," Zak said, straightening to his full height as though his size would stop the danger. It hadn't so far.

"Thank you." I touched his arm. "That's sweet, but it's time for you to move on with your life. And we'll be fine."

I retreated to my office, pondering the meaning of the notes. I'd interpreted the first as a push to investigate Tamara's death. The second was almost a shove.

Who wanted me to investigate, but didn't dare say so directly? Who cared about Tamara—and justice—enough to prod me from the shadows?

Tariq? Another employee? But while her coworkers had expressed sadness, I'd detected no deep, personal grief. And though one or two sounded willing to believe Alex guilty, no one gave off vigilante vibes.

I called Spencer to report the Hamlet note. She promised to send an officer ASAP.

Meanwhile, I had a coincidence to probe. I dialed another number.

"Thanks for taking my call. I'll be quick. You told me the Tamarack space had electrical problems. Can you be more specific?"

"Lights going on and off," Danielle replied. "A fan that ran backward. A curious smell, like burnt cinnamon."

Other than the smell, it sounded a lot like what we'd experienced. "Tamara ever say anything about Ashwani Patel?"

She hesitated. "He—didn't want us to lease the space. Mucked up his plans for expansion. Pipe dream, if you ask me. His food is too traditional for the modern urban palate."

"But Indian food's hugely popular." At least, judging by

how well our curries and garam masala sell, not to mention turmeric, cardamom, and even *bhut C*.

"Your modern foodie doesn't want to step out in the evening to eat the same samosas or curries over rice that she can get at any food truck. She wants sautéed arugula and spinach with paneer and roasted cashews. She wants Indian food with a Pacific Northwest accent—seared halibut with black chickpeas and a yam curry."

Talking to chefs always makes me hungry.

"Updated classics," she continued. "A little familiarity, a little adventure. If you're going to commit to pricey real estate in the heart of the city, you've got to satisfy those eaters."

As Tamara had hoped to do. "She ever mention ghosts? Or a tiny Indian woman who works for Patel? Elderly. Wears a sari and a bindi—the dot on the forehead."

"Ghosts? That old rumor. I'm sure Patel spread it himself," she said with a wry laugh. "I stopped by his place a couple of times to give him updates, assure him we'd be good neighbors. But I never saw a woman like that."

"Doesn't matter," I said. "One more question. What do you know about his ex-wife, Ashley?"

She was silent, no doubt thinking. "I heard she left town, ages ago. Sorry, but I've got to run. If I think of anything else, I'll let you know."

I thanked her and hung up. A hot, sour sensation dripped down the back of my throat and grabbed at my chest.

All this talk about curry and Ashwani Patel gave me heartburn, and I hadn't eaten a thing.

Twenty-four

Columbus didn't find all the spices—or gold—he originally claimed, but one spice he did find, the aji, or chile pepper, proved so popular, and so easily grown in so many parts of the world, that it has traveled even further than he did.

"A LIGHTLY SMOKED PAPRIKA," I TOLD THE CUSTOMER planning her first paella party, "recreates the traditional flavor of cooking over an open wood fire. Combine it with Hungarian paprika and a sweet Spanish variety, plus a hint of rosemary, to give the stock a rich, full flavor. And the saffron threads—"

The door opened, and in walked Officer Hot Wheels.

"I'm only here to collect the evidence," Tag said, the glasses still on.

"It's a full sheet of paper," I said, acutely aware that my customer had gone silent. "Won't it get crushed?"

"I know how to transport evidence, Pepper." He glared at me. "It will be perfectly safe."

"Let's see if we can finish up that list." Kristen swooped in to rescue my customer. "Oh, this will be divine," I heard her say as I led Tag to my office. "And you've already got your fish . . ."

Hands gloved, Tag inspected the note, the letters thick, black, and ominous, and slid it and the envelope into separate plastic bags. "Who handled these?"

"Sandra touched the note. She and the customer touched the envelope."

He shot me a dark look. "Not you?"

"No. When she realized what it was, she left them both on the desk and told me about it when I came in." The bitter taste returned to my mouth, and I swallowed hard. "Tag, I am so tired of this. We finally managed to get to the point where we could talk without every conversation turning into a battle, and now—"

He snatched off the glasses, grabbed my shoulders, and kissed me. Hard.

And heaven help me, I kissed him back.

After a long, long moment, we unlocked lips. I tried to step away, but the door and Tag's arms kept me within kissing distance. "Pepper, you don't know how much I wish I could turn time back."

I put my hands on his chest, his warm, broad chest. "It's not going to happen, Tag. We need to move on."

"Why? Why can't we give it another try?"

Because maybe we never should have been together. Because I'd finally managed to erase the black mark I'd felt on my forehead ever since I'd stumbled over him and Miss Meter Maid in the darkened corner of a trendy hotspot on my way to the restroom.

Because I like my new life. I like who I am on my own.

Arf nosed my leg. "My dog needs to pee. Let me get his leash and we'll walk out with you."

Tag tucked the evidence into his bike bag, and we headed up Pine, stopping to let Arf do his business in an alley. A hint of sunshine made faint shadows of us on the sidewalk. My heart was thumping, and not from the uphill climb. I was a bit ashamed of myself for questioning him on the evidence transport; he's a good cop and I know it.

"Tag, I know you don't like me asking questions about cases, but—"

"I don't want you in danger." A slight tremble betrayed his emotion.

"—it's about Tamarack, the restaurant Tamara Langston was working on. Where she was killed." I went on as if he hadn't spoken, gesturing as we walked. "The man who runs the Indian place next door, Ashwani Patel. Apparently, he'd planned to rent the space himself, and was pretty resentful."

"How do you know this?"

"Danielle Bordeaux. Patel and his wife started the restaurant. When they split, she disappeared. Left town."

"You're the one in favor of moving on."

I ignored the barb. "Last Saturday, I stopped in, and the moment I introduced myself, he got all hostile. Then a strange thing happened while he was talking to a customer."

"Wait, go back." Tag rolled the bike forward slowly. "Too many cooks. You're saying that Tamara, the victim, was opening her new place with Danielle Bordeaux? The restaurant owner? Howard used to work for her. Did Patel work for her, too?"

"Alex worked *for* Danielle? I didn't know that. He started the Café a good ten years ago. She mentioned knowing Patel but didn't say they'd ever worked together."

He tilted his head, one eye winking shut, a habit I found oddly sweet. "What if Tamara wasn't the target? What if the killer was after Danielle?"

"There's no mistaking one for the other. Danielle's a good five or six inches taller, twenty years older. Both blondes, but that's it. Tamara spent a lot of time at the site. Planning, envisioning. And scoping out the electrical problems.

Danielle dropped in occasionally." She could have been the target—but that still raised the question why.

"What electrical problems?"

I told him what I knew. "But the strangest thing happened when I stopped in Patel's last weekend. This tiny, ancient Indian lady sits behind the takeout counter. Her sari's the same shade as the walls. You'd hardly notice her. She told me there was a ghost hanging around, a *bhut*, and pointed next door." I stopped, grabbing his arm and forcing him to face me. "A *bhut*, Tag. It's the same word as in *bhut capsicum*, the ghost peppers that killed Tamara."

"Oh, c'mon, Pepper. Vinny doesn't have you believing all this ghost stuff now, does he?"

"Tag, you're not listening. This isn't about ghosts. She was trying to tell me something. About Tamara's death. I think she wanted me to focus on the ghost peppers."

"You're not making sense."

Maybe not, not yet. But I knew there was a connection. Patel told the customer he'd taken ghost chiles off the menu, and I had to admit, he could have been at Big Al's to pick up anything, not necessarily to restock *bhut C* after using his supply to kill his next-door neighbor. And anyway, why would he have attacked Tamara?

Some connection I couldn't quite grasp . . .

"You want to take Vinny and Hal to Tamarack and see what we can find?" Tag's tease interrupted my musing.

I laughed. "Not a bad idea."

Tag's big hand encircled my upper arm. "Yes, it is. It's a terrible idea. Anything that brings you in close contact with a suspected killer or takes you back to the murder scene, at midnight or in broad daylight, is a terrible idea." He stopped in the middle of the sidewalk, tightening his grip and stepping closer. My throat clamped shut, certain he was about to kiss me again.

Talk about a terrible idea.

* * *

MOVIE Night is the Best. Idea. Ever.

Most weeks, anyway. Usually, I adore gathering for girls-night-in to eat, chat, and watch a movie. Or just eat and chat.

But recent events had thrown me off-kilter, and what had seemed like a plan when I shopped the Market and plucked spices off the shelves now resembled one of those cook's challenges on TV, where contestants are given three ingredients, a pantry, and half an hour to stun the judges. In a good way.

"Stress is simply unfocused energy." Alex's kitchen mantra appeared unbidden in my brain. "Focus on creating flavor."

Gad. As if things weren't crazy enough—I was channeling Alex Howard.

Well, no matter what else you might say about him, the man can seriously cook.

First up, a champagne Negroni. Tag's mother believes no refrigerator is properly stocked without at least one bottle of champagne. You don't need a trust fund or a second mortgage to follow that rule—there are some decent sparkling wines under fifteen dollars. I pulled one out of the meat cooler, uncrimped the wire cage, then put one hand on the cork and twisted the bottle.

Voilà! A satisfying pop. I poured the Campari, sweet vermouth, and champagne over rocks and added an orange twist. One sip and I felt like a master chef. Or bartender. I stuck the bottle in the ice bucket and set out glasses and ingredients for Negronis and Cosmopolitans.

How had Danielle described her ideal diner? Modern, urban, with a taste for international.

That's me all over.

Inspired by my recent restaurant visits, the menu was all appetizers. Last night, I'd roasted almonds and cashews with garam masala and amchur—dried mango powder—for the

Indian touch. I set bowls of fragrant nuts out in the living room. "Don't touch," I told Arf, curled on his bed with a chew toy. "Or you'll be sad."

He barely glanced up. That's how much the males in my life listen to me.

Next, swaying to the strains of another new discovery, the Portland Cello Project, I chopped fresh chives and mint from my deck garden and blended them with goat cheese. Mixed crab cakes and a carrot and red cabbage slaw. For fun, I popped open a jar of the apricot-currant chutney Laurel and I had made last fall. The downstairs door bell sounded, and I pressed the button to buzz in my friends.

"So that's how you stay in shape," Seetha said. "You run up and down these stairs every day."

"And hike up to the Market and walk the dog," I said. Kristen slipped him a liver chew. She knows how to handle men.

Surveying the bounty on my counter almost made me drool. Laurel brought a bowl of Ripe's Greek salad. Seetha unpacked a colorful fruit salad with a honey-lime poppy seed dressing.

"Dang, I love friends who can cook."

"I'll drink to that," Kristen said, raising her Cosmopolitan in a toast. "And to Tamara. Murder sucks."

My eyes stung, and not from the spicy food.

"What's the movie tonight?" Laurel asked, sinking into my red leather chair, a champagne Negroni in one hand, nuts in the other, and my dog at her feet.

"I can't decide between *The Lunchbox* and rewatching *Chinatown*."

"Egad, you are in a mood," she said.

"'You've got a nasty reputation, Mr. Gittes. I like that in a man.'" Kristen's imitation of John Huston as Noah Cross set me laughing so hard I started coughing.

"Might be a good night to stream *Pride and Prejudice*,"

Seetha said. Jane Austen, our go-to when nothing else seems right.

My phone signaled a text. "'Scuse me." I took my phone and drink to the kitchen, where I scrolled through Callie's message. *Holy cow.*

"Speaking of nasty reputations," I said, rejoining the group and scooping up a few spiced nuts. "What do any of you know about Ashwani Patel or Ashley Brown? His wife, or ex-wife. The more I poked around, the more curious I got, so I called Callie this afternoon. She finally finished her rush and had time to do some research. That text was from her. There's no paper trail—well, electronic trail—of Ashley after she left him, two years ago."

"What are you saying, Pepper? That something happened to her?" Seetha said from the couch.

That same vapory chill I'd felt so often in the last week washed through me now. "No reason to think that, but it's like she just—vanished."

"Better have some of this goat cheese before it vanishes." Kristen smeared the herbed goat cheese on a garlic crostini.

"Callie find any family?" Laurel asked.

"The curse of a common name." Not a problem for any of us.

"I met him once. A year ago, right after I moved here," Seetha said, a hint of her Boston upbringing in her voice. "A neighbor invited us over. You know, they're both Indian—fix them up. The blind date—the American version of the arranged marriage."

"Don't dis it," Kristen said. "That's how I met Eric."

"And how I met Tag, so draw your own conclusions. Tell us more about him."

Seetha shook her head, her shiny black hair brushing her shoulders. "Nothing to tell. I never saw him again. The subject of his ex-wife never came up."

"Did he talk about expanding his restaurant?"

"Oh yes. He talked and talked." She sipped her cocktail, remembering. "He said he had some money coming, and then he would expand. I got the impression there might be problems, but he was so full of himself—honestly, I didn't care enough to ask questions."

That creased my brow. It fit what Danielle had said—that she and Tamara had come between Patel and his plans. I itched to claw through the documents Callie had sent.

"Seetha, what do know about *bhuts*? Indian ghosts."

I heard the ice hit the table and the glass crack as it struck the floor before I saw what had happened.

"Oh cra—" Seetha unfolded herself and stood, the cranberry red of her drink sliding down her jersey tunic and dark pants. "Pepper, your couch. Your rug. I am so sorry."

Ever the mom, Kristen dashed to the kitchen for a damp cloth. She dabbed at the red rivulets running down Seetha's hands and ankles—cranberry-tinted gin, not blood—then I led her to the bathroom. Flicked on the light and we locked eyes in the mirror.

Neither of us said it, but she was white as a ghost. I found a dark-colored towel for her and left her alone.

In the living room, Kristen and Laurel had already sponged most of the spill from the caramel-colored couch and the rug. Not everything in my place is the product of a day-off treasure hunt. I'd spotted the kilim in the bargain pile at a local branch of an import chain when I swung by to check out their spice blends.

We slid the couch back and wiped the floorboards. Then we each made ourselves another drink and settled back to wait.

Seetha emerged a few minutes later. Laurel raised her glass in question, and she wrinkled her nose. "I think I've done enough damage for the night."

"Don't give it another thought. We're more concerned about you."

She sighed and sank back into the couch. "I told you about my grandmother, right? The one in India who faked a heart attack to lure my mother back home?"

Laurel filled in. "She expected your mom to stay in Delhi and raise you kids there, leaving your father and her career behind, but the ruse didn't work. Then years later, when she did get sick, your mother almost didn't believe her."

Seetha nodded. "After my grandmother died, my mother started seeing *bhuts* in our house. In Cambridge, Massachusetts. Where my grandmother had never been, in a country she refused to visit."

For a moment, the oxygen seemed to leave the room.

"I started seeing them, too." The confession drew her back in time, and she stared at the unlit fireplace in the corner. "Ever since, they've come and gone. Nothing for months, a year or two, and then, there one is. What triggers them, or what they want from me, I don't know."

A less benevolent version of the medieval chants that play in my head?

"And now?" I said, not entirely sure I wanted to hear the answer. "When did this one appear? What does it look like?"

"Like they all look. They're white and they float." Her voice floated, too, as though it had lost its connection to her body and was drifting around the room, searching for a place to land. "Some of them carry a scent or a sound."

I pictured the ghosts we made as kids, wadding up a white Kleenex to make the head, then draping another over it and tying a string around the neck. Drawing eyes and a mouth with black and red markers.

"It started Wednesday," she said, looking me straight on. "Last Wednesday, and nearly every night since."

The scent of hot oil grabbed my attention, and I jumped up, stifling a yelp. Laurel stood at the stove, frying crab cakes. I cradled my throat in the vee of one hand and breathed out and in, out and in.

We migrated to the kitchen and set out slaw, chutney, and salads, none of us wanting to venture far from Seetha's side.

It couldn't be coincidence that her *bhut* had first appeared the night a woman had died in a building next to an Indian restaurant. But Seetha had never met the woman, and she'd never been to the restaurant, although she had met the owner. I'd found the body, but was Seetha's connection to me strong enough for the *bhut* to bother her?

Maybe so. Maybe they picked her because she believed and I didn't.

Or at least, I didn't used to.

Twenty-five

There are five elements: earth, air, fire, water and garlic.

—Louis Diat, 1885–1957,
chef at the Ritz-Carlton for forty-one years

KRISTEN STAYED LATE TO HELP ME CLEAN UP, THOUGH there wasn't much to do. Seetha had ridden over with Laurel, and I was glad she had safe passage home.

They'd both skipped dessert, a foreign concept to me.

Dishes washed and leftovers tucked away, we carried mugs of decaf and white ramekins of crème brûlée to the living room. "Every time we get together," Kristen said, "we get another nugget about Seetha, but we never see the whole picture. Ohmygosh, this is fantastic. Orange, cinnamon, and—what else?"

I thought about Danielle Bordeaux, who acted so open and friendly yet revealed little about herself. Or her former employees, never mentioning that Alex Howard had worked for her. Seetha, in contrast, appeared proper and reserved. But every now and then, she dropped a little bomb.

"Thyme," I said. "We still don't have any idea why she moved out here—"

"Can't get much farther from Boston," Kristen said,

"except for Alaska. And I can't see her driving a snow machine."

Seattle became the jumping-off point for Alaskan travelers during the Gold Rush, and is still a haven for Easterners eager to leave the past behind. "But I think she gave us a clue to what haunts her."

"You asking about *bhuts* set her off," Kristen said. "That was weird. I've never seen her so rattled."

"Been a rattling kind of day. First, the note, then Tag . . ."

"What? What happened?"

I felt my cheeks go as red as the leather chair I'd curled up in. "When he came by to pick up the note, he—he kissed me and—"

"Pepper. Do. Not. Do. It. Do not get involved with him again." She set her empty dish on the crate and leaned forward, hands in prayer position. "Nothing wrong with having dinner with your ex. Better to be friends than enemies. But don't let it go any further. Please."

"I won't. I swear." I ran a hand through my funky hair, not improved by the day under a ball cap. "But thirteen years means something."

"Not to him. He already proved that. The man does not know the meaning of commitment."

"Wait. Are you talking about Tag, or Alex?" I warmed my hands on the mug. "Why do I have such rotten judgment about men? I love my life, but it gets a little lonely."

"Your judgment is perfectly fine. You left Tag. You broke it off with Alex. You just need confidence." She stood. "Go bowling with Ben. Have fun. But don't be desperate. That's what leads to bad judgment."

After Kristen left, I took Arf for a spin around the block, then climbed into my jammies. Made another cup of decaf, said no to a second dessert, and opened Callie's finds on my laptop—easier to read the tiny legal print there than on my phone.

Over the years, Ashley Brown and Ashwani Patel had left a rubble of trouble, blazing a maze of deceit. I simply hadn't known where to look. Once she had Ashley's name, Callie had uncovered business licenses for three separate restaurants. Collections suits by unpaid vendors—meat, produce, and spices. If I could whistle, I would have—how on earth had Jane let them run up a bill that high? For all her customer savvy, Jane was a hippie at heart, uninterested in the financial side of the business. That's why I'd had to install an inventory system when I took over, and why it had been fairly easy to turn a profit, once we turned the organizational corner.

But she wasn't, apparently, the only soft touch. Eviction notices from two landlords claimed months of unpaid rent. I dug out a notepad and jotted down the dates and addresses, making a rough chronology of their business history. Claims by the state for unpaid overtime and stolen tips. Suits by linen services, a janitorial supply company, and an electrician.

That one gave me pause.

But the real shocker was that Ashwani Patel's name was nowhere to be seen. After his wife left, he'd hidden transactions behind half a dozen corporate names, no doubt counting on superficial credit checks or suave explanations.

The scum had even continued to rack up debt in her name. Callie had dug up her credit score—how, I didn't know; Callie never crosses an ethical line, but she knows how to tap-dance them. It looked like my last bowling score.

Good for you, Seetha. I may have rotten taste in men, but you knew a stinker when you met one.

I kept scrolling. Callie had found inspection records from the Health Department—his places had always squeaked by—and announcements of the new restaurants. The first incarnation, the Blue Poppy, had been profiled by a hipster blog shortly after it opened. I recognized the location from the photograph, a hole-in-the-wall off Madison, on the edge of super-trendy, super-expensive Capitol Hill.

But that wasn't all I recognized.

I zoomed in on the photo of the smiling couple, arm in arm beneath the vivid blue sign. Ashwani, tall, dark, and self-satisfied. And wearing a chef's coat in her signature green, Tamara Langston.

I inhaled sharply. Arf raised his head. "It's okay, boy."

But it wasn't okay. If my eyes weren't fooling me, Ashley Brown had disappeared and returned as Tamara Langston. Risen from the ashes, so to speak.

So why on earth open a restaurant next door to her once-and-former husband? Or whatever he was.

I tried to blow up the photograph for closer inspection, but no luck. I toggled to the daily paper's website. Ponied up to get the archived story pairing Tamara's picture with Alex's, already behind the paywall. Chalked it up as a business expense. Split the screen and put the two shots side by side.

Changing hair style and color is easy, as I can attest. Disposable contacts make new eye color a cinch. Eyebrows can be pretty distinctive, but I recalled reading an article ages ago that said earlobes are our most distinctive facial feature. Unless you hide them behind hair or under a hat, they can give you away.

I pulled up the magnifying glass app on my phone and peered closely. Reached over and switched off the lamp. I had to squint, and I couldn't be positive without showing the pictures to someone who knew both women. But I'd bet my bottom dollar that the missing had been found.

Dead, but found.

"Oh, Tamara. What were you doing, playing with fire?"

Ashley and Ashwani. Tamara starting Tamarack, next door to Tamarind.

All her hopes and plans, whatever they'd been, up in smoke.

* * *

NO *bhuts* disturbed my sleep. I hoped they'd been equally kind to Seetha.

Despite the late night, I was rarin' to go Wednesday morning, bolstered by the discoveries that could help identify Tamara's killer. Or Ashley's, if my theory was correct.

Buoyed by optimism, Arf and I jogged up the Market steps. The air smelled of a coming rain. At the top, near the bakery, I glanced toward the North Arcade. I saw no one unusual, but a jolt zipped up and down my spine, as though I'd touched a hot wire.

As I've said, if the Market had a middle name, it would be some version of wondrous strange. The Shakespeare quote jumped into my brain unbidden, triggered by what Reed had dubbed "the Hamlet note."

I ordered hot drinks for my staff and a box of cinnamon rolls, and asked for a candle in one. No reason cupcakes should have all the fun.

A few minutes later, I picked my way down the cobbles to the shop, juggling leash, bakery box, and drink holder. Sandra had already turned on the lights—working fine, thank you—and both Reed and Kristen had arrived.

"Hey, I know my watch has been acting funny lately, but is yours running fast?" I handed Kristen her cappuccino.

"Ha-ha. I wouldn't be late for Zak's last staff meeting. Besides, after last night, you and I have lots to talk about."

Sandra's eyebrows shot up, and Reed, fiddling with the sugar, looked up. The front door opened. Zak strode toward us.

"My last Wednesday. My last week."

"Hey, man. Don't be down. You landed your dream job," Reed said, and I knew that in the not-too-distant future, Reed would leave us for his own dream job, whatever it might be.

"Yeah, but you guys have been so great. Tory and I will never forget any of you."

"Forget us and I'll haunt you," Sandra said. She dealt out napkins and opened the bakery box. I picked up my latte and frowned, reading the note scribbled on my cup.

NF2L. Never the same woman twice.

Nonfat double latte, I understood. But what did the silent, pale-faced barista mean by the rest? My appearance and my outfit didn't change much day to day. My mood, on the other hand, could be a little shaky before coffee.

I took a long sip and pushed the questions aside.

"So Eric made coffee for me this morning," Kristen said, her fingertips on my arm. "He always does when he gets up first. But instead of dusting cinnamon on top, he grabbed the cumin by mistake."

Sandra gasped. She has a more developed palate than Kristen and makes the occasional snide comments about Kristen's taste. (Impeccable in everything else, but then, having tweens at home can downgrade one's food choices.)

"I didn't want him to know it was awful," Kristen continued, "because he was being sweet, so I pretended I was in Casablanca."

"Remember who started the trend when Starbucks features it," I said.

After our meeting—short on substance, long on reminiscing with Zak—we got ready to open, then I retreated to my office. Caught Callie on the first ring.

"Hey, thanks. I owe you. But you raised more questions than you answered."

"Welcome to a researcher's life."

"Am I reading this right? You found absolutely nothing on Tamara Langston before two years ago?"

"Right. It's as if the woman sprung into life when she moved to Seattle," Callie said.

"The flip side is, everything you found about Ashley

Brown ends at exactly the same time, except for the credit record."

"Also right. Until then, I found her all over online. She shared recipes, entered baking contests, ran 10Ks and half marathons, and then, poof! Nothing. Ohmygosh, Pepper! Are you saying what I think you're saying?"

"Yep. One more search, if you have time. You sent me a photo of Ashley and Ashwani at the opening of Blue Poppy. See if you can find more pictures of her—at races, charity cook-offs, whatever. I know the name might hold you back—"

She snorted. "And I thought Caroline Carter was a common name."

We hung up, and I followed a train of thought that occurred to me as I drifted off last night. It was remotely possible that Ashley-now-known-as-Tamara had gone along with what Ashwani was doing in her name. A twisty-turny type of fraud. But why? The real puzzle was the location. Why give her restaurant a similar name to his and open next door? She'd insisted on that location, despite Danielle's doubts.

The light dawned. Her motive had been revenge. His had been rage.

First, I called Jane. "Pick your brain? I'm going over a list I found of former customers, wondering if I might bring them back in the fold."

She gave me the scoop on a Madison Park bistro and an upscale joint in Lake City. Then I asked about Ashwani Patel.

A long pause. Then, "Oh, my dear." Said ambiguously, as both endearment and exclamation of concern.

"I'm afraid I may have made things worse for her." She paused. I waited. "They came to me when they opened their first restaurant—a flower name."

"The Blue Poppy?"

"That was it. They'd used their cash on the build-out, so I carried them for a while. They'd let the account build up for a few months, then bring in a check for the full balance and a wonderful take-out meal for the staff. It became a routine."

Depending on the size of the bill—and the skills of the chef—that might not be such a bad deal.

"He's one of those overbearing men with sweet wives. You wonder how they stand it, if their husbands treat them privately the way they treat them—and everyone else—in public. But you try to stay out of it." She paused, and I pictured her in her island paradise, staring out at the ever-changing winds upon the ever-changing waves. "She went from being a vibrant, confident blonde to a mousy thing you barely noticed. After Blue Poppy came Mon—not Montlake . . ."

"Mantra?" One of the corporate names Callie had uncovered.

"That's it. They went upscale but kept the take-out service. For financial security, I imagine, but I thought it was a mistake. Blurring their identity. What your generation would call diluting their brand."

An evil to be avoided. Thanks to Jane's sketchy bookkeeping, none of this showed in the few financial records she'd left behind. "What happened?"

"That failed, too, so they started a third place, Tamarind. One day, they brought in a check to pay off a big tab, and a huge feast of a spread. He asked my opinion, and I gave it to him. The butter chicken was tough, and the spicing was off—he'd let his curry go bitter. The samosas, on the other hand, were delectable. Perfect pastry. And she made a carrot cake using Indian spicing, a cross between a halvah and a cake, with cardamom and nuts and an edible silver star on top. Divine."

Bring in a recipe once, and forever after, Jane would recall what you'd made. She couldn't remember to update personnel files, but she knew what spices you'd needed for which dish for your book club two years ago.

"I'm afraid I'm too blunt sometimes," she continued. "He

was the cook; she was the baker. When I gushed over the cake, he scowled and dismissed it as not traditional. Acted as if it were her fault that I praised her dish and not his."

"Like she was showing him up." I bit my lower lip.

"Exactly. They left, and I saw them outside—him yelling, her cowering. I wanted to intervene, but what could I say that wouldn't have made things worse?" She paused, and I heard her sipping tea. "Not long after, I heard she'd left him. Left town. I felt guilty—I never saw him hit her, though I suspect he did. If his ego was too fragile for honest criticism, he shouldn't have asked for it. And he certainly shouldn't have blamed her."

"Straws and camels' backs," I said. "Sounds like your compliment gave her the courage to leave. Check your e-mail in about five minutes and call me."

I sent her the two photographs—Ashley and Ashwani outside the Blue Poppy, and Tamara Langston from last week's newspaper. She wouldn't have seen the story—her indifference to business extended to the daily news as well.

Then I called the electrician who'd sued Patel for nonpayment.

"Deadbeat. First he wouldn't pay, then he had the nerve to say my work was substandard. I've been wiring commercial kitchens and restaurants in this city for twenty-five years. My work is second to none."

Why was I not surprised? "Were you working on the build-out next door? For the new restaurant called Tamarack?"

"Yeah. Screwy deal. We scoured that place from top to bottom. Couldn't recreate the problems, couldn't find the cause. With these old buildings, you don't always know what's in the walls—"

As I was discovering, myself.

"—but if there's something wrong there, we'll fix it."

"One more question. Did you ever talk with the little lady who works out front, at Patel's place? His grandmother, maybe?"

"Never saw her."

I thanked him and hung up, grabbing the phone a minute later on the first ring.

"Are they twins? Cousins?" Jane's voice was tremulous, high and worried. "Pepper, what's going on?"

I only wished I knew.

Twenty-six

In Tudor England, nutmeg—bought from Venetian merchants who acquired it in Constantinople from traders who got it who knows where—was used to treat colds and flatulence. But when physicians prescribed nutmeg pomanders to treat the plague, the seeds of Myristica fragrans became precious as gold.

—Giles Milton, in *Nathaniel's Nutmeg, or,*
The True and Incredible Adventures of the Spice Trader
Who Changed the Course of History

THE POSSIBILITIES SCREAMED THROUGH MY BRAIN. I could take the fuzzy picture to Zu Wang or the house-painting neighbor and ask if Tamara was Ashley Brown reincarnated. Show it to Danielle, to the women in the salon, or if I was ultra, uber brave, to the little woman I thought of as the crazy Indian grandmother. The woman who'd first told me about *bhuts*.

But the face in the photo was so small and shadowed.

And I could think of only one person—besides Patel—who'd known them both.

* * *

NOT long before I met him, the local paper ran a feature on Alex, showing the great man posing in the restaurant and in the kitchen. After this ordeal—assuming he came through unscathed—they might want to do another, focusing on his office. If *GQ* had a design section, he would be the poster boy. Other folks worked here, too—after all that had happened, I'd dared come up only because Ops, her assistant, and the accountant would be close by. But in style, the place was all him. And the decorator.

He gestured to the dark cherry Windsor chairs paired in front of the very tasteful cherry desk—not too large, but not too small—and glanced briefly at his own padded brown leather chair before taking the seat next to mine. A photo on one of the matching bookcases behind the desk stood out: Chef Alex Howard attending the James Beard Awards dinner, the year he was nominated for Best Chef Northwest. I had never seen him so genuinely happy.

"How's business?"

"Good, good," he said, rapid-fire. "Never thought I'd miss the kitchen so much. Or all the idiots who work for me." He grinned, but his heart wasn't in the gibe.

"According to everything I've heard and dug up, Tamara worked in just two restaurants in Seattle, both yours. A bit of a surprise."

His face remained neutral, but a vein in his neck throbbed.

"Alex, did you know when you hired her who she was?"

I'll give him credit for this: Most people would have acted astonished, pretending they didn't know what I was asking. Not Alex.

"Of course I did. That's why I hired her. Pepper, you know the restaurant community. Everyone knows everyone. Oh, not the diner or pizza people, or the brand-new prep cooks."

He waved a hand at those unseen worker bees. "But if you've cooked in this city at this level for six months or more, I want to know you, so I can steal you away."

The heavy double doors opened, and a young woman brought in a coffee tray, the French press working its magic. She set the tray on a cherry buffet along the redbrick wall and left. Alex rose and poured for us both. He handed me a hot cup and sat, cradling his own. Murder is a chilling topic.

"She couldn't have reinvented herself without our help," he said. "She didn't want to be driven out of town—her town—because her husband turned out to be a creep."

"Did you hire her as Ashley Brown, or as Tamara Langston?"

"Tamara. She changed her name legally, but not in Seattle, because she didn't want him to find her. She was living in Snohomish County and working in my Eastside bistro. Worked like a fiend, learning every station." He eyed me over the rim of his cup.

"But you said everybody knows everybody. He was bound to find out." Had Danielle known, and not told me? Had Spencer and Tracy discovered the switch? "Especially when she opened up next door. That, I don't get."

"Me, neither." He squinted, beating his chin with the side of his fist. "Part of the reason I thought she would stay is that we sheltered her—Ops, Glassy, and me. We kept her secret. We didn't put her picture on our website. We didn't brag that our new sous had run three Seattle restaurants, that she was a prizewinning pastry chef, that she knew Indian food inside out but could conquer any cuisine."

"Right. The article about Blue Poppy exclaimed over her deft touch, and said she combined Indian spices with French pastry sensibility. And Jane called Patel's food bland and overcooked but raved about Ashley's baking. That was years ago, but Jane thinks she might have set him off."

"A man who will hit a woman is only looking for an excuse," Alex said.

I shuddered, knowing he was right. "A lot of women don't report abuse. Even if she had, it would have been as Ashley Brown, so the detectives wouldn't connect her to Tamara. Or Tamara to Patel."

He fixed me an intent stare, an I-need-you-to-understand stare. "I admit, I lost it when I discovered she'd decided to leave. I'd gone out on a limb for her. My whole organization had. And she didn't bother to tell me."

"Maybe she wanted to protect you."

He jerked his head back, his eyes hooded in disbelief.

"Maybe she finally felt strong enough personally and professionally—as a full-service chef, not just a pastry cook—to do what she really wanted. To challenge him," I continued. Laurel had often lamented that women with chefly ambitions get shunted onto the pastry track, which never garners the same respect as meat or fish. "Maybe she wanted to get all her ducks in a row before telling you, so that you couldn't stop her. So *he* couldn't stop her."

"But why go to Danielle?" An unfamiliar note of hurt crept into his voice. "If she wanted to prove that she could survive his abuse and come back stronger, why not let me open up next to him, with her at the stove?"

"Because she wanted to do this on her own. You didn't want a partner. I don't mean this as criticism, Alex, but every restaurant you run is all you." He opened his mouth to protest, but I held up a hand. "Yes, you've got your long-trusted managers—Ops upstairs, your front of the house manager, Glassy at the bar. You treat them well and trust them to be professionals. But it's always *your* world. Tamara wanted to create *her* restaurant." I remembered her standing in my shop, talking flavors and sketching ideas for presentation. I remembered her lying on the floor of the unfinished space.

"She needed financial support and experience behind her. Danielle could provide that. But she trusted Tamara's vision. She didn't need to take over."

Alex set his cup on the floor. Elbows on his knees, he rested his forehead on his arms. When he sat up, his eyes were filled with sadness and, perhaps, if I weren't imagining things, a hint of regret. "I'm an SOB sometimes, aren't I?"

I smiled, but without humor. "Meanwhile, Patel was continuing his spendthrift ways, running up bills his restaurant couldn't pay, setting up fake corporations and using her name. Any idea whether she knew?"

"She never said." He sat upright, leaned back, and crossed his arms. "Patel's not the first guy to play the corporate name game, but sooner or later, they get you. Some little thing trips you up. A waiter gripes to the labor department about the house keeping the tips, or a cook bitches about no bathroom breaks, and ka-boom. You think he killed her?"

I stood and took a few steps before answering. "I've spent enough time around lawyers to argue both sides of that. If he truly didn't know she was still around until she showed up with plans for a hot new restaurant next door—"

"One that would have put him out of business," Alex said, "by being a hundred times better."

"—then seeing her would have been like seeing a ghost." Is that what the old woman meant when she'd hinted at a *bhut*?

Alex angled in the chair to face me. "He got enraged, confronted her, and things got out of hand. I always heard he had a volcanic temper."

I gave him the look the kettle gave the pot.

He colored, understanding. "Beyond the heat of the kitchen. That's part stress, part showmanship. I mean real anger. Violent anger."

"Or he planned to kill her, to stop her." I paced under the watchful eye of a hand-carved raven mask, a Northwest tribal totem. "But that doesn't explain the choice of weapon.

And, I'm thinking out loud here, but if he was relying on her credit and reputation to stay afloat financially—"

"Right," Alex said. "Why kill the cash cow?"

"Or the credit cow. But maybe that didn't matter. It was Tamara Langston who died, not Ashley Brown. Common name, easy to fool people." I stopped and faced him. "Ah. That's it. What if she tumbled to his scheme and threatened to expose him?"

"I'll ask around. Talk to my suppliers and see what they know about Patel. See if they'd heard from her."

"Careful. Word might leak back to him and tick him off," I said.

"Good." Alex rose. "If he thinks people are onto him, he might get scared and make a mistake."

"Alex, the cops think I told the reporters that she was killed with *bhut C*. It was you, wasn't it? Through your staff."

His eyes flicked almost imperceptibly at the door. *Oops.*

"Why? Didn't you think that would make them focus on me?"

"No." He sounded surprised. "You would never betray confidential details. I thought that would make them look elsewhere, try to figure out who else had inside info." His voice took on a rare tenderness. "It was the only way I could think of to clear you from suspicion."

Sure as sugar, I hadn't expected that.

"PEPPER." The sound of my name penetrated my mental fog as I neared the Spice Shop.

Knock me over with a feather. "Danielle. What brings you down here?" Heaven help me, my first thought sprang from my business brain, wondering if we still had a chance to become her supplier. My second thought, mercifully, came from my empathic brain, which told business brain to shut up.

"Can we talk?" In her dark pants and stacked heels, her

teal raincoat open, she looked at first glance like any other well-moneyed woman on a mission, but it didn't take long to detect the worry in her hazel eyes.

A few minutes later, after I'd checked in with my staff, we settled at a table on the main floor of Lowell's, overlooking the Great Wheel on Pier 57.

"This place never changes," she said. "How long's it been here—fifty years? Sixty?"

The waitress, who could have been an original employee, slid steaming mugs in front of us and whipped her order pad out of her apron pocket. Snooping had made me ravenous. "Two eggs over easy, hash browns, and toast. With butter and cinnamon sugar."

"Cinnamon toast," Danielle said. "Sounds heavenly."

While patience is not my middle name—nor my first, though they start with the same letter—waiting was getting easier. When someone is dying to talk to you, give them space and you'll learn the most astonishing things.

Danielle's jaw moved as she wet her lips, then turned her attention to the black leather bag on the chair beside her.

It was as if the dead had come back to life. On the table between us lay Tamara's bright green notebook. Who knew what secrets lay etched on its ivory pages?

"She left it in my office last week. Wednesday morning, a few hours before . . ." She swallowed hard and reached for her coffee. "I found it this morning. At first, I assumed she'd left it by accident, but if she knew someone was after her . . ."

Hard to believe it had been a full week since Tamara's death. "Did you call the police?"

She pursed her lips, her eyes downcast. "I—I should, I know, but I wanted to tell you first."

I pulled a napkin out of the stainless steel dispenser, covered my fingers, and drew the notebook toward me. Inside the cover, Tamara had written her name and the address in Wallingford. One by one, I turned the pages with the napkin. Notes for recipes, lists of ingredients, flavor combinations. *Black chickpeas, citrus-cilantro dressing?* one read. She'd made sketches for how to plate an entrée— the relationship of garnish to sauce to filet of halibut. A graceful pencil drawing showed a cocktail glass next to the words lime—*wedgy, not too thick.*

A fat section held tasting notes from restaurants she'd visited, each entry dated and detailed. From the classic Metropolitan Grill and the Dahlia Lounge to the quirky Oddfellows Café. Specialty spots like Salumi, serving the best cured meats around, and her favorite cupcake shops.

Alex may have worked hard to keep Tamara-Ashley undercover, but she'd ventured far and wide in her search for the flavors of the city. All, I knew, with the aim of bringing her own vision to life. Or to the plate, which to a chef is the same thing.

Our breakfasts appeared, and the wordless waitress topped off our coffee. I kept turning pages. Finally, I found what I hadn't realized I'd been searching for: proof that Tamara had figured out what Patel was doing to her. To Ashley.

But she wasn't Ashley anymore. She had made herself into someone new.

I studied the lists of vendors, dates, and collections claims until the aroma of cinnamon toast finally got to me. I pushed the notebook aside. Picked up a slice, but before the first bite, asked two questions. "Did you know who she was? And why she was so insistent on opening next to Tamarind?" Surely, the similarity of names—Tamarind, Tamara, Tamarack— betrayed her plan, no doubt sparked by the Ashwani-Ashley coincidence.

"Not at first." She paused, thinking, then appeared to make a decision. "Not until I talked to Glassy."

"Glassy?" I said around a bite of toast. "Alex's bar manager? She wanted to hire him away and you told her to stay away from him."

She reached for the notebook. I shot out a hand and grabbed her wrist. Pushed the napkin dispenser across the table. She covered her fingers, then flipped to a page I hadn't seen. Across the top, Tamara had written two names, connected by an arrow that went both directions. And above the arrow, she'd placed a question mark.

She'd been asking about the connection between Alex and Glassy.

I picked up my fork and pointed the tines at her. "Spill."

I ate. She talked. We drank more coffee. People came and went around us, and she talked.

And when she was through, I understood more than I ever had about people I thought I knew and people I'd just met.

But I had serious questions about people I thought I knew very well.

Twenty-seven

Monastic gardens were not simply places in which to toil, to grow plants, and to dispel idleness, "the enemy of the soul": they were also secluded open-air temples in which to celebrate and worship the Creator, and a daily reminder of the mortality of all living things in which God may be glorified.

—Rob Talbot and Robin Whiteman,
Brother Cadfael's Herb Garden

IN MY KIDHOOD, WHEN OUR FAMILY AND KRISTEN'S LIVED together in the house her great-grandparents built, the house my father still calls "the group home," a poster on the wall in the third-floor meditation room said, DON'T JUST DO SOMETHING. SIT THERE.

I honestly did not know what to do after Danielle left. But the lunch crowd was beginning to arrive, and I couldn't just sit there.

Outside the restaurant, the North Arcade bustled, the foot traffic driven under cover by a middling rain. So much for my plan to walk until a real plan occurred to me.

Instead, I headed Down Under. First to the bookstore—I

spread my business around—to see if the singing bookseller had taken in any spice references I had to have or any medieval mysteries I hadn't read. He hadn't.

I pressed my nose to the window—metaphorically speaking—of a painter's studio, closed for lunch. Poked through a couple of clothing shops—cute stuff, perfect for spring, but I wasn't in a spring mood. Stood on the ramp, not knowing whether to go up or down, wanting nothing more than my dog, a blankie, and a good cry.

This was the first time in memory that roaming the Market had not cheered me up.

"Pepper! I was hoping you'd swing by."

Holy marjoroly. I was so not in the mood for Mary Jean the Chatty Chocolatier. But I was trapped.

And dang, were her chocolates good. Turned out to be exceptionally pleasant to perch on a comfy stool in the corner of her shop, rich, cocoa-y scents swirling around me, nibbling a chocolate honey truffle. Damp customers drifted in and out as she described her philosophy of chocolate and her products.

"Pepper owns Seattle Spice Shop, up on Pike Place," she said. "Freshest spices and best selection in the city. She works with the police on murder cases! We're plotting deliciosity." She practically rubbed her hands together.

A cloud lifted. How could it not, in the presence of such exuberance?

I might not know what Brother Cadfael would do, but it was clear that when it came to blending chocolate and spice, Mary Jean and I were on the same page.

I spent the next hour in my shop, fielding questions, helping Zak pack orders for mailing, and tackling a million other projects. Do not go into retail if you can't multitask. Then I closeted myself in the back office to make phone calls and ask questions. As I'd learned in HR, and again when Ops gave me info on Tariq, if you ask nicely, people will tell you almost anything.

But now it was time to follow Cadfael's lead and take my discoveries and my doubts to the law.

Detective Cheryl Spencer and I might never develop the camaraderie the old monk and young Sheriff Hugh Beringar shared, but no matter. What mattered was that she would listen and take me seriously.

"Yes," Spencer said, closing the homicide detectives' office door on the buzz and chatter of SPD HQ. "Ms. Wang did mention a notebook. Lime green, spiral bound. Detective Tracy took a CSU crew back to the house to search again."

Thank God for small favors. I pushed a brown paper bag across the scarred but tidy desk, a picture of her daughter its only personal accessory. Spencer peered inside, shot me a glance, then tugged on disposable gloves. Slid out the notebook, swathed in napkins. Tilted her head in a suppose-you-tell-me-what-this-is-all-about look.

"In trying to build a case against Tariq Rose, I may have stumbled over the truth. Open the notebook to"—I gestured and she flipped a few more pages—"right there."

She took a minute to read. "Okay. Clear as mud."

"Does the name Ashley Brown mean anything to you? Or Ashwani Patel?"

She frowned. "Brown, no. Patel owns the Indian restaurant next to the construction site where Tamara Langston was killed. We interviewed him. Nothing useful."

"Patel came to Seattle about ten years ago, from San Jose. Handsome, big personality, mildly exotic. Bounced around a handful of restaurants. Competent, but nothing special." I paused to unearth a water bottle from my tote and took a long swig. "Unlike Ashley Brown. Young, blond, just shy of pretty. Pastry chef in a joint where Patel worked the line."

"You said this had to do with the Langston murder."

Spencer lowered her chin and leaned back in her chair. It creaked.

"Patience, Detective. And requisition a squirt or two of WD-40."

She suppressed a smile.

"They got married. They quit their jobs to start an Indian take-out joint on Madison called the Blue Poppy." I laid a folder on her desk and opened it to a printout of the blog post Callie had found, along with two other photos of Ashley that she'd dug up this morning. "They were ahead of their time. The Capitol Hill renaissance hadn't reached that stretch. Roadwork blocked access to their entrance for months. They'd sunk all their cash into the place and didn't have the cushion to ride it out. Common problem in business, often fatal."

"I don't remember it. How was the food?"

"Closed before I got there, but I hear it was hit-and-miss." Her dishes hit; his missed. "They regrouped and tried again, farther north. Place called Mantra. Takeout plus dinner service. Classic Indian fare."

"How'd it do?" She picked up a travel mug emblazoned GOD FOUND THE STRONGEST WOMEN AND MADE THEM COPS, and took a sip of tea. My tea—I recognized the sharp orange scent mellowed by a hint of allspice.

"Better, by all accounts. But by those same accounts, their relationship was going downhill. He was an abusive bully. At first, she stood up to him. But it got worse, and he wore her down. Beat her up."

Spencer flicked her eyes toward her computer. "I don't suppose I'll find any reports."

"Could be helpful, if you do." I took another swig of water, knowing I was about to ask Spencer to take a leap of faith and do the investigation I couldn't, to confirm the tapestry I'd woven out of fact, rumor, logic, and innuendo. "A former employee I talked to this morning told me Ashley received a small inheritance from an aunt. They used it to make one more run, and opened Tamarind."

Spencer set her cup down and reached for a three-ring binder labeled with a case number. "Patel's place. We questioned the whole staff, but I don't remember her."

I reached for my file, open on the desk, and slid the photos of Ashley Brown aside. Underneath lay the newspaper photo. Spencer leaned in for a closer look.

And let out a long, low whistle.

"She disappeared a little over two years ago. He told everyone they'd split and she'd left town." I relayed Jane's story of seeing Patel light into Ashley outside the Spice Shop, towering over her, fists looming. "At first, I thought he might have killed her and hidden her body in the walls between his restaurant and the space next door. Then he got the crazy little lady who works for him to spread stories about *bhuts*—"

"Boots?"

"Hindi for 'ghosts.' Same word as in ghost peppers, *bhut capsicum*," I said. At that, Spencer gave up all effort at self-control. She twirled her eyes and wagged her head like this was making her crazy.

"Ashley went underground," I continued. "Moved to another county and changed her name. Gave all the required notice to creditors, but didn't let Patel know."

"That's no crime. That's smart."

I sat up a little straighter, stretching my spine. "She got a job working for Alex Howard and set about making herself into a culinary star. Howard and his organization sheltered her."

"They knew?" She sounded skeptical.

"Yes. Alex Howard is an SOB, by his own admission, but he is capable of a good deed. What he didn't realize was that she—Ashley-turned-Tamara—had a plan of her own. She'd discovered that Patel was using her name to get credit and defraud suppliers. New ones, who didn't know his track record. Worked for a while because her name is so common." I pointed to the page in Tamara's notebook. "She decided to come back. To rise from the dead."

"To make herself a *bhut*," Spencer said. "To kick his ass."

I sat back. "Exactly."

"If she'd filed for divorce, she'd have to give him notice. Safer to disappear." Spencer reached for her phone. "I'll pull in all the resources I can. But it's going to take time to verify enough of this to get a warrant, so we can confirm the rest. If the money trail leads to banks or crosses state lines, we'll need to alert the feds."

A bubble of dismay rose in my gullet. "You're talking fraud. Identity theft. What about murder? He had motive, means, and opportunity." I told her about hearing Patel tell the customer he'd stopped serving dishes with ghost peppers. At the time, I'd chalked it up to not feeding the frenzy, but now I suspected he'd used them all up, killing Tamara. My chest tightened and my voice rose as I begged her to call Big Al and find out if Patel had refreshed his supply.

Then I told her I'd smelled cinnamon and pepper in Tamarack when I'd found the body. "When you work with spices all day like he does—like I do—they waft off you."

She sniffed twice in my direction, then pushed back her chair. "Your sense of smell is not enough to prove murder, Pepper."

"Everything I've given you is circumstantial." I put the legalese in air quotes.

"We can charge on circumstantial evidence, even convict on it. But it doesn't add up yet." She came around the desk and put her hand on my shoulder. "This may be the break we need. At the very least, the fraud investigation will allow us to focus on Patel. We'll search for abuse complaints and interview friends, employees, anyone who knew one or both, including your Jane. I promise you, Pepper, we will stir up his life until the evidence boils to the top."

I left HQ unsure whether to rejoice that they were going after Patel, or bemoan that we still couldn't prove who'd used my peppers for murder most foul.

After unburdening his conscience to the law, Brother Cadfael went to the Chapel to unburden his spirit. Me, I stopped for a triple shot.

Because unlike Brother Cadfael, I hadn't shared all my suspicions with Detective Spencer. Some things a woman has got to handle for herself.

Twenty-eight

※

Lead me not into temptation
I can find it all by myself

—Lari White, "Lead Me Not"

TAG'S STOMACH IS NOT NECESSARILY THE MOST DIRECT
route to his heart, but it's a good place to start.

I'd gotten back to the Market in time to score two beautiful duck breasts from my favorite butcher and a dozen ador-
able kumquats. I was glad I'd resisted the temptation to dip
a spoon into the leftover crème brûlée.

It wasn't hard to convince him to come over. I'd apolo-
gized for my impatience earlier in the week, and for doubt-
ing his intentions. And then I'd told him I had all the
ingredients for his mother's variation on duck à l'orange and
would he please come help me eat it?

I buzzed him in and poured two glasses of Côtes du
Rhône red, a stellar complement to the sauce. His feet
echoed on the plank stairs, and Arf rose at the sound, nails
clicking as he trotted to the door.

"Hey, boy." Tag reached down to scratch behind the official greeter's ears. His eyes sparked and his lips parted
slightly as he handed me an enormous bundle of early spring

flowers: lilacs, deep pink double peonies, and branches of plum blossoms from the garden behind our old bungalow. Similar bouquets had cropped up in the Market stalls the last couple of weeks, and I was glad I hadn't bought one on my afternoon shopping spree. There are advantages to knowing someone well. Even if not quite as well as I'd thought.

Tag and Arf played tug-of-war with the stuffed duck toy Tag had brought while I found a cut glass vase—a wedding present—for the flowers.

"You look terrific," he said when I interrupted their play to hand him a glass of wine. I'd dressed for the still-young season, hoping to encourage more spring weather, in a sap green smock dress and white leggings, my feet bare, toenails freshly pinked. I'd wrapped a pink-and-green stretchy headband from a Market vendor around my spikes—not because Tag razzes me about my hair, but because the colors made me happy.

"Not too shabby yourself." He wore slim navy pants that emphasized his long legs and a white crewneck sweater, a wide navy stripe down the arm. Sleeves pushed up, as always. Navy sneakers with a wide white rim. His dark blond hair, freed from his helmet, flopped over his forehead in what could be style or a missed haircut. "To spring."

"To spring," he repeated and raised his glass, bright blue eyes peering over the rim.

Careful, girl, I told myself as I picked up a plate of crackers and baked Brie. *You're on a mission here.*

We stepped out the window to the veranda and settled at the bistro table. The herbs had gone hog wild in the past week's alternating rain and sunshine. My neighbors' Japanese maple had sent a few branches over the metal grate between our spaces, creating a lovely unplanned awning.

"Nice." Tag glanced around. Then he gestured to the Viaduct with his glass and said, "Except for—*that*."

"I never minded the highway being there, but now that

they're going to tear it down, I wish they'd hurry up. Although, when they do, the noise and dust might mean moving out for a while."

The look in his eyes reminded me I still had his spare key, and I almost regretted the direction I knew this conversation had to take. *Later.*

We sipped, nibbled, and chatted—easy talk about life and work, but not The Case. Stories, musings, memories. The kind of conversation we'd always been good at, and that I'd missed. To my surprise, when the ducks came off the grill and I suggested we move inside, he asked if we couldn't eat on the veranda—a loft feature he'd ridiculed in the past.

"Your cooking is better than ever." He wiped up the last bit of sauce with a hunk of bread. "The upside to hanging out with all those chefs."

We took our dishes in. I got out dessert and started coffee, the aroma nearly as strong as the lilac scent perfuming the loft. "Your garden is beautiful. I peeked when I picked up the tickets."

"A man needs a refuge." He rested his hands on the butcher-block counter between us. "Pepper, I need to tell you—"

My chest tightened, and I held up a hand. "Tag, don't. I'm savoring this friendship between us. Let's keep it on this level. I don't want to scrap and battle with you, but getting back together romantically is not in the cards."

His jaw worked, and his fingers tensed. "Is that decaf? Maybe I can catch a couple hours of sleep before my shift."

I settled on the couch, but he took the rocker, a sign that he was struggling to digest my message about our relationship.

"Tag, I learned something today that we need to talk about. Something about the past that I never knew." Across the room, the rocker stopped. I ignored the anxiety threatening to stab me just below the ear and plunged on. "I don't blame you for not telling me. But it's influenced how you've treated me the last few months. It's about Alex Howard and Detective Tracy."

Tag's face froze, and his square jaw looked a little blunter.

"I don't understand all the details about the scam Alex was running," I said. "Or who all was involved. He—"

"He was stealing." Tag spat it out. "He was supposed to be running the joint for the owner. Instead, they made drinks but didn't ring up the sales. The servers took cash, made change themselves, and kept forty percent. Howard and his crony bartender split the rest. Money that wasn't theirs."

"Crony"—never a word with positive implications.

"You and Tracy were partners on the investigation, and it went wrong."

He stood. Arf stopped chewing, on alert. "Where did you hear this? Mike Tracy didn't tell you. That scum Howard, to make me look bad?"

"Sit down. I'm not finished." He sat, and I swallowed my astonishment. "Danielle Bordeaux knew I was asking questions about Tamara's murder. She discovered physical evidence. And yes, I've turned it over to Detective Spencer. But she also told me about her history with Alex. He was her chef. His scheme fell apart when she came into the restaurant unexpectedly and caught a server making change out of her own pocket. Danielle also said she'd told Tamara about it."

"To get Tamara to quit working for Alex."

"No." I reached for my coffee and took a sip. "Tamara wanted to hire Glassy away from Alex. That was too much for Danielle. Scuttle is they're clean now—"

"Don't you believe it." He rolled his coffee mug between his hands.

"—but thick as thieves." I couldn't resist saying it. "Danielle is convinced that because no charges were ever brought—"

His head jerked up.

"—anything negative she said about them would sound like sour grapes. Now that they're successful." *Holding on to your anger,* she'd said, *is like drinking poison and expecting someone else to die.*

"Tag, I know you only want to protect me, and I'm grateful. But if I'd known why you didn't trust Alex—"

"I couldn't tell you, Pepper." Tag stood again, but this time there was no menace in it, and Arf kept working his new toy. "All I could do was try to warn you away from him. And try not to show my relief when you broke it off."

He paced in front of the fireplace. "Tracy was investigating the liquor suppliers, and I was responsible for tracking down the witnesses. Just when I thought I had 'em, the girl disappeared."

"What?" I set my mug on the packing crate and leaned forward. "Who?"

"Howard paid her to disappear. I'm certain of it. Mike—Detective Tracy—blamed me for losing her." His Adam's apple bobbed. "Remember how every time I tried for a promotion, it got blocked? That was Mike."

"You said you liked patrol, you were happy there."

"Eventually I decided the streets are the better place for me. I look better in bike shorts than in suits, anyway."

A bad feeling sidled up the back of my skull. "What was her name? The girl. A server? Tell me it wasn't Ashley." I'd thought she was too young, but maybe not.

He shook his head, the long lock in front flopping back and forth. "Melissa? Melinda? It's been fifteen years, but I thought I'd never forget."

The creepy-crawly feeling grew claws that stabbed me. "I don't know what she called herself then, but now she goes by Lynette," I said.

He gaped at me. The story of how Lynette had ratted Tamara's plans to Alex—leading me to fire her and to feel responsible for Tamara's death—was barely out of my mouth when he charged toward the door.

"I am going to get that son of a bitch once and for all."

"Tag, no! Wait! He didn't kill her." Words were no use. I scrabbled for shoes, a jacket, keys, and a leash.

He was a block away, striding up Western, when Arf and I caught up to him.

I grabbed his arm, out of breath. "Tag, wait. Call it in. Handle this the right way. Don't make things worse by charging into his restaurant making accusations you can't back up."

He stared up the street, still enraged, but at least he'd stopped moving and taken out his phone. "After everything I told you, how can you believe the man innocent?"

"The evidence Danielle brought me and I took to Spencer? It points to Ashwani Patel."

"Who?" He cocked his head, brow wrinkled.

"Short version, Tamara Langston's ex-husband. I'll let Spencer give you the long version. By now, she knows a lot more about it than I do."

"It'll be the talk of morning briefing, I bet. Not sure I'll be able to wait."

Arf barked, one single note. "Long as we're out, might as well walk the dog."

Tag put his phone away and slung his arm around my shoulder. I liked the feeling more than I wanted to admit. We strolled up to the park, then followed Arf's lead and started down Pike Place toward the shop.

We were two hundred feet away when Tag snapped into alert mode.

"Is that smoke? Holy shit."

"What? What's wrong?"

He thrust his phone at me. "Call 911. Your shop's on fire."

He was off and running before the words registered.

My shop, my shop. My hands shook as I punched in the numbers and reported the emergency. Sirens seemed to pierce the air almost instantly. I looped Arf's leash around a post outside the North Arcade and dashed forward. Flames licked the outside wall.

Tag beat back the fire with his gorgeous white sweater.

I tore off my jacket and tried to join him. "Stay back, Pepper. I don't want you hurt."

"I don't want you hurt." My voice cracked and broke.

The first engine pulled up, and firefighters jumped out, hoses in hand.

"Officer Buhner, West Precinct," Tag told the first man to reach him. "It could be electrical." The other man spoke into a handset, and Tag stepped back to let his brothers in service take control.

We watched from across Pike Place, where I crouched next to Arf and Tag stood behind us. A crowd of diners and drinkers and moviegoers had gathered in the streets, the evening clear and dry. Southish, behind a makeshift barricade, a group had emerged from who knows where, loud and teetery, making raucous comments despite the smoke and flames.

A movement in the crowd drew my attention. A slender woman, dressed to kill in a short red skirt and a black blouse with a plunging ruffled neckline, black lace stockings, and red stilettos. I squinted, craning my neck for a better view. Glitter and flash, and something familiar.

Was it who I thought it was?

Wrong hair.

She tossed her head, laughing, but her gaze never left the fire.

A wig. *That's what the barista was telling me. The changeable lady, never the same woman twice.* Not me, as I'd assumed, but the actress who could change her appearance in the blink of an eye. Who'd once been a waitress in a bar managed by Alex and Glassy. Who'd learned about electricity and staging fires while working on theater sets.

Who'd left me threatening notes written with a marker she'd stolen when I fired her.

"Tag, it's her. Lynette. She set the fire; I'm sure of it." I didn't dare tip her off by pointing, but she noticed us notice her, and terror swept across her heavily made-up face. She kicked off her heels and took off down the street. She had a head start, but Tag was faster. I jumped up and down, trying to get the attention of the patrol officer who'd taken charge of the scene.

"The shirtless man," I yelled, out of breath. "It's Officer Buhner in pursuit of a suspect. The woman who set the fire."

He barked into his radio. I watched Lynette bob and weave, Tag gaining on her, though the crowd slowed him. She ducked behind the Triangle Building and disappeared from sight. Tag kept up the chase, and I kept jumping up and down, pointing. The Sanitary Market and Post Alley shops are a warren of hallways and doorways and dead ends, but Tag knew them better than almost anyone.

More patrol officers arrived, but before they could join in, Tag appeared on the sidewalk, a crooked grin on his face, a bedraggled Lynette in tow, her stockings torn and her wig gone.

Dang and blast the man. He'd ripped off his sweater to put out a fire. He'd chased an arsonist through a jeering, uncooperative crowd. He'd ventured into the back alleys of the Market without backup, gun, or radio, and emerged triumphant.

And he had never managed to look so good.

Twenty-nine

Justice may be blind, but she has very sophisticated listening devices.

—Edgar Argo

"CAN YOU BELIEVE IT, ARF?" I WHISPERED INTO THE SOFT fur behind the dog's ear an hour later. We were sitting on the living room floor in my loft, me in my jammies, he working on that fool stuffed duck.

I'd given Tag my jacket, but he gave it back when the patrol officers who took charge of Lynette—or whatever her name was—handed him a blanket. We'd given our statements in the back of a patrol car, and after the firefighters had assured me, for at least the fifth time, that the fire was really, honestly, truly out, an officer drove us home. All the damage was external—the fire had not broken through the thick outer walls, but it easily could have, if Tag hadn't spotted the flames in time.

Tag had trudged up the loft stairs behind us, then stood in the doorway. I'd smiled at his smudged face, his filthy chest, and reached for his hand to draw him closer. "Don't just stand there. Come on in."

"Pepper," he'd said, his voice catching. "It's late. I work

early. And I don't want you to do anything you'll regret, in the heat of the moment. Because if we ever have a chance of getting back together, it's gotta be real. It's gotta come from your heart *and* your head."

I admit, I was stunned. Who'd a thunk it? The guy had been after me almost since the day I left him. In the last few months, he'd been in serious courtship mode. He'd treated me at my favorite restaurants. Taken me to the Mariners' opening game, getting great seats on the third base line, buying kosher dogs and microbrews. Brought me flowers from the garden that had once been ours. But I'd kept my distance.

And then, when I change my mind, he leaves. Either he'd grown a conscience when I wasn't watching, or I was some pathetic freak. "Take care of our girl," he'd told the dog, and walked away.

"What does it all mean?" I asked the dog. He kept right on chewing.

Images of the evening rolled through my brain: orange flames licking the pink stucco, crowds gathering in the street, the Public Market sign glowing red against the night sky.

"That's it, Arf. I know what to do about the sign." I'd fallen hard for Fabiola's idea of a lighted sign featuring our new logo—a vintage shaker pouring salt into the ocean.

But the Historical Commission had told me repeatedly that signs hanging from the awning had to be rectangular and made of wood, as they were when our building was erected in the 1930s. Other buildings had shaped signs, or neon, but ours never had, and we couldn't make that change now.

But I had a new plan. We could paint the logo on a standard exterior sign, and hang an LED version, the modern green equivalent of neon, inside the front window. Smaller LED signs could shine out the clerestory windows, making spice a beacon for day or night.

Funky. Vintage, but modern.

"That's us to a T, right, Arf?"

He was too busy chewing his toy duck to say so, but I knew he agreed.

I woke the next morning knowing I should feel like everything was resolved. But instead, I had the nagging suspicion I'd overlooked something.

The shower is the perfect place to wash away unwanted thoughts. Or to think them through. Ashwani Patel had killed Tamara, formerly known as Ashley. I knew that. Alex, while far from innocent, was not a killer.

What puzzled me was this: Tamara had asked Glassy to manage the bar at Tamarack before learning from Danielle the reason why he would never leave Alex Howard's employ. The two men were bound at the hip, less by trust and affection than by mutual dishonesty. If one lost sight of the other, both were at risk of betrayal. The thefts from Danielle's restaurant corporation—the stolen drinks scheme—had been years ago. The statute of limitations was long expired.

But while the threat of criminal charges was long gone, and Danielle had vowed to keep to the high road, each man still had the ability to destroy the other's life. Or at least, his ability to work, and to some men, that's the same thing. Certainly it was to Alex, and maybe Glassy, too.

Glassy had sworn that he'd kept Tamara's planned defection a secret. But what if he had told Alex? Talk about their scheme had long died down, become nothing more than vague rumors, the facts known only to a few old hands.

But what if Alex feared that Danielle might start the talk back up again? She had become an even more powerful player in the Seattle food scene than he. As far as I knew, she had never used her suspicions about the uncharged crimes against him.

What if he believed that was about to end? That she had revealed the history to Tamara, who saw the stories as leverage against him and Glassy? What if he'd decided to silence Tamara as a message to Danielle, not knowing Tamara had a different target—Ashwani Patel.

I stepped out and toweled off. *You're spinning your wheels, Pepper. Looking for motives that aren't there.*

And as every police officer I knew would tell me, motive doesn't prove a thing.

WHEN I got to the shop, it was abundantly clear that everything was not resolved.

Orange cones and yellow crime scene tape marked off part of our exterior wall. The fire marshal had come and gone, and the electrician and a Market carpenter had ripped out a huge chunk of stucco to get at the damaged wires and framing.

"So, what she did was this," the electrician said, and explained how Lynette had set an electronic ignition switch, connected to a small timer, on the exterior wall where the power entered the building. She'd used a box of trash, mostly paper, to both hide the contraption and make sure the fire got a good start, then retreated to a nearby drinking establishment to wait.

And when the sirens called, she couldn't resist coming back to watch.

"So you're telling me the smoke and char make it look worse than it is," I said.

"No. I'm saying you were damn lucky. Five minutes later and the fire would have broken through to the interior."

Talk about a heat index. If that fire had reached the shop, more than our paprika would have been smoked. Someone would have seen the flames before long—a late-night diner, a security officer. Still, we could have been ruined—a Market institution destroyed, half a dozen people left unemployed, our customers set adrift.

It's okay, Pepper. The danger's over. "What about today? Do we have power?"

"Yes. Inspector needs to sign off before we close it up, but he's on his way. Some plaster repair, a little painting, and you're all set." He reached for a tool. "Miracle, if you ask me."

Those old medieval harmonies began to play, and I sent the Universe a silent thank-you.

Inside, I flicked the light switch, holding my breath momentarily. The chandeliers sparkled, the red lamp shone, the tiny green power button on the electronic scale glowed.

All was well. Or would be, when we found the right hires. Before I knew it, Zak would be gone.

Once again, I found myself explaining near-disaster to my staff and springing for treats.

"So Lynette was behind all the electrical problems?" Kristen bit into a *pain aux raisins*.

"Not the first incident, last week when the ceiling lights flickered. That was probably caused by work up the hill at the kitchen shop—our power supply is linked to theirs. When she read in the paper that Tamara had been killed while looking into electrical problems at the construction site, the lightbulb went off. So to speak."

"And she's a vengeful witch who knows how to grab an opportunity when she sees one," Sandra said, her tone bitter.

More than you know. Plenty of time later to tell the staff the full extent of Lynette's misdeeds. If we ever knew the full extent.

Midmorning, Spencer and Tracy come in with more questions about Tamara, aka Ashley, and Patel, and to take a formal statement about the fire.

"You are a magnet for trouble." Tracy plucked a pastry out of the box. "You were right about the domestic abuse. Ashley Brown filed two reports, then retracted them—not uncommon, sorry to say. Without a cooperative victim, prosecutors were SOL."

"We've got our best records people sniffing down that money trail you found," Spencer said. "You, and Tamara. Her notes will be an enormous help."

"When do you expect to file charges?"

"Early next week, with any luck." Her eyes narrowed. "You keep away from him. We don't want to alert him, and we don't want any more incidents."

On that, we were in complete agreement. "Before you interview Lynette, there's something else you should know."

I'd lain awake a good part of the night, trying to decide how to tell Tracy about Alex and Lynette without raising his ire at Tag. "You distrusted me because you distrusted Tag. I only learned about the bar tab scam yesterday. You blamed Tag for losing a witness and tanking the investigation. But he's made up for it."

Tracy wiped the last crumb off his chin. It landed on his lapel. "How do you figure that?"

"Actors spend years in and out of disguise. Change their hair and voices, use makeup and costumes." I described seeing Lynette in the Market several times since I'd fired her, each sighting coinciding with an incident—the ghost notes, the electrical problems, even the falling produce crates. "She wanted to scare me, and it worked. So did her disguise. In the months she worked here, Tag never recognized her, and you won't, either."

He stared at me, openmouthed. I resisted the urge to brush the crumbs off his jacket.

"Are you saying that your disgruntled employee and arsonist is Melissa the missing waitress?"

"One and the same."

"What are the odds," Spencer said, "of wrapping up two cases at the same time involving women passing themselves off as someone they aren't?"

Tamara created a new identity to escape the past. Lynette used a changing appearance to fool the world and enable her petty vengeance. Alex and Glassy had reshaped themselves from thugs into successful businessmen.

In a million different ways, we all create ourselves every day.

AFTER his fireside heroics, Tag had been given the day off. Turned out that after leaving me, he'd gone back to the fire scene to make sure my shop was safe. The man took seriously that old police motto "To Serve and Protect."

Especially the protect part, especially when it came to me.

He deserved a day of rest, but I worried about him. I kinda missed seeing him wheel through the Market.

The UPS man brought the day's deliveries, and Zak and Kristen started unpacking.

"Oh, they're here!" Kristen exclaimed. "Aren't they the perfect wedding gift?"

Heart-shaped white porcelain espresso cups and round saucers, in a boxed set. I'd seen a pair at Fabiola's last fall, but it had taken us months to track down a supplier. Now all we needed were hordes of brides and wedding guests, to make the registry pay for itself.

A fair amount of detailery had piled up while I was out investigating. I returned Tessa Spencer's call and set up an interview. She sounded ideal, and another connection to the SPD couldn't hurt. Responded to more calls, texts, and e-mails—amazing the ways technology has created for us to get behind.

I crossed Pike Place to see Herb the Herb Man and confirm plans for our annual seedling sales. He'd provide the potted seedlings, we'd provide a rolling wire rack to sit outside during the day, and our customers could buy fresh herbs to grow themselves. A nod to the Spice Shop building's history as the Market's original Garden Center, and a benefit to us all.

Sandra held out the phone when I walked back in. "A reporter. One you want to talk to."

"Buy you lunch and treat you to a free concert?" Ben said.

"Not sure I can get away," I said.

"Go, go, go," Sandra said in a stage whisper.

"He's so young," I whispered back.

"Give him a shot," she mouthed.

"Meet you at the fountain," I told him.

"CLOSE call at your shop." Ben sat next to me on the ledge around the International Fountain. "But you're safe, thank God."

His gaze wasn't exactly scorching, but it definitely raised my temperature. He wore a soft gray T-shirt, black jeans, and high-top sneakers. Arf promptly rested his head on Ben's knee. I almost hadn't brought the dog, after what happened the last time we came to the Center, but those big brown eyes had swayed me.

"I think my heartbeat's finally back to normal," I said.

Two women sat next to me. "Wait till you see this bowl," one told the other. "Chihuly. It's like a bolt of lightning struck a flower and made glass."

"I want you to know," Ben said, "I called because I wanted to see you, not because I'm digging for news. And—here's this. Hot off the presses."

He handed me a copy of his paper, open to a quarter page photo of me in the shop. I almost didn't recognize myself. Ben watched, a tell-me-you-like-it look on his face. I started reading, speaking a few of the best lines out loud.

"'In the urban theater that is the Pike Place Market, Seattle Spice is a kaleidoscope of color and aroma, presided over by the Mistress of Spices, the tangy and bewitching Pepper Reece.'"

"'Tangy and bewitching'? What were you smoking when you wrote that?"

"I'm a serious journalist. Every word is true." Tiny crinkles formed around his eyes.

"'The shop feels like a party. "We don't cater to food snobs, although they're welcome," Reece says, handing out samples of tea and setting out bowls of cinnamon bark for customers to try. "We think good food is for everyone, and that eating should be fun."'"

"I can't believe this," I said, tucking the folded paper in my bag. "Thank you. Let's grab lunch before the concert."

"They've got food booths at the music venue. Part of the International Festival," he said, standing and reaching for my hand. "It's India Day."

Half sitting, half standing, leash in hand and mouth open, I must have looked like an idiot.

"I thought you like Indian." He sounded apologetic.

I took his hand and clambered over the ledge. "I do. But I don't know anything about Indian music, so let's go listen."

The festival was surprisingly well attended for midday, midweek. We queued up at the Curry in a Hurry truck, and I worked to vanquish my unease.

No use. As we neared the order window, a tall, dark-haired, man flipped chapatis on the griddle, his back to us. *Patel.* A blonde who reminded me of Tamara-Ashley took our order, giving me the willies. I'd glimpsed her behind him, the night of the murder. Did she know she was working for a man who'd borrowed money in his dead wife's name to keep his restaurant afloat?

Everyone in line wanted to pet the dog. Mr. Ambassador quickly became the subject of casual Q&A. "Airedale, or Welsh terrier?" "Airedale." "How old is he?" "Five, the vet thinks." "Can I pet him?" "If you don't mind being licked to death."

A male voice boomed out our number, and we stepped forward to take our plates.

"Thanks." I smiled up at the face of a killer.

Recognition struck, and a bead of sweat rolled down Ashwani Patel's cheek.

Thirty

In ancient Rome, wealthy mourners added spices to funeral pyres to represent the triumph of life over death and disguise the smell of burning flesh. After the death of his wife Poppaea—from his kick to her stomach— Emperor Nero horrified accountants, politicians, and traders when he heaped a year's worth of cinnamon and cassia on her funeral flames.

—Jack Turner, *Spice: The History of a Temptation*

"THE SITAR, I RECOGNIZE," I SAID AS WE SAT ON THE SLOP-ing lawn, plates in hand. "But what are the other instruments?"

"The man facing the sitar player has a sarod. You'll hear them throw the melody back and forth. The drums are called tabla."

A swath of dark red fabric caught my eye, and I craned my neck to see around the barefoot men sitting on the portable stage. "What about the tiny woman in back, plucking strings?"

Ben leaned to one side, then the other. "I can't see her, but it's probably the tambura, a four-string drone that fills in the bottom. Like a bass, but without the chording."

Turned out he knew quite a bit about Indian music.

Between pieces, he explained the theory of the raga, a melody improvised on a basic scale, chosen to fit the time of day. "The heart of classical Indian music. This is Bhimpalasi, played from noon to two P.M."

When the last piece ended, the musicians rose and faced the audience. Smiles on their faces, hands in prayer position, they bowed deeply, then left the stage, the little lady in red trailing behind the men.

A dozen singers took the stage. "Folk music," Ben said. "I've heard this group before. Mostly Bengali songs, from Pakistan and North India."

"I need to talk to her." The impulse was irresistible, and inexplicable. I scrambled to my feet and took off, the dog behind me.

"Talk to who? Pepper, wait," Ben called as I threaded through the crowd, hoping I wasn't too late to catch her.

I worked my way to the side of the stage, turning my head, twisting my neck, searching.

A rope strung between two metal posts barred backstage access. I rose up on tippy toes, trying to spot the little lady. The white-clad backs of the sitar and sarod players blocked my view as they chatted in a mix of English and Hindi.

The tabla player, also in white, appeared out of nowhere. "May I help you?" His lilting accent emphasized the word "help," but I did not know what help I needed.

"I was hoping—I wanted to talk—"

"What are you doing here?" Patel's brusque baritone broke in. "Haven't you done enough damage, getting Tamara fired, getting her killed? Don't think I don't know you sold that murderer the weapon."

"There you are."

I smelled her before I saw or heard her. She smelled like cinnamon.

Her hand reached out for mine, the fingers strong, their touch soft. "I knew you would come. We know things they don't." The little lady's dark eyes shone up at me, the ruby red bindi on her forehead glinting in the midday sun.

"Can we talk? Are you able—" A single bark interrupted me. "Arf! No!"

"He is a bad man." She pointed, and I followed her gaze. "Not the very worst, but a very bad man."

Ashwani Patel raised a hand as if warding her off. His nostrils flared. and his full lips drew back, exposing gritted teeth. He lowered his hands and shoved me into the barricade. I went down hard, the skin on one hand ripping open as the heel scraped the rough concrete.

Through gaps in the crowd, I saw Patel turn, probing frantically for a way out. A young woman in a lavender sari pushed a double stroller across his path. He swung his arm and knocked her aside. She staggered backward, crying, "My babies!" The stroller rolled down a slope toward the stage, and a young man dashed after it.

"Stop him!" someone yelled.

The crowd parted, a natural reaction to the chaos as bystanders tried to suss out what was happening. Patel spotted the opening and sprinted toward the Armory.

"Are you hurt?"

A hand touched my shoulder, and I looked up into the concerned eyes of the Indian drummer.

"You look like you've seen a ghost," he said.

A furry muzzle poked me in the neck, and I struggled to rise.

The drummer held out a hand. "Are you able—?"

Arf barked once.

I unhooked his leash. "Cain!" I said, and patted him firmly on the rump. His brown eyes searched my face, as if to be sure I meant the command. "Cain!"

And off he went, darting and weaving silently through the crowd, making his way more easily than any human could, a terrier in pursuit of a rat.

I got to my feet and pushed after him. People moved out of the way, and one or two grabbed for him. Silently, I urged him on.

Tall enough to stand out as he ran, Patel glanced back. At one point, I thought he saw me, and at another instant, he noticed the dog. Panic filled his eyes and he stumbled, then recovered and pushed forward.

"Pepper!" Ben yelled from somewhere in the distance.

And then I lost sight of our quarry. There were too many people, too many men who could have been Patel. I slowed, gasping for breath, sending mental messages to my dog to keep the scent, to keep up the chase.

There he was. To the left, a dark head moved quickly, raggedly. His pace faltered. The limp, or years of eating rice and chapatis, catching up with him.

He veered toward the International Fountain.

"Son of a borage." On a day this gorgeous, the lawn around the fountain would be jammed with lunchers, festivalgoers strolling casually, kids with painted faces carrying balloons twisted into shapes of puppies and kitties and elephants, kids high on sugar and sunshine and the pure joy of play.

Behind me, Ben shouted my name again. Off to my right, I heard footsteps pounding. Through a break in the crowd, I spied Patel, his leg dragging as he ran along the ledge surrounding the fountain. Voices commanded "Stop! Police!" It's instinct—at least, for most of us—to stop at those words, but I plowed on, knowing they weren't meant for me.

The woman I'd seen earlier showing off her Chihuly find drifted into view. Patel pushed her out of his way. She shrieked, and the sounds of breaking glass shattered the air. Colored shards flew in all directions.

Patel jumped over the ledge. Behind him, a tan-and-gray streak made the same jump, far more gracefully.

"Doggie!" a child cried.

I darted through an opening and ran into the shallow

bowl that held the fountain, angling down its sloping sides. Dodged a trio of boys oblivious to the chaos. Wove past older kids and adults who'd noticed man and dog and paused to watch. Patel kept going, slowed by that bad leg.

Ten feet in front of me, Arf leaped into the air. His big jaw grabbed the seat of Patel's pants. Down the man went, tumbling, rolling toward the giant silver dome, the dog so close he almost appeared to be pushing him. Patel came to a rest, and Arf stood guard, barking like I had never heard him bark.

Before I could decide how to corral the man, two Center police officers grabbed Patel's arms and yanked the sputtering chef to his feet.

"Arf, hush. It's okay now." I snapped the leash onto his collar and started up the side of the bowl, my bloody hand throbbing.

And then the music—the music I hadn't even heard, over the pounding of my heart—the music changed. "The Ode to Joy" rang off the stone and glass and concrete, and the water spouted far and high and drenched the officers and their captive, the soaring notes a triumph of good over evil.

Or, at least, of dog over man.

"Good boy." I sank to the stone ledge and wrapped my arms around my panting, soaking, wet dog. "Good boy."

"I knew you wouldn't have taken off without good reason. When I saw him shove that mother and then you chasing after him, I grabbed the nearest cops." Ben sat beside me on the ledge.

"I didn't kill her," Patel repeated, water puddling around his feet. He tried to cover his backside where the terrier had torn his pants, but the handcuffs made it impossible. "Whatever else I did, I didn't kill her."

"Save it for the detectives," one of the officers told him. A patrol car rolled up to the intersection between the fountain and the Armory, followed by an unmarked vehicle, and the officers loaded him into the back of the patrol car.

"What was I saying about you attracting trouble?" Detective Tracy said a few minutes later after he and Spencer wrapped up a quick chat with the cops on the scene. This morning's croissant flakes had vanished from his sport coat, replaced by chocolate sprinkles.

"I prefer to think I'm attentive to details."

"Run through them for us," Spencer said, so I replayed the scene, from recognizing Patel in the food truck and spotting the little lady from his restaurant onstage, to my dog giving chase and catching his man.

"You trained him to attack at the phrase 'Cain and—'?" A note of admiration snuck into Tracy's question, but he stopped when I held up a finger.

"He came that way. He'd bark, once, at the oddest times. Then last Saturday, we were here at the Center. A little boy named K-A-N-E ran out in traffic. The dog chased him and saved him." I rubbed behind Arf's right ear, the fur still damp. "The parents were yelling the boy's name. It wasn't until today that I realized he also barked at A-B-L-E, and put two and two together."

"This little lady, she's the one who told you about the *bhuts*? The floating ghosts?" Spencer said.

"Right. And she's the one who got me thinking about Patel."

"He says he didn't kill her," Ben said.

"They all say that," Tracy told him.

Broken glass glittered. The bowl hadn't been a genuine Chihuly—the souvenirs sold at the Garden store are made by Northwest artisans based on the great sculptor's designs and specs—but it had shattered like one.

A shiver raced up my spine as my conviction that Ashwani Patel had killed Tamara-Ashley shattered, too.

"Ben, would you take Arf to the shop? Detectives, we

need to swing by the First Avenue Café. I'm about to solve your case for you. For real, this time."

"ALEX is at the Eastside joint today." My sous chef pal ground out his cigarette in the puffer zone behind the Café.

"It's not Alex I'm looking for."

Prep hadn't started yet, and the side door was locked. And I didn't want to appear at the front door with two detectives close behind me.

"Thanks again for those bones," I said as he let us in. "The dog's in heaven."

"Boss was a bit peeved when we didn't have enough for a stock he'd planned, but hey, plans change." He winked and headed for the kitchen.

"Well, well. Look who the cat dragged in." Scotty Glass's eyes narrowed as he gazed past me.

I slid onto a barstool. My companions kept to their feet. The mirror behind the bar reflected Spencer checking out the space. She was not sizing it up for its dining potential.

"This is Detective Spencer. I believe you know Detective Tracy."

"We are acquainted," Glassy said, his tone wary, the words drawn out.

"I watch a lot of movies," I said. "The way I see it, this is a buddy movie gone wrong."

"Is that so?" He picked up a bar towel and polished a heavy glass goblet, as bartenders do in the movies.

"Every friendship is a story. Kristen and I have been friends since before we were born. Our parents shared a house, and we were due on the same day, though I showed up two weeks before she did."

"Sounds kinda kinky," he said.

"Laurel and I knew each other casually for years, but we bonded over tragedy. Then there's you and Alex."

Glassy set the goblet on the counter next to a dozen others, ready for service, and tossed the towel over his shoulder. In the mirror, I saw him reach for a half-round mezzaluna and begin cutting limes in half.

Beside me, Tracy coughed. A hurry-up-and-get-this-going cough.

"You had a nice gig," I said. "You worked for a chef-owner who spent most of her time in the kitchen. She hired good people and got out of their way."

I forced myself not to watch as Spencer's mirror image strolled casually to the servers' station at the end of the bar.

"Then she decided to expand and hired another chef to run the kitchen while she focused on her new place. That chef, being a bit of a schemer himself, quickly realized that you were running the bar like it was your own, letting the servers make cash sales without ringing them up and splitting the proceeds. He wanted in. You had no way out."

A small electric juicer whirred, and citrus scent sparked the air.

"When Detective Tracy and Officer Buhner came calling, you and Alex formed a united front. The servers disappeared, after you slipped them extra cash to start over in Portland or Denver or wherever. But one stubborn gal wouldn't go. She'd had enough small roles in local theater to think she could make a career on the stage if she stayed in Seattle. So you and Alex paid her off, and Lynette—I think she called herself Melissa back then—took a short vacation. Long enough for the cops to lose track of her, but not long enough to lose her theater connections."

"You want a drink to wash down that tall tale?"

"Like that Negroni you poured me last week, to warn me to keep my mouth shut?"

"She's got it about right, doesn't she, Glassy?" Detective Tracy took a step closer. "You and Alex Howard are tied at the hip. You've got to keep an eye on each other, or risk losing everything."

"I don't know what you think we did way back when, but you can't prove any of it."

"Oh, but we can, Mr. Glass," Spencer said from her post at the end of the bar. "You of all people ought to know you can't trust someone you're paying to keep quiet. This Lynette, she saw the end of the gravy train and started singing. And you know how actresses love a spotlight and an audience."

"Your trouble's getting deeper," Tracy said. "Ms. Reece here figured out that when Tamara Langston asked you to join her new operation, you knew she was bound to discover the real reason you would never leave Alex Howard's company. Not out of loyalty—you don't have any, not really."

Glassy's jaw tightened, and he rolled one shoulder back and forth. In the mirror, his fingers twitched.

"You got it wrong," he said. "Alex is my best friend. He wouldn't know how to betray me."

"You knew Tamara well enough," I said, "to know she couldn't be bought. She'd started to unravel Patel's scheme of using her name and credit to prop up his failing business, and she asked you for advice. You made a big show of helping Alex shelter her, but you had to get rid of her."

"What better way," Tracy said, "than to force your way into the construction site and kill her there, to cast blame on Patel?"

"How would I do that? She died of some obscure pepper sold by your little storyteller here." His glance darted nervously around the room.

"We called Big Al on our way here," Spencer said. "We knew Howard had an account there, but he insisted he bought all his spices from Ms. Reece. Her records show a regular pattern of sales that supported his claim. Seems you've been buying ghost peppers in his name, supposedly for your special hot Bloody Mary. Bought about a decade's worth in a few weeks."

Tracy held up a pair of cuffs. "Scott Glass, we're here to arrest you for the murder of Tamara Langston, also known as Ashley Brown. Put your hands on the bar where we can see them—"

The mirror told me he was on the move. Glassy flung the bowl of lime juice at Tracy. He ducked, and it flew over his shoulder, clattering onto a table behind us. Glassy leaned across the bar and reached for me with his left hand, the mezzaluna glinting in his right. I twisted away, and his hand grazed the top of my head, the thick fingers scrabbling for my hair, too short to hold on to.

I grabbed a goblet from the top of the bar. Threw it at Glassy. He ducked. I grabbed another and another. Threw like the baseball player I was named for, spit and fire, salt and pepper.

The swinging doors to the kitchen opened. "Hey, I found another bag—"

"Stop right there," the two cops shouted in unison, guns out.

The frozen bones crashed to the floor as the sous chef raised his hands.

"Down on the floor, you scumbag." Gun in hand, Spencer dashed behind the bar. Out of the corner of my eye, I saw the terrified sous drop to the ground. Spencer grabbed Glassy's wrist, and the knife clattered to the floor. Tracy joined her, gun trained on the big bartender, as his partner snapped on the cuffs.

My breath rattled my teeth, and I set the last goblet back on the bar. I slid off my stool and approached the sobbing sous.

"I didn't do anything," he said, not yet grasping that the target of the operation was the man behind the bar. "I'm innocent."

I reached out and helped him to his feet. "You're innocent, but he's guilty, guilty, guilty."

Guilty as cinnamon.

Thirty-one

*There's rosemary—that's for remembrance. Pray you,
love, remember.*

—Ophelia to Laertes, *Hamlet*, Act IV, Scene 5

SPENCER AND TRACY HAULED SCOTTY GLASS OFF TO
jail. I asked a patrol officer to drop me off at the Center. I
had a little lady to find, and to thank.

The crew of Curry in a Hurry were hitching their wagon
to a battered white pickup when I reached the lawn. Gone the
crowds, the children, the music of a happy day. Gone, too,
the sunshine, as a pale gray blanket rolled in off the Sound.

"I had no idea," the blond woman said after I told her
about Tamara-Ashley and Patel's elaborate schemes. She
wrapped her arms around herself.

"If it's any consolation, at first I thought he'd killed her,
but now we know Scotty Glass overpowered her and forced
her to breathe a bag of ghost peppers."

"You dodged a bullet," a male employee said. He bent to
plug in the trailer's lights, and I gave her a questioning look.

Shock and pain flooded the face so much like Tamara-
Ashley's. "We were engaged. We—I just bought this food

truck. I'd planned to sign half of it over to him as a wedding present."

"I'm so sorry. I was hoping to catch the little Indian woman who sits out front in the restaurant. The woman who played the tambura onstage."

Her brow wrinkled. "No little Indian woman works for us."

"She's tiny." I held a hand below my chin. "Not five feet tall. Dark hair, pulled back. Wears a jeweled bindi, and every time I've seen her, she's worn a deep red sari. I assumed she was his grandmother."

"He has no family," the blonde said. "And I've never seen anyone like that in the restaurant."

The other employee straightened. "Me, neither. I helped the musicians set up. It was just the three guys. They don't use a drone player."

In a distant corner of my mind, a solo monk began to chant. Other voices joined him, melding together in harmony, and if I were a swearing woman, I would have sworn I heard a tambura join in.

"RUB a little chile pepper into that scrape on your hand and it won't scar," Sandra said, a twinkle in her dark eyes.

"You even think about pouring capsicum in my hard-earned wound and you'll be out on the street so fast your head will spin right off your neck." The cuts and scrapes I'd gotten when Patel shoved me to the ground stung, but were nothing a fresh, fat cinnamon roll couldn't cure.

"You wouldn't dare. You couldn't run this firetrap without me."

She had me there. "Patel's fiancée says he's deathly afraid of dogs. Got badly bit as a kid, teasing a neighbor's Doberman. That's what gave him the limp."

"And the limp slowed him down enough for Arf to catch him?" Reed said.

"I had no idea Arf could run that fast." The hero of the story lay beneath the table in the mixing nook working on a bone. Thanks to the sous, we had a year's supply to stash in the freezer. "Just don't mention any biblical brothers around him."

Outside, the Market carpenters were repairing the burnt plaster. Our electrical system had been given the all clear. I'd get our new signs ordered. The herb seedlings were already selling well, as were the aprons and mugs bearing our logo, delivered this morning. I filled my mug with spice tea and raised it in a toast.

"Here's to the little lady in the sari, whoever—whatever—she may be."

FRIDAY morning, I stopped for coffee at the bakery at the top of the Hillclimb. "How did you know?" I asked the shy barista who'd left clues I hadn't understood on my coffee cup.

She pulled the steam arm, and it spit and hissed.

The counter girl handed me my change, and I dropped it in the tip jar. "Mouth shut, eyes open. That's her."

I looked at my cup. No note this time. The barista had drawn a smiley face. I caught her eye and smiled back.

My crew and I got the shop ready for the day, then three of us piled in the Mustang and headed north.

"We're playing hooky," Kristen sang, off-key. "Lookie, hooky, cookie."

A killer, an arsonist, and a fraud-wreaking identity thief were behind bars. How could I not sing along? Mount Rainier dominated the skyline behind us, and Mount Baker towered in front, their glacial peaks sparkling. Girls on the road. Plus dog.

"Pepper, look." Lunch had gone down easy—open-faced Dungeness crab salad sandwiches and glasses of Pinot Grigio on a deck overlooking Padilla Bay. We were ten feet inside the third junk slash antique shop of the day in Anacortes, not far from the Naval Air Station on Whidbey Island, when Kristen grabbed my arm. Secondhand shops near military bases are jackpots for international prize hunters like us.

"Holy macaroni." Electric, like the old one, and slightly larger. Brass exterior, ceramic insert. Not a crack to be seen.

"Not much call for those," the shop owner said. "Too big. Came from a tea shop in Victoria. I can give you a good price. The Russians call it a samovar."

And I called it perfect.

OUR first customer Saturday morning was Danielle Bordeaux. "What a tangled mess. I knew I shouldn't have hired Melissa—Lynette to you—in the first place, but I never imagined a mistake fifteen years ago would lead to all this."

"Funny, isn't it? We convince ourselves they'll work out, we can train them, yada yada yada, and those are always the hires that bite us in the bittersweet. Danielle, when you called Glassy last Friday, after I came into your place—"

"I thought he was covering for Alex," she said. "That he knew Alex had killed Tamara. And I told him to stay away from you, or I'd take the gloves off."

"You weren't afraid that Glassy would come after you?"

"He's been in my kitchen. He knows what I can do with a knife." Her lips curved in a wry twist, and I almost laughed out loud.

"We're having a memorial service for Tamara at the restaurant next week," she continued. Makeup hadn't covered the circles under her eyes. "I hope you'll come. I'm pulling the plug on Tamarack."

"Did the building have electrical problems?"

"No. You were right. It was Patel. He got in through the shared access in the basement, to try to run Tamara off. Ashley, to him. She had a great idea, but the best concept won't fly without the right chef. And I'm losing my taste for growing the business."

"If you change your mind, give me a call. I'm thinking of hanging out a new shingle: Pepper Reece, Spice Merchant and Ghostbuster."

She left carrying a box of tea and a Spice Shop mug, on the house.

As always, the spring sunshine brought Seattleites out in droves, and we hustled all morning. I'd learned my lesson about hiring in desperation, but we desperately needed help.

"Cinnamon?" a woman said, reaching for a jar of our custom blend. "I always think of that as a fall spice."

"It's a spice for all seasons. You can make do without Celtic salt and smoked salt, three kinds of paprika, and all those exotic chile peppers." I'd debated long and hard whether to keep carrying ghost peppers, aka *bhut capsicum*, wondering if they were worth the trouble. But then I realized I was trying to make myself responsible for something that had nothing to do with me. I pictured the bumper sticker: BHUT C DOESN'T KILL PEOPLE—PEOPLE KILL PEOPLE. And I doubted Tamara would want me to banish them from our shelves. "But you can't make decent toast without cinnamon."

Spencer and Tracy came in to give me an update. While they were there, Tag appeared, wearing off-duty jeans and a blue Henley.

"Sorry about your white sweater," I said.

"A worthy sacrifice." He gave me that heart-melting smile, but the air between us had changed, and I suspected I wouldn't be seeing as much of him in the future.

"All these years, I blamed you for losing a witness. Not only did you have nothing to do with it, she was under our noses the whole time." Tracy extended his hand.

Tag took it, and they shook. "Thanks. But if I'd been quicker on the uptake back then, Tamara Langston—or Ashley Brown—might still be alive."

"You're the one always telling me we aren't responsible for other people's choices," I said.

"Speaking of choices," Spencer said. "My daughter decided to be a nanny in Switzerland for a year. It's a great opportunity, but she could have learned a lot about retail from you."

The compliment almost made up for the loss.

Sandra and I took advantage of a brief lull after lunch to polish our ideas for the Market's spring festival. The time I'd spent investigating had left us seriously behind.

"One more thing, boss." An impish grin crossed Sandra's face. "We have a gift for you."

She handed me a package wrapped in brown paper and kitchen twine. A teeny warning bell went off in my brain. *The Complete Idiot's Guide to Private Investigating.* "Between this and the adventures of Brother Cadfael, I'm sure I'll learn everything I need to know. Thanks."

"And this." She drew a small item out of her apron pocket. A new watch battery.

"Thanks." My phone buzzed, and I glanced down at the text. "Dinner and bowling?" it read. "This time, you choose the food."

I texted Ben back. "Staff party at Zak's gig tonight. Join us?"

The reply was nearly instant. "It's a date!"

A nice, safe group date.

But I had one more question. "How old are you?"

A moment later, the reply: "The curse of a youthful face. Forty-one. Do you mind dating an older man?"

Turns out this don't-judge-a-book bit goes both ways. I decided to keep my age—and my misread of his—secret a little while longer.

Midafternoon, Reed stuck his head in the office to let me know there was a customer out front asking for me.

"Pepper. I came to apologize for all the trouble I've caused."

"Thanks." I couldn't say "no apology needed" and mean it, even if that was what Alex wanted to hear.

"Everything Glassy did was wrong, from paying off Melissa—Lynette—to silencing Tamara. But he was right about one thing: We really were friends." His throat seemed to collapse on the words, and every handsome feature radiated sadness and regret. "I realized pretty quickly after we met that you didn't know about the past—that for reasons of his own, your ex would never tell you. I'm far from perfect, but I'm not the man I was back then."

I nodded. I'd known that. My judgment wasn't as flawed as I'd feared.

"I'm taking a break for a few months," he continued. "Travel, try to figure out what matters to me, what's next."

"What about the restaurants? All your employees?"

"Barbara—Ops—and my executive chefs will hold down the fort. We're taking over Tamarind, Patel's place, so those jobs are safe, too." He held a shopping basket in one hand, a few bags of cinnamon sticks inside. "Help me choose gifts for my staff?"

"With pleasure." We picked out cookbooks, pepper mills, salt cellars, and for a newlywed server, the heart-shaped espresso cups. Every employee got a package of cinnamon sticks and a jar of my favorite Puget Sound sea salt. (Despite my wisecrack that morning to the cinnamon buyer, I really do believe every kitchen needs honest-to-goodness genuine sea salt.)

I walked him outside, hopeful that the time away would be everything he wanted. There's a subtle difference between creating yourself, as we all do every day, and creating an image to live up to, as he had. He gave my cheek a good-bye kiss, and I turned back to my shop. Plucked a pot of rosemary off the rack and took a good whiff. A good addition to my deck garden.

"You're the owner, aren't you? Are you still hiring? My sister saw your sign."

A pleasant alto caught my attention. The speaker was a woman about thirty, with smooth, dark skin and an engaging expression, her hair swept up in a lobster roll.

Afterword

Death by ghost chile is remotely possible, but highly unlikely. If it were to happen, the action would probably be as Dr. Locke described. The peppers can be highly inflammatory; if you decide to cook with them, try making the oil Pepper and Alex concocted, or follow your own spice merchant's recommendations. Start small, and glove up! And whatever you do, don't get them anywhere near your eyes. As anyone who's ever made salsa can attest, even the oils from the mildest peppers can sizzle those tender tissues!

Recipes and Spice Notes

The Seattle Spice Shop recommends . . .

Pepper recommends keeping a jar of an all-purpose curry close at hand for spicing up vegetables or sprinkling on deviled eggs. This recipe has plenty of flavor and not a lot of heat.

CURRY

1 tablespoon coriander
1 tablespoon turmeric
1½ teaspoons cayenne
1½ teaspoons ground cloves
1½ teaspoons ground cinnamon
1½ teaspoons ground ginger

Mix together and store in a tightly closed jar.

Makes ¼ cup.

Optional additions: *cumin, cardamom, yellow mustard, or black pepper*

For a quick side dish, add a tablespoon to cooked garbanzo beans along with lemon, cilantro, and a diced tomato.

GARAM MASALA

Another blend that varies with the cook. Pepper and Sandra created the Spice Shop's Garam Masala to contrast with the hotter curry. It's especially yummy on shrimp or roasted nuts (recipe below).

  4 teaspoons ground fennel seeds
  2½ teaspoons cinnamon
  2½ teaspoons ground caraway seeds
  ½ teaspoon black pepper
  ½ teaspoon ground cloves
  ½ teaspoon ground cardamom

If your spices are whole, grind them in a coffee grinder. (Clean it first by grinding a tablespoon of rice to a fine powder and wiping out the grit; this also sharpens the blades.) Mix together thoroughly in a small bowl. Store in a tightly closed jar.

Makes about half a cup.

At home with Pepper

FALAFEL BURGERS WITH LEMON-TAHINI SAUCE

Pepper finally persuaded the owner of her favorite Middle Eastern restaurant to share his recipe, though she prefers pan grilling to deep-frying, for a healthier option and a cleaner kitchen. These burgers are equally good with or without the pita—she often serves them on a salad of greens, tomatoes, black olives, and sliced red onions, drizzled with the lemon-tahini sauce. Panko bread crumbs are a Japanese style, coarser than typical bread crumbs, readily available in the baking aisle of most groceries.

FOR THE LEMON-TAHINI SAUCE:

⅓ cup tahini
¼ cup lemon juice
3 tablespoons plain yogurt (Greek yogurt is too thick; choose a thinner variety for a pourable sauce)
1 clove garlic
Salt and freshly ground pepper

FOR THE FALAFEL BURGERS:

2 14-ounce cans garbanzo beans, aka chickpeas, rinsed and drained
½ red onion, diced
2 tablespoons fresh flat-leaf (Italian) parsley
6 fresh mint leaves
2 cloves garlic
Grated zest and juice of 1 lemon
1 tablespoon ground cumin
2 teaspoons ground coriander

1 teaspoon paprika
1 teaspoon salt
½ teaspoon pepper
1 egg, lightly beaten
½ cup panko bread crumbs
Nonstick cooking spray
4 whole wheat pita breads, toasted, cut in half, and
    split to form pockets
½ red onion, thinly sliced
2 Roma tomatoes, sliced
2 cups salad greens or romaine leaves, torn into bite-
    sized pieces
Mint sprigs, for garnish

Make the sauce: Combine the tahini, lemon juice, yogurt, and garlic in a blender or a small food processor. Puree until smooth. Season with salt and pepper to your own taste.

Make the burgers: Combine the garbanzo beans, onion, parsley, mint, garlic, lemon zest and juice, cumin, coriander, paprika, salt, and pepper in a food processor. Process until smooth. Place the mixture in a large bowl. Add the egg and bread crumbs, and stir to combine. Form into eight patties.

Heat a frying pan over medium and coat with cooking spray. Cook the burgers, carefully turning once, until golden brown, about 4 minutes a side.

To serve, put each burger in a pita pocket, top with a generous helping of sauce, and fill with red onion, tomato slices, and greens. Garnish the pockets or plate with a mint sprig.

Serves 8.

A classic from Ripe

ARUGULA FENNEL SALAD WITH DOUBLE MUSTARD VINAIGRETTE

Laurel adds a little heat to her lunch-goers' day by garnishing this salad with a very hot chile. The pepperoncini in the salad itself are mild, made milder by pickling, so no need to worry about entering the ghost realm prematurely!

FOR THE SALAD:

½ pound baby arugula
1 small fennel bulb, with fronds
½ English cucumber
4 small pepperoncini
¼ cup fresh flat-leaf (Italian) parsley
¼ cup fresh dill

FOR THE DRESSING:

1 heaping teaspoon grain mustard
1 teaspoon Dijon mustard
Juice of 1 lemon (3 tablespoons)
2 tablespoons olive oil
Salt and pepper

Make the salad: Wash and spin arugula and place in a serving bowl. A large, flat bowl is ideal.

Remove the outer layer of the fennel bulb and chop off the top with fronds. Chop 2 to 3 tablespoons of fronds for garnish. Cut off the tough, flat bottom end of the bulb, and cut the bulb in half. Lay each half on your cutting board, cut side down, and slice thinly.

English cucumbers typically come wrapped in plastic; unwrap yours, scrub it with a vegetable brush, and peel it in ¼ inch strips, leaving ¼ inch of peel, alternating with ¼ inch of flesh, continuing around the cucumber. Cut it in half lengthwise and slice ¼ inch thick.

Remove and discard the seeds from the pepperoncini, then slice as thinly as possible.

Roughly chop the parsley and dill.

Add all the vegetables and herbs to the salad bowl except the fennel fronds, and toss to combine.

Make the dressing: Stir the mustards and lemon juice together in a small bowl or measuring cup. Add the olive oil in a stream, whisking the ingredients together until the dressing thickens or emulsifies. (Pouring the oil in gradually keeps it from separating.) Season with salt and pepper to taste.

Toss the salad with the dressing. Garnish with the fennel fronds.

Serves 6 as a side salad or first course.

Breakfast on the houseboat

These baked sausages and muffins are excellent alongside eggs scrambled with green onions, red bell pepper, and the Seattle Spice Shop's Herbes de Provence (recipe in Assault and Pepper*).*

SPICY MORNING SAUSAGE

A tip from Laurel: Let the sausage sit on the counter, wrapped or covered, for about thirty minutes so your hands don't freeze when you mix it!

  1 pound lean ground pork sausage
  ½ teaspoon salt (kosher or flakes pack the best flavor
      punch)
  1 teaspoon red pepper flakes
  1 teaspoon fennel seeds, toasted (see below)
  ½ teaspoon cayenne
  ½ cup panko bread crumbs
  ½ cup grated Parmesan
  Nonstick cooking spray

Preheat the oven to 400 degrees.

Toast the fennel seeds by heating them in a small, heavy frying pan over medium heat, about five minutes, stirring often. They will turn golden brown and give your kitchen a lovely fragrance.

In a large bowl, break up the sausage with a spoon or your hands. Mix in the salt, pepper flakes, fennel seeds, cayenne, bread crumbs, and Parmesan. Form into small patties, about two inches across and half an inch thick.

Spray a glass or ceramic baking dish with nonstick cooking spray. Lay the patties in the dish, an inch or two apart. Bake about 20 minutes or until golden brown but slightly tender to the touch in the middle. You may want to stick a knife in one to make sure they are thoroughly cooked and hot.

Makes about 12 patties. They reheat nicely and freeze well.

DATE-BRAN MUFFINS

¼ cup chopped dates
½ cup hot water
1½ cups wheat bran
1 cup whole wheat flour
1 teaspoon baking powder
½ teaspoon baking soda
½ teaspoon salt
1 teaspoon ground cinnamon
½ teaspoon ground nutmeg
½ teaspoon ground cloves
⅓ cup vegetable oil
1 egg
1 cup buttermilk
½ cup chopped dates, or more
Nonstick cooking spray

Pour hot water over the ¼ cup dates; set aside. (Do not drain.)

Preheat oven to 400 degrees.

In a large bowl, mix wheat bran, flour, baking powder, baking soda, salt, and spices.

Pour the date-water mixture into a blender or food processor. Add the oil, egg, and buttermilk, and blend about 1 minute, until smooth. Pour into the flour mixture, along with the ½ cup dates. Stir until blended. The batter will be thick and lumpy.

Coat a muffin pan with nonstick cooking spray. Spoon batter into prepared muffin tin. Bake 20 to 22 minutes or until a knife or toothpick inserted in the center comes out clean. Allow muffins to cool in the pan about 5 minutes before serving in a pretty bowl or a basket lined with a colorful napkin.

Makes 12 muffins. These freeze beautifully.

Cocktail hour

SCOTTY GLASS'S COSMOPOLITAN

Pepper's old standby

FOR EACH DRINK:

    1½ ounces citrus vodka
    1 ounce triple sec (Glassy prefers Cointreau)
    ½ ounce fresh lime juice
    Dash of cranberry juice, for color
    Lime wedge, for garnish

Pour the liquor and juice into a shaker two-thirds full of ice. Shake about fifteen seconds, or until your hands are cold, then strain into a chilled martini glass. Add the lime as garnish.

NEGRONI

Pepper's new love

FOR EACH DRINK:

    1½ ounces Campari
    1½ ounces sweet vermouth
    1½ ounces gin
    1 orange twist (a strip of peel, about ½ inch wide and
        3 to 4 inches long, twisted to release the oils)

Pour the liquor into an ice-filled rocks glass, and add the peel. Best drunk outdoors on a deck overlooking water or a freshly mowed meadow. Or anywhere, actually.

For a Negroni Sbagliato, substitute champagne or sparkling wine for the gin. Drink lore says a bartender created it by grabbing the wrong bottle; sbagliato means "mistaken" in Italian. An inexpensive sparkling wine, on the dry side, like Freixenet (pronounced "fresh-eh-net") Brut from Spain or Yellow Tail from Australia, will do nicely. Plus the wine will add a touch of that international flair Danielle advises! No need to worry about opening the bottle. Just uncrimp the wire cage and remove it, place one hand over the cork, and turn the bottle, *not the cork, until you hear that satisfying pop.*

Spice up your life with Pepper and the Flick Chicks

It wouldn't be Movie Night without tasty treats . . .

SANDRA'S SPICY ROASTED NUTS

A bowl of spiced nuts is perfect with wine or cocktails. Sprinkle a few nuts on a plate of butter chicken or other dishes as a garnish. Make your own garam masala (recipe above), or find it and amchur, dried mango powder, in spice shops and Indian groceries. Variations abound; for a hotter flavor, substitute curry powder or cumin for the garam masala. (A note from Pepper: When my author couldn't find amchur, she ground dried, unsweetened mango slices in her coffee grinder. Perfect!)

1 pound raw almonds or cashews, or a mix
2 tablespoons canola oil
1 tablespoon kosher salt or another crystal variety
1½ teaspoons amchur, or mango powder
1 tablespoon garam masala
1½ teaspoons ground cayenne

Preheat the oven to 375 degrees.

In a large bowl, stir together the nuts, oil, salt, and spices. Spread the nuts on a baking sheet and roast about 10 minutes, stirring once to cook the nuts evenly. (If the edges of the nuts start to brown, pull them out to avoid burning.) Place the baking sheet on a rack; the nuts will continue to brown slightly as they cool.

Remember what Pepper says about spice blends: They take a few hours to marry and mellow, so these are best made ahead. They'll keep several weeks if stored in a tightly sealed container.

Makes 1 pound.

ORANGE CINNAMON CRÈME BRÛLÉE

On this, Pepper and Tag agree: the very best crème brûlée ever.

2 cups heavy cream
½ cup white sugar (divided use)
Zest of 1 orange, removed in wide strips with a peeler

1 cinnamon stick
6 to 8 strands of fresh thyme
4 egg yolks
½ teaspoon vanilla extract
4 teaspoons turbinado sugar, for topping
Strips of orange peel or thyme sprigs for
    garnish (optional)

Preheat the oven to 325 degrees.

In a small saucepan, combine the cream, ¼ cup sugar, orange zest, and cinnamon stick. Roll the thyme strands back and forth between your palms, over the pan, to release the essential oils, then toss the thyme into the pan. Whisk to combine. Bring the mixture to a boil, then remove from the heat and strain into a bowl to cool. (This step infuses the cream with the aromatics—the zest, thyme, and cinnamon.)

In a large bowl, whisk together the egg yolks, remaining ¼ cup sugar, and vanilla. When the infused cream is cooled to the touch, slowly pour it into the egg mixture and whisk to combine. (Cooling the cream avoids curdling the eggs.)

Place four 4-ounce ramekins or custard cups in a large baking dish or roasting pan. Carefully fill the ramekins with the custard mixture. Place the dish in the oven and carefully pour hot water into the pan, till it reaches about halfway up the sides of the ramekins.

Bake until the custard is set around the edges and slightly jiggly in the center, about 35 minutes.

Remove the baking dish from the oven. Lift out the ramekins—tongs work nicely—and cool on a rack at room temperature. (Don't leave them in the hot water, as the heat would continue to cook the mixture.) When cool, move ramekins to refrigerator to chill for at least an hour before the next step. Just before serving, sprinkle a teaspoon of turbinado sugar evenly over the top of each dish. Caramelize the sugar with a kitchen torch. The sugar will harden, turn golden, and become crunchy. If you don't have a torch, broil the dishes 2 to 3 minutes until the sugar forms a crisp, golden top. Garnish with a curvy strip of orange peel or a sprig of thyme.

Serves 4.

Readers, I'm always delighted to hear from you. Drop me a line at Leslie@LeslieBudewitz.com, connect with me on Facebook at LeslieBudewitzAuthor, or join my seasonal mailing list for book news and more. (Sign up on my website, www.LeslieBudewitz.com.) Reader reviews and recommendations are a big boost to authors; if you've enjoyed my books, please tell your friends. A book is but marks on paper until you read those pages and make the story yours. *Thank you*.